DON'T YOU WANNA STAY

KAIT NOLAN

For Erin Nicholas,
This is all your fault.
Kisses!
Kait

A LETTER TO READERS

Dear Reader,

This book is set in the Deep South. As such, it contains a great deal of colorful, colloquial, and occasionally grammatically incorrect language. This is a deliberate choice on my part as an author to most accurately represent the region where I have lived my entire life. This book also contains swearing and pre-marital sex between the lead couple, as those things are part of the realistic lives of characters of this generation, and of many of my readers.

If any of these things are not your cup of tea, please consider that you may not be the right audience for this book. There are scores of other books out there that are written with you in mind. In fact, I've got a list of some of my favorite authors who write on the sweeter side on my website at https://kaitnolan.com/on-the-sweeter-side/

If you choose to stick with me, I hope you enjoy!

Happy reading!

Kait

CHAPTER 1

*I*t was the cast-iron skillet that saved Deanna James from certain death.

In sheer instinct, she flung it up to block the projectile hurtling toward her head. The thing struck hard, sending reverberations down her arms, even as glass shattered and sprayed her with heavy glass shards and bright yellow crumbs.

"What the hell is wrong with you?" From inside the room, an unfamiliar voice dripped with shock and an accent that was more Motor City than Music City. "You asked for cornbread! That was freaking cornbread!"

"Jiffy Mix *is not cornbread!*" the country music diva shouted, then let out a noise that was...not musical.

At the banshee shriek, Deanna hunched in the doorway and dared a peek around her makeshift shield at the woman in the trailing silk robe, her glossy mahogany hair piled on top of her head in a cluster of fat rollers that spoke of the pageant queen she'd once been. Mercy Lee Bradshaw. Reigning princess of country music and current pain in Deanna's ass. Mercy Lee's nostrils flared and her cold blue eyes bored like lasers into the guy huddled behind a chair to the left of the doorway. This young man's ignorance, and a call from Mercy Lee's manager, Gavin Waters, were the reasons Deanna had fought her way through the ungodly and perpetual construction to downtown Nashville, after work on a Friday.

"Now, honey, be reasonable." Gavin's tone set Deanna's teeth on edge. Clearly, he knew nothing about women, and he sure knew nothing about cornbread. That knowledge had prompted Deanna to grab her grandmama's skillet on the way out the door a mere five minutes after she'd gotten home. Dealing with the hissy fits of entitled celebrities was not an eight-to-five job. Given what Mercy Lee paid the boutique PR firm, Deanna's bosses had decided that pacification was now part of her job description.

"Reasonable? *Reasonable?* I gave them the recipe *in advance.* For cornbread. My granny's cornbread. *Real* cornbread. Not this... this... sweet monstrosity." She waved a manicured hand toward what remained of the cheap ceramic baking dish of Jiffy Mix cornbread at Deanna's feet. "I'm not asking for $900 titanium straws like Beyonce or a booze slushie machine like Kanye. It's a simple and easy request. No cornbread. No performance. How is that not reasonable, Gavin?"

Mercy Lee's obsession with her grandmother's cornbread wasn't remotely the strangest celebrity rider Deanna had dealt with in her career. In truth, she had to agree with the woman on the fundamental point that Jiffy Mix was some sad Yankee's interpretation of cornbread. But it wasn't worth the publicity nightmare that was going to ensue if Mercy Lee didn't walk out on stage as contracted, or if she trashed any more of the venue dressing room in her outrage. Containing that prospective PR furor was why Deanna was here.

"Okay, look. Everybody just calm down." Stepping gingerly over the cornbread carnage, she lowered the skillet and brushed off the shrapnel. "You're going to get your cornbread. I brought my own personal cast-iron skillet, and a runner should be here any minute with the rest of the ingredients. If somebody will point me to the kitchen, I will make it myself to ensure it's done right. But I need you to finish getting ready to go on. It's curtains up in half an hour."

The country diva folded her arms. "I'm not going on until I've had my cornbread."

Deanna struggled to keep her temper level. She didn't get paid enough for this shit. "I understand your frustration. But you and I both know, it's going to take longer than thirty minutes to preheat the oven, cook the bacon, and get the cornbread baked."

"Then I go on late. That's the deal. You know how I feel about this, Deanna."

Yeah. She did. It was why she had Suellen Bradshaw's cornbread recipe committed to memory.

Mr. I-Thought-Jiffy-Mix-Was-Cornbread spoke up. "Now hold on. I've got a sold-out show out there. They're all waiting on you."

Gavin opened his mouth, but Deanna held up a hand to forestall whatever he was about to say. "What is your name?"

"Tony Moretti."

"Tony, where is Nina?" The venue manager had to be MIA. No way would this have happened on her watch.

"Out with the stomach flu. She left me in charge." And after Mercy Lee got finished, the wet-behind-the-ears rookie would probably be lucky to still have a job.

Not my problem.

"Okay look, Tony, here's what we're gonna do. You're going to take me to the kitchen. Meanwhile, you're gonna find someone to go on before Mercy Lee as a surprise warm-up act to buy us some time."

"Where am I gonna find somebody this close to showtime?" Tony demanded.

"This is Nashville. You can't throw a rock without hitting an aspiring musician. If you don't have someone readily available, I'm sure Gavin can help you come up with some options. He has a stable full of artists at his disposal." Deanna very deliberately did not think about one particular member of that stable. It wasn't her business anymore.

"I'm on it." Gavin already had his phone out, furiously texting someone.

Tony cast a glance at Mercy Lee that said everything they were all thinking—with probably considerably more profanity—but he wisely kept his opinion to himself. "Sorry for the misunderstanding."

Mercy Lee just sniffed.

Sending up silent prayers that the situation wouldn't devolve, Deanna followed Tony through the bowels of the building.

Once they were well out of earshot, he glanced at her. "Are they all that crazy?"

"If you think this qualifies as crazy, you're in the wrong business. Talent and fame often come with entitlement, eccentricities, and bad attitudes." And sometimes those things came even in the absence of talent *or* fame, as Deanna well knew.

"I'm just in it for the music."

"So says everyone in the beginning."

By the time they made it to the commercial kitchen, usually manned by whatever personal chef or caterer was attached to the talent, the runner had arrived with the ingredients Deanna had ordered. She paid the kid and got to work, sending Tony back to deal with finding interim entertainment and cleaning up the mess from Mercy Lee's Jiffy Mix protest.

Once the oven was preheating to 450 and the bacon was sizzling on a low flame, she set to measuring and mixing the remaining ingredients. After the chaos of traffic and the shitstorm she'd walked into upstairs, the empty kitchen was a welcome break. It had been a helluva week, and she'd been looking forward to a quiet night at home with a bath, a glass of wine, and some HGTV while she added to her never-ending Pinterest boards. Instead, here she was, babysitting yet another entitled celebrity.

Fishing out the bacon, she swirled the hot grease around the perimeter of the skillet to coat the edges and added the requisite amount straight into the buttermilk batter. Once it was stirred in, she poured the batter into the skillet, satisfied with the pop and sizzle that would make a proper crust, and slid the whole thing into the oven. Nothing left to do but wait.

She could've headed back upstairs to check on the status of the warm-up act, but that would require she have further interaction with the circus, and she'd had enough already. Instead, she grabbed the bacon and munched as she slipped out her phone to see if she'd managed to head off the damage. When none of her alerts for Mercy Lee's social media referenced the Jiffy Mix incident, she opened Instagram for a little bit of dreaming.

Almost her entire feed was made up of old houses in need of saving. If there was an account that curated them, Deanna followed it. The houses were all over the country, in all kinds of styles and various shades of disrepair. Many were in foreclosure. Plenty were under threat of being torn down. The idea of being able to one day buy one of these historic gems and bring it back to life was her dream. New construction simply didn't have this kind of history and personality. She wanted to own a piece of that. Maybe because she wanted to rewrite her own history.

A picture caught her eye. The shot was terrible. Too dark and the angle was a little funky, with part of the house obscured by the message *Save This House* photoshopped across the image. But Deanna opened it anyway, trying to get a better glimpse of the antebellum house set at the end of an avenue of old-growth trees. It was white—or had been, in some long-ago incarnation. A quartet of columns marched across the front, giving presence to what looked like a square box of a house with a second-story gallery. There was no way to tell how far back it went. She swiped through the other two pictures—one of some body of water visible from the house, and one of what might once have been a truly magnificent stairway inside that now had paint peeling in strips from every tread.

She scrolled down to the description.

Save this antebellum beauty in Hamilton, TN.

A frisson of excitement shivered down Deanna's spine. Hamilton was one of the bedroom communities of Nashville. Maybe she'd actually get a chance to *see* this one. She favorited it to look at later.

Her phone began to ring. She tensed, expecting Gavin again, but saw her mother's name flash across the screen, even as muffled strains of music sounded from the distant stage. Obviously Tony and Gavin had sorted something out, and she had further reprieve from the crazy.

"Hey, Mom."

"Hi, baby. What are you up to tonight?"

"Putting out fires. The usual. I'm hoping to head home in a little while to get some chill time in. I was just looking at photos of this really cool old house outside Nashville."

"You and your old houses." Deanna could practically hear her mother shaking her head. "You know those things are just money pits. You're not in a position to do something that foolish." She didn't actually say *since your divorce,* but the words hung between them, nonetheless.

Deanna deflated. "I know, I know. I've used up my quota of foolish." Like she really needed *that* reminder of the years she'd wasted on Blake. But she understood that her parents only wanted the best for her, and the best included not making impulsive decisions. She'd more than learned her lesson on that score.

Wanting to shift the conversation away from her, she asked, "How did Dad's doctor's appointment go?"

"Oh, fine. His cholesterol is down. He's hoping that means he doesn't ever have to eat oatmeal again."

They continued to chat about safer topics until the timer went off, signaling the cornbread was done.

"Listen, Mom, I've gotta go. Give Dad my love, okay?"

"Will do. Talk soon."

Removing the pan of perfectly baked buttermilk cornbread, Deanna hunted up a knife and plate, slicing and arranging the whole thing to Mercy Lee's exacting standards. Then she carried the plate of steaming cornbread and the fresh package of sweet cream butter up to the dressing room.

Mercy Lee pounced as soon as Deanna came through the door, shoving a hunk of cornbread into her mouth and moaning. "This. *This* is cornbread." With barely more than a glance at Deanna, she yanked the plate out of her hands and carried it over to a table to slather on butter. Hearing male voices coming down the hall, and knowing she wouldn't get a proper thank you, Deanna brushed her hands off. "Okay, well, are you good to go now? Because it sounds like your warm-up act is finished." The music had stopped a couple of minutes ago.

Mercy Lee nodded, continuing to shovel in cornbread and guzzling water.

Celebrities were weird.

"I'm gonna go then. You have a good night." Deanna turned and walked straight into an all-too-familiar chest.

Her body recognized the hands that came up to catch her arms before she even dragged her eyes to his face. Blake Fucking Lucas. Her cheating bastard of an ex-husband.

"Whoa. Hey there, darlin'." Blake grinned that single-dimpled smile that had melted her heart and her panties back in college.

Setting her jaw, Deanna ignored Blake and looked to Gavin, who was right behind him. "Really?"

"You said you wanted someone available immediately."

She highly doubted there hadn't been other alternatives. "Fine. Whatever. The crisis has been averted and Mercy Lee is ready to go on. I'm going."

"Oh now, don't be running off so fast," Blake wheedled.

Deanna glanced down to where his hands were still curled

around her upper arms. "If you don't take your hands off me right now, I'm going to take them off at the wrists."

He let her go, lifting his hands in the universal sign of no threat.

She wished she had the skillet in her hand. Then again, the fact that she still wanted to bash him over the head with it almost two years after their divorce probably meant it was a good thing she wasn't armed. Shoving past both men, she stalked down the hall, yanking her phone out to send a text to the one person who could rectify her suddenly foul mood.

Deanna: **Close-encounter of the asshat variety. I need detox.**

Bennet: **I'll bring the wine.**

~

"This place is a dump."

Wyatt Sullivan smiled at his companion's assertion and continued to pick his way through the piles of old newspapers, boxes of jars, and other detritus filling the rooms of the 1980s split-level. "Ah, but it's a dump with potential".

"The potential for a CDC lockdown, maybe. What is that smell?" Simon demanded.

"My guess is a mouse nest somewhere. But look." Moving to a corner, Wyatt shifted a pile of wilting boxes and used a pocketknife to pry up the moldy shag carpet. Beneath were dull oak floors. "These can be refinished. I'm betting they run through the entire first floor." Letting the carpet drop, he straightened. "You have to learn to look past the surface to the bones beneath."

"I know, I know. Fixtures and paint can be changed. This isn't my first rodeo with you. But why is it you always seem to go for the really horrible places?"

"Because I can see what most people can't. This place belonged to somebody's relative. Obviously, they were a hoarder. Whoever inherited the house doesn't want to deal with the mess, so they're willing to make a hell of a deal to get the property off their hands as is. If the bones are good, that means bigger profit on the flip."

"I get all that. But dude—you live on site while you flip. How can you even consider doing that in a place like this? Obviously there's mold." Simon tugged his T-shirt up over his nose, as if that would help.

"I can couch surf for a bit until we strip all that out. I admit it's not always ideal, but that's how I maximize profit and minimize cost. I'm not wasting thousands on maintaining my own residence, where I'd have to commute who knows how long across Nashville to the job site every day. That saves time, and time is money, too. It works for me." Though he had been considering investing in a small camper that he could tow behind his truck and park on site. Maybe if this next project was profitable enough.

"I feel sure it contributes to your perpetually single status."

Amused, Wyatt shot Simon a mock glare. "You saying I don't have game?"

"I haven't even seen you try to play."

Yeah, well... Wyatt had been burned on that front a long time ago and had little interest in trying again. He had options if he wanted short-term female companionship. He just hadn't pursued any in a while. Too much work to do. There was always the next flip, the next episode of his home improvement show, *DIWyatt*, to put together for posting on YouTube. Maybe he'd think about that after he'd reached his goal. After he'd proved himself.

"Right now I can't afford the distraction."

"You've always got an excuse."

Irritation prickled. "Better I avoid dating entirely than to make some poor woman feel like she's second fiddle to my dreams."

Simon went quiet for a moment as they made their way into a kitchen that probably merited hazmat suits. "I mean, that's fair, but don't you want someone to share it with?"

Did he want someone to love and support him in the thing

that meant the most to him? Of course. But Wyatt had stopped believing in fairy tales a long time ago. Rather than point that out, he hooked an arm around Simon's neck and gave him a noogie. "That's why I have you."

When he'd taken Simon on, it had been as a favor to his old foster mom, Joan Reynolds. A summer job. A way to keep him out of trouble and teach him a few skills. Three years later, Joan was dead and Wyatt had the chance to be the kind of big brother he'd been lucky enough to have. He hadn't imagined the boy would stick. But Simon had proved to be a hard worker and eager to learn. He was taller and broader now, no longer the whip-thin boy he'd been, but a leanly muscled man as tall as Wyatt. But there was still teenage boy in his laughing response to the head-lock—an elbow jab and long fingers reaching for Wyatt's ticklish ribs.

"Are we taking this monstrosity on?"

His use of "we" made Wyatt smile, even as his gaze automatically tracked over the ceiling and walls, noting small cracks and the evidence of a leak. "Maybe. Transforming this place would be something of a miracle. It's got that whole train wreck vibe that could really drive views." And views were income on his monetized YouTube channel.

They stepped outside. From the front of the walk, beside the gate of the chain-link fence sporting signs declaring *No Trespassing* and *Keep Out,* the realtor looked up from her phone with hope in her eyes. "Well? What do you think?"

Knowing how desperate Shelley was to get the listing sold, Wyatt conceded, "It's a possibility. I want to look around outside."

He shoved through an overgrown section of fence that was more vines than chain link. That would have to go. There was already little enough space to navigate between this house and the next less than fifteen feet away. The foundational plantings were massive and should've been ripped out decades ago. But what really concerned him was the huge old oak shading the house in the back. One good storm could send that big, beautiful bastard crashing through the roof.

Wanting a look at the foundation, he fought his way through the holly bushes that stood higher than he did, cursing as the prickly leaves scratched his arms. Low-tech alarm system at its finest. Crouching, he made his way along the base of the structure. About halfway across the east side of the house, he realized the roof didn't matter. A huge crack snaked up from the foundation, right where one of the gnarled roots disappeared beneath the house. Based on its location, it was likely running up into one of the overloaded closets, which explained why he hadn't spotted the problem inside.

Shoving back out of the bushes, he rejoined Shelley and Simon out front. "No go. There are foundation problems. That big ass oak is gonna have to go, and the house will need releveling." Foundational issues were too costly and time consuming to tackle for a flip with his small operation.

Undeterred, Shelley insisted, "I'm sure the sellers will deduct that from the cost. They're eager to make a deal. I'm positive they'll negotiate."

"I'm sure they are, but unless they want to just hand me the deed, the answer is no. We'll keep looking."

"Thank God," Simon muttered.

Shelley's face fell.

Wanting to throw her a bone, Wyatt offered a smile. "If you find any others that fit my parameters, let me know. I'm happy to look."

She just nodded, casting a frustrated, disgusted glance back at the house.

"Thanks for your time."

They climbed into Wyatt's truck. As they waited for Shelley to lock the house—Wyatt wasn't about to leave her on her own in this neighborhood at this time of day—Simon stretched out his long legs.

"So now what? You close on the current flip tomorrow, right?"

"Yeah. First thing in the morning. I had hoped to move directly into the next project house, but I'll have guaranteed money in the bank. I can afford to take a bit more time to find the right next project." The show needed something with wow factor. Something that would get him noticed by the networks. The right house was out there somewhere. He knew it.

"What's the word from the buyer about the potential connection at CMT for the show?"

Curt Welling was some kind of mid-level something or other at CMT. He and his wife had actually found the house through *DIWyatt* and put in an offer before the property even went on the market. In the process, he'd mentioned that his boss was part of a team looking at producing some original content for the network in the home improvement arena. With luck, his enthusiasm for Wyatt's work would translate into a meeting with that team.

Wyatt shrugged with more nonchalance than he felt. "No word yet. I'm hoping he'll have something to say tomorrow." And if there was a part of him that was crossing his fingers and toes that he'd get the meeting and land a show, such that there was an actual production budget, well, he couldn't be blamed for hoping.

"They'd be crazy not to talk to you."

If only his little brother were in charge of the decisions. "Here's hoping."

"Since you're about to be flush and all, how 'bout you buy a brother dinner? It's the least you can do to make up for subjecting me to that shit show." Simon jerked a thumb toward the property they'd just walked through.

Wyatt laughed and pulled away from the curb. "I expect I can make that happen."

CHAPTER 2

*T*he piquant scent of Thai food greeted Deanna as she stepped into her apartment.

Bennet Hartley slid out of the kitchen *Risky Business* style in sock feet, leggings, and an oversized T-shirt that should have looked shlumpy but on her looked stylish. She held a full glass of wine in each hand. "I have been honing my list of insults since you texted. Dinner's just waiting to be plated, and there's Ben and Jerry's in the freezer. I figured you haven't had a chance to eat yet."

Tears of gratitude pricked the backs of Deanna's eyes as she accepted a glass, wrapping Bennet in a one-armed hug. "I will never ever regret giving you a key to my place."

"I got you, girl. Go pajamaficate, then we can have an insult the asshat contest the way we did all through your divorce."

Deanna drained half the glass where she stood. "How much wine did you bring?"

Bennet's laugh warmed the cold that had lodged itself in the pit of Deanna's stomach since the run-in with Blake. "I came with an overnight bag and hangover preventatives."

"God, I love you. Maybe we should become lesbians."

"The world cannot handle that much fabulous in one couple. Besides, you are a legitimate morning person, and I'm pretty sure that's grounds for murder in some states."

"Only if I don't come armed with coffee."

Bennet angled her head in mock consideration. "You *do* make excellent coffee."

In the bedroom, Deanna stripped out of her work clothes in favor of yoga pants and her most comfortable T-shirt, the Five Finger Death Punch one that Blake had hated. She no longer lived her life based around his whims and wants.

It did no good to berate herself for all the years that hadn't been true.

By the time they settled at opposite ends of the sofa with bowls of extra spicy basil fried rice and more wine, Deanna felt some of the rough edges of her day smoothing out. Or maybe that was just the alcohol hitting her very empty stomach.

"So how exactly did you run into the spineless dick weasel?"

"Work. Of course." She explained her close encounter of the bastard kind.

"This is the first time you've actually had to deal with Blake the flake in over a year, right?"

"Yeah. Which is a minor miracle considering how small a world the music industry really is. Since he's now being repped by Gavin Waters, and since I'm now at the beck and call of Gavin's number one client, I suspect it won't be the last." With a grimace, she sipped more wine. "It's the epitome of irony that my deft handling of the whole potential clusterfuck of Kyle Keenan's surprise engagement meant I got switched from County Music's Captain America to Nashville's biggest diva."

"Being amazing at your job has its drawbacks."

"I miss Kyle. He was sane. And watching him with Abbey gave me fresh hope that love actually does exist." It was nice to know some men could and did keep their promises. Certainly she hadn't seen that kind of devotion from her ex.

"They are pretty damned adorable, and you just know their baby is gonna be the cutest thing ever."

"True story. They're really *nice* people. I miss nice people."

Bennet angled her head, considering. "I think it's less nice and more normal. You've been rubbing elbows with the famous and famous adjacent for a long time."

Deanna drained the last of her second glass of wine. "I have. And, God, I'm so tired of it. I'm tired of wrangling spoiled musicians and keeping their bad behavior or poorly thought out remarks from becoming a DEFCON situation. I'm tired of fixing other people's mistakes." Reaching for the bottle on the coffee table, she filled her glass again. "But I don't get to do anything else because my own mistake was so huge, I'll be paying for it via alimony for what feels like the rest of my natural life. Because Blake isn't going to marry again. Why would he? He can't keep it in his pants."

Bennet squeezed her ankle. "You never know. Maybe he'll hook up with Mercy Lee and be taken off your hands."

"I'd say from your mouth to God's ear, but I don't know that I hate her that much."

"She'd certainly be able to afford him and his expensive tastes better than you. And you don't need them to *stay* married. Just get married in the first place. That would terminate the alimony."

"True." Deanna lifted her glass. "To Blake and Mercy Lee. May they find they're the perfect combination of crazy for each other."

"Cheers."

They clinked glasses.

"You know what you need?" Bennet declared. "Hot guys in tool belts. That always makes you feel better. What are you feeling? Carter Osterhouse? Ty Pennington? The Property Brothers?"

"Oh, I've got a new guilty pleasure on that front. Remember, I told you I met Paisley Parish at Ivy's wedding?" Deanna grabbed the remote and flipped on her small TV, navigating to YouTube.

"I'm still jealous of that. I frigging love her books."

"Well, she's the one who told me about this." Hitting a few more buttons, she brought up her current favorite home improvement channel. "I give you *DIWyatt*."

Bennet leaned forward. "What have we here?"

"He's this contractor who specializes in mostly one-man flips. He'll take these absolute monstrosities and turn them into beautiful, functional homes. And it's not just video of the flip process, which you know I love, but also a ton of instructional videos about how to actually *do* the stuff."

"A glimpse behind the home improvement curtain."

"Exactly. This isn't a case of having a full production crew, round-the-clock contractors, and an army of volunteers. He's just one guy. From time to time, he'll pull in a few other folks, but by and large, he does all of this on his own. He makes it look easy and doable."

Bennet smirked. "*He's* doable. All that thick, dark hair and muscles."

Deanna tossed a pillow in her direction and made her laugh.

"Seriously, though. The fact that your commentary is all about his construction skills and not how that tool belt hangs on his hips is not what I was expecting. I thought you were just obsessed with the prettiness of the end product like the rest of us. I didn't know you cared about the actual process that goes in to this kind of thing."

"I *love* old houses. I love the idea of renovating something. Building something up that would otherwise be torn down. None of these modern, clean lines and no soul. A home should tell a story. Have a history." She swiped open her phone and pulled up the house she'd been looking at earlier. "It's my dream to be able to buy one of these houses and bring it back to glory. Someday I want to walk into my home and feel ownership—not just because it's my name on the deed, but because I put in the sweat equity to truly make it *mine*."

Bennet studied her with an expression that was part

impressed, part *Girl, you crazy*. "I had no idea you were this into the idea of home improvement. You never said."

Deanna swigged more wine and shrugged. "It's just a dream. Something I play with as stress relief. Pinterest boards and Instagram."

"Will you show me?"

Dragging out her laptop, she introduced Bennet to her many and varied Pinterest boards and the old house accounts she haunted.

"This is really good, Deanna. You have a great eye."

She liked to think so, but anybody could capture pictures on the internet. "It makes me happy."

Bennet fixed bright, dark eyes on her. "Have you ever tried to actually do anything like this before?"

"I tried to talk Blake into buying a fixer upper. The kind of place we could really put our mark on. He wouldn't hear of it. All he ever wanted was the new and the shiny. All our money ended up going toward this lavish lifestyle that was above our means because he was *convinced* it would help him be discovered. And instead, it landed us neck-deep in debt—or rather, it landed *me* neck-deep in debt, since he ran most of it up in my name. Between that and the alimony, I just don't have the money to put into a project like this."

"I mean, yeah, I get that. But why aren't you doing something like this as a career? Why stick with PR when you hate it?"

"I'm not qualified for home renovation and design. It's just something I'm playing with. There's nothing practical about it, and with the debt and the alimony, I don't have the luxury of making some kind of career jump." Topping off her glass with the last of their second bottle of wine, she settled back into the sofa. "I'm slowly building up savings. Maybe someday I'll actually be free of this anchor around my neck. In the meantime, I have wine, excellent friends, and HGTV. That'll have to be enough."

~

"AND JUST ONE MORE." Nyra Singh slid another sticky tabbed document in front of Wyatt.

He scrawled his signature for the hundredth time and felt his head ache as the letters of the contract swam on the page. This was the worst part of his business. He and the written word were not on speaking terms. Thank God Nyra was a trusted friend who could do the heavy lifting on this front and explain what was in the paperwork without him having to struggle through it all on his own.

He passed the contract across the table to the Wellings. Curt added his signature and dropped the pen, flexing his hand while his wife Megan signed the last line of the seemingly endless FHA loan paperwork.

"That is it. You're officially homeowners," Nyra announced. "I'll get all of this filed today and my secretary will have copies of all the paperwork ready for you to pick up tomorrow."

Curt wrapped his arm around Megan, and they both beamed at Wyatt. "We can't begin to thank you enough."

He grinned back, rising to offer a hand to the other man. "No thanks necessary. I'm delighted to know the house will be loved." It meant a lot that the property he'd poured his passion, blood, and sweat into would be a real home for this growing family. Just because he chose to live a somewhat itinerant lifestyle didn't mean he couldn't appreciate the value of a home.

Megan absently ran a protective hand over her small baby bump. "I love that we have a video record of the renovation from your YouTube channel, so we know what it started out as. Nobody would believe it used to look like *that*."

"Speaking of," Curt began, and Wyatt's stomach jumped. "I talked with my boss. He's interested in meeting with you, if you're game."

Holding in a whoop and a fist pump, Wyatt nodded. "I absolutely am."

"Fantastic. What is your availability?"

"I'm between projects for the moment. I'll make myself available whenever. Just name the time and place."

"Great! I'll text you the details as soon as I confirm."

"I'll be sure to be there."

After one last handshake, Wyatt handed over the keys and managed to wait until the Wellings had walked out of the office to do a little victory boogie.

This was *it*. His big break. He couldn't wait to tell Scott.

Nyra laughed. "Another successful sale down. I noticed there was an extra zero on that check from the last house you flipped. Getting bigger, better, and more profitable. Your brother will be proud."

Wyatt fought not to wince at the hitch around his heart at the mention of his brother. The reason for his whole career. The reason he even *had* a career. "Yeah, I think he'll be pumped."

"The funds should show up in your accounts tomorrow, split per your usual preference. I know you're eager to get on out to see him."

"I am, thanks."

She pressed a hand to his arm. "Tell him I said hi."

Wyatt gave her fingers a squeeze. "Thanks, Nyra."

The buzz of excitement kept him company on the drive to the other side of town. After a brief stop off to pick up milkshakes, he turned onto the campus of Fairland Village. The security guard at the gate looked at his decal and waved him on through with a smile. A tree-lined drive gave way to a cluster of buildings housing assorted therapy modalities, as well as apartments for the wide range of residents. It was, in a sense, a little self-contained village. As residential facilities went, it was a nice place, certainly better than some of the others they'd looked at. Here, Scott had access to round-the-clock care and top-of-the-line therapies and rehab specialists. Wyatt had been able to have him moved here two years ago on the profits from his flips. The progress he'd made in that time was sufficient motivation for Wyatt to keep funneling a portion of every single job toward keeping him here. By rights, part of the profits belonged to Scott, anyway. He'd been the one who'd taken the chance and bought the first house Wyatt had flipped. Before the accident and after, he'd always been Wyatt's biggest supporter.

The receptionist at the front desk beamed a sunny smile as he came through the door. "Hey there, Wyatt! I saw the latest episode. The house turned out great."

"Thanks, Jeannie. Just closed on it this morning."

"That's so exciting! What's your next project?"

He thought about spilling the beans about the upcoming meeting with CMT. Better not, just in case there was some kind of secrecy surrounding the network's potential move into home improvement television.

"Haven't settled on one just yet, but I'm hoping it'll be a bigger challenge." A full production show counted on that front, for sure. "Can you check the schedule and tell me where my brother is?"

Jeannie's fingers flew over the keys of her computer. "Looks like he's in with his occupational therapist."

Wyatt frowned. That was important rehab. The new therapist had started with Scott six months ago and was one of the biggest reasons for the improvement. "I don't want to interrupt."

"Oh, they should be wrapping in ten or fifteen. You go on back. I know Scott will want to see you, and he'll sure want that milkshake."

Following her directions, Wyatt made his way to the therapy room. The snarled curse stopped him from knocking on the door.

Inside, brow glistening with sweat, Scott flopped into a chair. "I'm never going to get this."

"You know how I feel about that word." The therapist's quiet voice was full of rebuke.

"It might as well be four letters," Scott said, clearly reciting an oft-repeated phrase.

"A huge part of your recovery is mental."

"I have a fucking traumatic brain injury, in case you've forgotten."

Unperturbed, the guy just packed up the light weights. "And look how far you've come in the last several months. You've been motivated. You believed you could improve, so you did. Why should that change now?"

"It's your fault. You made me believe I have a shot at independent living again."

"I believe you do."

Wyatt jolted. His brother might have a chance at a life on his own someday? It was an outcome he hadn't dared hope for.

"Then you're crazy."

"You've clearly had enough for today. We'll come back to this tomorrow. Meanwhile, I've got homework for you."

"Of course you do." Scott rolled his eyes. Or tried. It was more like rolling his entire head. "What is it?"

"Think about Chimney Rock."

Wyatt didn't understand what the man meant, but he didn't miss the pulse of tension that flared between them.

Scott blew out a breath. "I'll see you tomorrow."

The therapist turned and only then did either of them notice Wyatt. "You must be Scott's little brother."

"I am."

"Alton Howard. I've heard a lot about you."

"I wager maybe fifty percent is true."

"It's all true," Scott declared. "Best little brother ever."

"Now I know you've got a head injury."

Scott stuck out his tongue. "Is that a peanut butter milkshake?"

"Might be more like peanut butter milk at this stage. It kinda melted."

"It'll still taste good. Gimme."

Wyatt handed the cup over, making sure his brother had a good grip on it with both hands before letting go.

"I'll just let you two visit. I need to get ready for my next appointment. See you tomorrow, Scott."

Scott grunted agreement, attention apparently focused on the milkshake. But Wyatt saw the way his eyes tracked Alton's progress out of the room.

Rolling over one of the giant balance balls, he sat, sucking down some of his own milkshake. "So. How long have you been crushing on your OT?"

Scott's eyes flew to his. "I... I'm... I..." In his haste to rebut the statement, milkshake dribbled down his chin.

Since his hands were full, Wyatt dabbed at it with a napkin, adding conversationally, "I mean, he seems like a nice calm match for you in your surly bastard phase, and he's pushing you past what you think your limits are. Seems like a good fit."

Wyatt knew he'd hit pay dirt when Scott didn't shout at him for wiping his face.

"It's not like that. There's that whole therapist-patient thing."

"And if there wasn't that whole therapist-patient thing?"

Scott dropped his gaze and gave a rough jerk of his shoulders. "I'm a fucking mess."

"Seems like he's working to help you be less of one." He set his own milkshake aside. "I didn't know you were working on progressing to independent living."

"Didn't feel like mentioning it. It's a long shot. We all know that."

"But Alton thinks you could achieve it?"

"I'm pretty sure Alton is smoking crack. But I'm gonna try."

Wyatt didn't give a damn how the occupational therapist motivated his brother. Whatever he was doing was working. "Good for you." Not wanting to belabor the point, when Scott clearly didn't want to talk about it, he picked up his milkshake again. "In the category of other long shots, guess who has a meeting with an executive at CMT to talk about a real show."

"Seriously? How did that happen?"

Wyatt told him the story, no longer censoring his excitement. "I think this could really be my big break."

"That's fucking fantastic, bro. Really. I'm proud of you."

Throat going thick, Wyatt shrugged off the compliment. "There's that whole counting chickens thing. It may come to nothing." Not that he really wanted to entertain that possibility. Not when he was so close he could taste the success.

"Power of positivity, Wyatt. You go in there with your head held high. Don't take no for an answer. You're a fucking Sullivan. Sullivans know their worth."

Except he wasn't a Sullivan. Not deep down where it actually mattered. He knew well enough that Scott was worth ten of him. But mentioning it to his brother risked sending him into a conniption fit. Scott was the only Sullivan left who still counted Wyatt as family, and that meant he'd do whatever it took to make his brother proud.

CHAPTER 3

The Pyrex dish of Jiffy mix had hit her in the head. That was the only reason Deanna could come up with for why her skull pounded like a Nine Inch Nails concert. On a groan, she cracked open her eyes and spotted the wine bottles on the coffee table.

Oh right. That.

Bennet lay sprawled half on the other end of the couch, half on the lone ottoman, one arm thrown over her face. Her breath eased in and out on a little whiffling snore.

The room tipped in an alarming fashion as Deanna worked to shove herself vertical. Regrets. She had so very many regrets. The last time she'd drunk that much alcohol, she'd been celebrating the finalization of her divorce, and she'd learned then that she absolutely was *not* in college anymore. But she still remembered hangover protocol.

Electrolytes and grease. And maybe the entire contents of Old Hickory Lake.

But first she needed to pee.

After taking care of the essentials, Deanna staggered into the kitchen, pawing through the fridge for the coconut water she'd bought as a smoothie component and discovered tasted like ass. Beggars couldn't be choosers and all that. On a grimace, she guzzled it down, along with some ibuprofen. Another inventory of her fridge confirmed that nothing here fit the parameters of greasy breakfast. She wasn't sure she could cook just now, anyway. Maybe she could have something delivered. What time was it?

The microwave said nearly eleven. She was late for work. Thank God the firm allowed partial telecommuting now. So much of her job was on the road or out in the field. She'd work from home today so no one would see her looking like warmed-over death instead of a put-together professional.

"Please Lord, let none of my charges need anything today."

On autopilot, she put on the kettle for tea. Ginger wasn't her preference at this hour, but she figured it might settle her stomach. While the water heated, she ordered food for the two of them, then headed to her email to check for alerts about her clients on social media. She'd learned long ago that finding out about things early meant a better shot of controlling the narrative.

There was nothing about Mercy Lee and the cornbread debacle, but another subject line caught her attention.

Congratulations new homeowner!

Deanna frowned and started to delete the message unread. It had to be spam. She was as likely to have won a house as to be betrothed to an African prince. But some inner instinct urged her to open the email to check, just in case.

The message appeared to be the receipt from an online auction site. The picture in the listing was the historic home she'd been drooling over last night. And the total listed at the bottom? The entire contents of her savings.

The phone nearly slid straight from numb fingers as all the blood drained straight out of her head. Dizzy, she slumped against the counter. "No. No. No, no, no, no, no."

She had *not* drunk-bought a house, sight unseen. No way. She *wasn't* that foolish.

Ignoring the kettle that had come to a boil, she stumbled into the living room and dove for her laptop. Sure enough, her browser was open to the auction site. The listing of Blackborne Hall showed as sold. To her.

"Oh my God."

Bennet stirred. "Dee?"

Maybe the charge hadn't processed yet. If she could get in, put a stop payment on it... Frantic, Deanna logged into her bank account. But it was too late. Her savings showed a balance of three dollars and eighty-two cents.

Drowning in horror, grief, and dread, she sank back against the cushions with a groan.

"Are you crying?" Bennet levered herself up, scooping glossy black hair out of her face. "Honey, what's wrong?"

She made no effort to wipe away the tears steaming down her cheeks. "I bought a house last night." Saying the words aloud didn't make the situation feel any more real.

"You what?"

Reaching out, Deanna spun the laptop so Bennet could see. As her friend studied the page, a dim memory surfaced of marathoning *DIWyatt* and feeling invincible and capable, like she could do what he did. And in drunken, girl power fashion, Bennet had agreed.

"Oh, damn. This is bad. But maybe it's not final. Go check the terms of the auction site."

With a renewed spark of hope, Deanna clicked through, searching for some kind of escape clause. But that spark winked out almost immediately as the fine print made it very clear that all sales were final. There'd be no getting out of this.

"What the hell am I going to do? I can't afford a house!"

"I mean, apparently you could. That's a hell of a price for that much square footage and land."

Deanna couldn't even think about that. This wasn't the well-planned purchase and renovation she'd dreamed of doing. This was a disaster. "It's a project house."

"You wanted a project."

"Not *now*. Even if I could do the work myself, I have literally no money to renovate."

"Okay, so you sell it yourself."

"That listing had been up for something like two years, with multiple price reductions. I can assure you that it needs more than a thorough cleaning and a few coats of fresh paint." She buried her face in her hands. "How could I be so *stupid*? I couldn't afford to make another mistake, not after Blake. And here I've leapt without thinking—again."

"Maybe your family could help?"

Deanna whipped her head up and instantly regretted it as the room spun again. She fought back a wave of nausea. "No. *No*. They can't know. They already treat me like an irresponsible idiot. I can't give them this kind of ammunition."

"Fair point." Bennet laid a hand on her shoulder. "We'll figure this out. It's old, right? Maybe there are some historic home restoration grants or something. There's an answer out there somewhere. We're going to find it."

Deanna wished she had Bennet's faith. She was pretty sure she'd just ruined her life. Again.

"The meeting was a disaster." Wyatt punctuated the statement with a jab and a right cross that sent the heavy bag swinging.

Mateo Guerrero slid in behind the bag to stabilize. "What happened?"

Wyatt attacked the bag with renewed vigor. "I don't even know why the guy met with me. As a favor to Curt, maybe. I barely got a chance to say a word because this asshole is too busy telling me that while my skills with actual renovation are impressive, my following isn't big enough. The show isn't a unique enough premise. There's no story. No hook. I'm just small time and not ready for the big leagues." The next punch sang up his arm as it connected.

"Dick," Mateo pronounced. "Keep your wrist straight and fix your stance."

Wyatt did as instructed. When a former MMA title holder corrected your form, you listened.

From the next bag over, Griffin Powell glanced up. "Do you know what kind of car he drives?"

"No. Why?"

"Too bad. We could have put sugar in his gas tank."

Levi Roth grinned from where he braced the bag for Griff. "Or egg the paint."

The two men exchanged a look that made it abundantly clear that they'd gotten up to a whole host of troublemaking during their time with Joan. Wyatt was almost sad he'd missed it.

Mateo glanced over, one black brow winging up. "I thought you quit that shit after you got arrested back in high school. The Marines was supposed to be your straight and narrow."

Griff's grin flashed white in his close-cropped ginger beard, transforming his usually serious face. "I know a lot more about not getting caught now."

"I was good enough not to get caught in the first place," Levi boasted.

"You were fucking lucky is what you were," Griff told him.

"Keep telling yourself that, bro."

Wyatt's mouth kicked up on one side in a reluctant smile. What would it have been like if he'd stayed with Joan instead of being adopted by the Sullivans when he was twelve? If these three had been his brothers growing up? He wouldn't have had the same opportunities he'd had in a suburb of Nashville if he'd stayed in Eden's Ridge. But in the end, what had those opportunities mattered? He'd have been surrounded by a big, messy family that likely would have been as loving as they were maddening. And he'd have had longer with Joan, who was the best mom he'd ever known. Certainly she'd been more comfortable in the role than Marjorie Sullivan ever was.

But... he wouldn't have had Scott. The idea of that made his chest ache even as he acknowledged that his big brother might have been better off. Might still be the golden boy attorney on a fast track to greatness instead of living in a residential rehab facility for the traumatic brain injury that had effectively stolen his life.

A voice in the back of his mind whispered, *It should have been you.*

Shaking off the thought, Wyatt dragged his attention to the two men cheerfully suggesting various forms of payback. The great thing about having been one of Joan Reynolds' fosters was that they always considered you family. God knew, there were countless others she'd taken in. Her adopted daughters maintained the tradition of an annual family reunion now that they'd converted the house into an inn, which meant he'd reconnected with others who'd gone through her care. Some, like Mateo, he'd known before. Others, like Griff and Levi, he hadn't. But all had helped supply that sense of family he'd lost since the accident.

He needed that now more than ever.

"Earth to Sullivan."

Wyatt blinked at Mateo, realizing he'd missed everything his brother had said. "Sorry. What?"

"I asked what you were going to do now."

Wasn't that the million-dollar question?

"I don't know." With another series of irritable punches, he admitted the fear that had been dogging him since he left the producer's office. "Maybe I've gone as far as I can go with this. Flipping houses for a moderate profit and being a substitute bartender when things are lean." His college girlfriend and his parents had told him he'd never amount to anything. Maybe that was true after all.

"You actually giving up?" Levi asked.

"I don't know. Maybe." Though he couldn't imagine doing anything else. Not really.

Velcro shrieked as Griff unfastened his gloves. "That sounds like the chickenshit response."

Bristling at the insult, Wyatt couldn't help slapping back. "Because you've got your life all figured out since you left the Marines?"

"I'm doing okay. I made enough money as Kyle's bodyguard on tour that I can afford to take time to figure out my shit while he retreats from the public eye to do the daddy thing. And anyway, we're not talking about me. Are you really gonna let some network blowhard reduce what you've done almost single-hand-edly to nothing? Because fuck that shit. You've worked hard, and it shows. I bet his pansy ass doesn't have a single callus on his hand."

"Not from work anyway," Levi snarked.

He had busted his ass to become a master of his craft. It was good honest work, and no one got to diminish that. "You know what? You're right. Regardless of what he thinks, I love what I do, and I'm damned good at it." He might have all kinds of self-esteem issues, but none of them centered around building and restoring things. That he'd always been good at.

"Damned straight," Mateo agreed. "You just need a new project. Something you can really sink your teeth into."

"I need something bigger. Something that shows more of my capabilities and skills. Something I can document from start to finish and prove I'm not just small time. I just haven't found it yet."

"Well, when you find it, if you need another strong back, I've got some downtime. Griff's not the only one at loose ends. I know my way around a construction site," Levi offered.

"Appreciate that, man. I don't know what it'll be or when, but I'll keep you in mind."

"You came all the way down here to Hamilton. Maybe you should go check in with Carson at Reclamation Station while you're here," Mateo suggested. "I know how much you love that place."

It was true that the hardware salvage store was practically Mecca for Wyatt. A huge chunk of what he knew about restoration had come from old man Carson during all those summers he'd worked on salvage jobs with him. Carson usually had his finger on the pulse of what properties were about to be destroyed that had materials worth saving. Maybe he'd know of something that would be a suitable candidate for a more involved flip. If nothing else, Wyatt knew he could get on as hired labor for a deconstruction job or two while he waited for the next right project to appear.

"Yeah. I think that's a good idea."

Mateo slapped the heavy bag. "Good. Now that your head's clear, it's time to work. Hands up. Combinations."

CHAPTER 4

"*A*re you sure you don't want me to come with you? I can be there in forty-five minutes, as soon as I wrap the edit on this wedding video."

Deanna was already shaking her head, though Bennet couldn't see her over the phone. "No, there's no need for you to come all the way out here."

"Are you already there?"

"GPS says I'm a mile away." The closer she got, the tighter her hands clamped around the steering wheel.

"I can't believe you managed to stay away the last few days."

"That's more a matter of heading off the latest potential PR disaster where one of my clients decided it would be a good idea to pick a fight with fans on social media than lack of desire. Plus, I didn't get the keys until today." She'd needed those for it to feel really real. The deed with her name on it had gone a long way on that front, as well. Whatever she was into, she owned this place outright. The idea of that was still sinking in.

"Well, I'm available for whatever. Moral support. Hugs. Alcohol."

She cringed. "I may never drink again. That's what got me into this mess."

"Fair point."

The GPS's robotic voice filled the confines of the car. "Turn left in one hundred feet."

Deanna's pulse jumped, part dread but also part excitement. "Nearly there."

A board fence that might once have been white gave way to a tree-lined drive.

"Turn left."

On a deep breath, she turned, her tires crunching on gravel.

"You have arrived at your destination," the GPS announced.

"Well?" Bennet demanded.

"I'm not actually there yet. The driveway is pretty long and there are a lot of trees."

Almost as soon as she said it, the tunnel of trees opened up to what was technically a yard. Or had been in some long ago decade. Beyond it was the house, half swallowed by overgrowth. She pulled to a stop and took it in, noting the heavy columns holding up the massive front porch and second-floor gallery. At least she thought that was what lay under the vines. No wonder the pictures had been dark and crappy. There was no way to get decent shots of the full house for all the vegetation that had encroached.

"Deanna! Are you there?"

"Yeah. I'm here." She couldn't take her eyes off the house itself. Big and boxy, it was two stories of what had once been antebellum splendor. Now it was.... Well, it was hard to tell what it was.

"Well?"

"It's..." *Beautiful. Full of personality. It needs me.* "Big."

"Does it look... safe?"

Valid question given its age. "I don't think its going to collapse on me when I open the door. I'm gonna call you back later." She wanted to be alone with her thoughts this first time she took in the place.

"Take pictures!"

Deanna grunted a noncommittal noise and hung up.

Stepping out of the car, she approached the house. A breeze whispered through trees, and only the distant whine of a lawn-mower reminded her she hadn't stepped back into the past. Beyond the eight-acre lot, the rest of the world waited. But right here and now it felt like the house held its breath, waiting to be judged and found wanting. Or maybe that was just her.

She circled the perimeter. Several shutters were missing from the multitude of windows, and most of those that remained were missing louvers or were hanging catty wampus on a single hinge. But she could see how they'd have lent a stately grandeur and balance to the facade. Two chimneys anchored either side of the house, and a ramshackle structure that might optimistically be considered a sun porch was tacked on one side. Beyond it, she could make out the glint of water through more overgrowth. That turned out to be a choked and overgrown pond. Not somewhere she was venturing without long pants and sturdy boots. In the summer heat, snakes would be out.

Continuing on around the perimeter, she noted some kind of outbuilding set among more trees about fifty yards from the back of the house. A barn or carriage house. She'd check that out later. What she could see of the roof looked pretty good to her inexpert eye. No missing shingles or obvious dips. The siding that should've been white was dingy gray with mold, at least where the paint wasn't peeling. But her mind scrubbed it clean, reattached the shutters, cleared out the encroaching flora and replaced it with neat landscaping. In its day, Blackborne Hall was a beautiful house.

And it was hers.

Spinning in a circle, she began to grin. All of this was hers. Yes, the property looked a bit like something from where *The Wild*

Things Are, and bringing this old girl back to glory would take forever. But she wanted it. Wanted to do the work and put her stamp on the place. It could be her labor of love.

Of course, she'd have to give up her apartment to do it. The money currently going to rent would go at least some way toward repairs each month. No matter what she'd told Bennet, part of the house was bound to be habitable with a good cleaning and some paint. She could rough it and do the work. And have something of her own. Something untouched by Blake.

With a surge of renewed hope, she unlocked the front door and stepped inside. A garish, patterned wallpaper hung in tatters from the walls, missing in places where someone apparently started ripping it out. But oh... the staircase. She laid her hand on the newel post, running her fingers over the gorgeous millwork hidden beneath about a million layers of paint. The paint could be stripped and sanded, the treads re-stained and it would be a showpiece. It was a staircase meant for making an entrance. Her mind already filled in fresh greenery garlands on the banister for some future Christmas, and she could practically hear the notes of some classical Christmas album playing in her head.

The front parlor showed signs of rodent infestation. In a place this big, in this kind of condition, she might want to consider a cat. Except she wouldn't want one to get trapped somewhere in the chaos of renovation once that started. So maybe she'd just buy some traps and start there. The enormous windows were coated in a thick layer of dust on the inside and what was probably several seasons' worth of pollen on the outside. They obscured the view and the light. But that plaster ceiling medallion was gorgeous and in remarkably good shape. It needed a lovely, elegant light fixture to go with it. Something that fit with the picture in her head for how the rest of the room might be, with luxurious custom curtains and comfortable furniture arranged around the restored fireplace.

As she continued moving through the house, she made a

mental note of the signs of rot and mold, but they took a backseat to all the beautiful architectural features that just couldn't be found anywhere else. The picture rail and wainscoting in the dark dining room made the vines growing through a broken window worth dealing with. The built-in bookcases in what might once have been a study gave her fantasies of cozy winter days reading in an overstuffed chair, despite the abrupt way the room seemed to have been divided. In the room beyond that, which served no purpose she could discern, a wavy mirror propped against one wall looked like it might lead to another world. Everywhere she looked, she saw potential.

Then she found the kitchen.

"Oh, God."

It was… bad. Some previous owner had done a partial demo in here. Walls gaped open, revealing pipes and electrical wires. The brick floor was uneven and cracked in several places. A noxious odor made it clear some kind of wildlife was in residence. One entire wall showed clear signs of water damage, including the obvious evidence of mold, and it looked like all the cabinets were a lost cause. One of them looked in danger of crashing to the floor at any moment. As she gingerly opened a cabinet door, she was pretty sure she saw something scurry behind the avocado green fridge. The source of the smell? Or something else?

A little desperate, she tried to find something good about the room, some glimmer of hope.

The antique faucet looked cool. She wondered if it was the original brass fixture. Moving to test the water, she twisted one of the knobs. With a horrifying shudder, the faucet began to groan and spit, until a stream of foul looking water gushed into the sink. No telling how long it had been since any of this plumbing had been used. Deanna reached to turn it off, and the knob spun right off into her hand.

Dumbfounded, she could only stare at it for a moment as water continued to beat into the sink. Maybe she could twist it back on? Fumbling with the knob, she attempted to reattach it with no success.

The phone in her pocket vibrated, propelling her into motion. No time for whoever was on the other end of the line.

"Shut-off valve. Gotta find a shut-off valve."

But there was none under the sink. None of the plumbing down there looked like what she grew up with. A further search of the surrounding rooms turned nothing up. She didn't have the first clue where the shut off was for the main house, and even if she did, she didn't have a water meter shutoff key. Did a house this old even use something like that? That was a question for later. If she didn't do something, water was just going to keep on running.

What if the pipes were bad? What if this constant stream of water meant the leak got worse and did more damage? What if something straight up exploded and flooded the house while she was out trying to find help?

Bowing under the weight of all the what ifs, Deanna acknowledged the truth. This was all another gigantic mistake. She was in serious trouble, and no amount of dreaming was going to save her.

WYATT STEPPED inside the twenty-thousand-square-foot warehouse that made up Reclamation Station and paused for a few moments, soaking up the scents of wood and metal and dust. This place was his own personal Cave of Wonders, and he was Aladdin, more than willing to get lost in here for hours, exploring the myriad of treasures. But this wasn't a pleasure trip. At least, not to start. He needed to speak with Carson first.

Ignoring the lure of the rows of salvage doors and the siren song of all the bins of antique cabinet hardware, Wyatt made his way down the center aisle. In the center of the warehouse, a two-story office had been erected. The lower level had wide counters and pass-throughs where employees could help waiting customers. Up a set of spiral stairs was the office proper, where Carson liked to look out through the reclaimed windows on his little kingdom. The whole thing had a kind of treehouse vibe that delighted Wyatt. It was a unique showcase of upcycling and reinvention.

Carson Colwell himself was behind one of the ground-floor counters. An old man of indeterminate age, with a shoe-leather face half hidden by a wiry silver beard that he'd grown long to make up for his balding pate, he habitually wore red suspenders with everything. Today it was a pair of ancient painter pants and a gray T-shirt with the Restoration Station logo. Wyatt had always privately thought of him as Santa's redneck cousin. But the rosy cheeks and unquestionable belly didn't diminish his capability at all. The man had probably forgotten more about historic restoration than Wyatt could ever hope to learn.

"Wyatt Sullivan! Haven't seen you for an eon. How'd that Craftsman flip go?"

"Just closed on it a few days ago for a tidy profit."

"Good, good. What can I help you find today? What are you working on?"

"Nothing at the moment. None of the properties I've looked at have been the right fit." Not having one lined up was making him twitchy. "Your ear is always to the ground. You hear about anything interesting coming available?"

"Well now, most of what I've been hearing lately are folks looking for contractors to do renovations on their current homes."

Certainly Wyatt was more than capable of that, but there was the matter of where he'd live for the duration of the project. There was only so much couch surfing he could reasonably do, and he wasn't ready to make the jump to a travel trailer or some kind of property of his own.

"No enticing candidates for flips?"

"Not off the top of my head. At least not the kind you like."

Meaning none with much historic interest. Not that he couldn't work on a newer house, but those were less interesting to both him and to his viewers. If nothing else turned up in the next week, he'd consider it for the sake of keeping the momentum going on his income, but it wasn't his first choice.

"Well, something is sure to come up. Meanwhile, do you suppose you could use me on any deconstruction jobs? I find myself with idle hands."

"I can always use somebody with the skills to tear down without breaking. There's this property out in—"

"Excuse me, I really need some help." At the desperate tone, they both turned, and Wyatt lost his breath.

Her hair fell in burnished gold waves down her shoulders. Fine-boned features were set in lines of panic, but that did nothing to detract from the picture she made in that tidy little skirt and blouse that absolutely didn't fit this place. Slim hands moved restlessly as she spoke.

"—I literally had to leave my house with the water still running in the kitchen because this broke off, and I couldn't turn the faucet off or find the main shut-off valve." She held out a faucet knob to Carson. "I'm praying I don't get back to find a flood. Help!"

Damsels in distress were Wyatt's kryptonite. "Just curious. Why did you come here instead of calling a plumber?"

Irritation rolled off her in waves as she turned heated hazel eyes his way. "Because I have no idea if a regular plumber can work on antique plumbing, and—" Her eyes widened as she fully focused on him. "You. You're DIWyatt."

Delighted to be recognized, he offered a smile. "I am." But his good humor disappeared in short order as her gaze narrowed.

"This is all your fault."

Too surprised to be offended, he only blinked. "Come again?"

She waved a hand in his direction. "You… with all your videos and your know-how. You make all this shit look easy, when it's totally not."

The profanity made him like her more, even if he didn't understand what she was talking about. "Well, I—"

But the woman simply rolled right over him, words spilling out in a torrent, as if now that she'd started, she couldn't turn them off any more than the faucet she'd apparently broken. "I thought I could do this. I thought I could take on a restoration slowly, in my own time, and I just can't. I'm not even started, and I'm going to lose my house and be excommunicated from the family and hear I-told-you-sos until I'm six feet under. And I never would have even *thought* about it if not for you."

Wyatt might have been offended at the accusation if she hadn't appeared so absolutely panicked and defeated. The whole point of his show was to empower people to do things themselves. He'd inspired her. That went a long way toward soothing the ego left wounded by CMT network execs.

Wanting to comfort, he took a half-step toward her, only just stopping himself from reaching out. "I'm sure it's not as bad as you think it is."

She sucked in a breath, and her eyes went shiny.

Oh fuck. Please don't cry. He absolutely, positively, could not handle a woman in tears.

"Look, I've got some time. Why don't I come out and help you with your faucet problem?" Even if he was only partly responsible for her biting off more than she could chew, it felt like the least he could do. Offering help was second nature.

"He's one of the best," Carson added. "He'll take good care of your house."

"You'd do that?" The look of hope on her face about cut him off at the knees, even as it made him feel ten feet tall.

"Sure. I can at least get the water shut off so you don't have to deal with flooding. Then we'll see what's what." Maybe he could give her a better evaluation of the project she'd taken on and make some suggestions about what was and was not a reasonable DIY fix.

On a long, slow inhale, she closed her eyes. The shoulders that had been halfway to her ears relaxed a little, and her hands unclenched. They were ringless, he noted, with a neat French manicure. Not someone who worked with her hands. Good to know.

"Thank you."

Wyatt held out his hand to Carson for the knob, then gestured toward the front of the warehouse. "After you Miss..."

"James. Deanna James."

CHAPTER 5

"*E*ureka!" Wyatt's muffled voice came from beneath the house, where he'd disappeared in search of the main water shutoff.

It never would have occurred to Deanna to check in the crawl-space. She wasn't squeamish about getting dirty, but belly crawling under there in the dirt, without a flashlight, unable to see what creepy critters with too many or too few legs occupied the dark was not something she had any inclination to do. And in her business attire from work, she certainly wasn't dressed for such an expedition.

Wyatt backed out of the dark hole of the crawlspace, and she tried not to notice how well those faded jeans cupped his ass. "If it were me, I'd absolutely put in another, more accessible shut off."

She wondered if he'd covered how to do that on his show. "How did the pipes look under there?"

"I didn't do a full inventory, but they didn't look as bad as you might expect. Somebody replaced the plumbing at some point. It's not new by a long shot, but it's not all galvanized pipe, so it's got life left in it, I think." He brushed dirt and cobwebs from his rich, dark hair and off his clothes. "Now, let's go see what's what."

Circling back around to the front, Deanna led him inside. "Welcome to Blackborne Hall. Or maybe hell. Jury is currently still out."

Wyatt tipped his head back and scanned the foyer. "I had no idea this place was here. When was it built?"

"I don't know for sure. Sometime during the 1850s. There may be more information on the place somewhere, but I haven't had a chance to track it down." Certainly, the documentation that had come from the auction was limited.

He said nothing as he took in the space. Was he seeing the faded beauty or the disaster zone?

Bracing herself for judgment, she led him into the kitchen, where the water had stopped gushing in the sink. There didn't appear to be fresh water anywhere else at first glance, so her fears of a flood faded. Small miracles.

Two steps into the room, Wyatt stopped dead. "Wow."

Her shoulders tightened. She knew it was a hot mess. If he said something about how foolish a purchase this place was—

"That pressed tin ceiling is gorgeous."

Looking up, Deanna saw what he did. She'd been so overwhelmed by the rest, she hadn't noticed it before. Paint was flaking off across the whole surface, but the actual pattern of the ceiling tiles appeared to be intact. The ornate design lent elegance to a room that was otherwise a complete disaster. This was the silver lining of the room she'd been looking for.

Without commenting on the rest of the mess, Wyatt moved over to the sink and examined the faucet. "Long run, you'll want to replace this, but I think I can get it functional for you for now."

"That would be much appreciated." Anything she could put off in favor of the more important stuff would help.

"Let me get a few things from the truck."

He strode out, leaving her alone for the moment. She looked back at the ceiling, wondering how tough it would be to get the panels down, strip off the old paint, and reattach them. The idea of it had fresh hope dawning. Or maybe that was Wyatt himself.

Of course, he understood. His entire show was about taking houses in terrible shape and transforming them. That was exactly why she watched it. So maybe they were kindred spirits on that front. It wasn't fair to treat him as if he was judging her by the same standards as her family. Nor was it reasonable to blame him for her poor decisions.

He came back into the room, wearing a tool belt that drew her eyes to his narrow waist and those long, powerful legs.

Eyes up top, James. You are not here to ogle this gift horse.

"I'm sorry," she blurted.

He glanced up. "For?"

"It wasn't fair of me to blame you for getting me into this mess."

His lips curved into an amiable smile. She'd wondered whether that was only for the show. Looked like it was just him.

"No worries. You're hardly the first person to panic over the true scope of a home renovation. I like knowing my show inspired you to buy this place."

"Well, it inspired me to think about it. It was copious amounts of wine that pulled the trigger on the auction." Deanna grimaced and wished she'd kept that part to herself.

"You bought this at auction?"

She appreciated that he didn't comment on the drunk part. "Online. I didn't really know what I'd bought until I got here. The pictures were terrible."

"You didn't even tour it first?"

"I'd intended to, in a get a clearer picture of whether buying and restoring a historic house myself was an attainable goal kind of way. Then I had a run-in with my ex-husband at work, and my best girlfriend came over with therapeutic wine, and when I woke up the next morning, I'd bought a house."

There was a beat of silence.

"Well, that's certainly one of the more interesting acquisition stories I've heard. What sort of work do you do?"

Really? He wasn't going to comment on the hazards of... any of that?

"I'm in public relations in the music industry."

"Yeah? Bet that's interesting."

"It's... something. A lot of the time I feel like a glorified babysitter for spoiled celebrities." As if she'd conjured one of them with the words, her phone rang. One glance at the screen showed her Mercy Lee was calling. Wincing, she sent the call to voicemail and waited for Wyatt to ask what famous people she'd met, as most people did. But he surprised her.

"So you've got some aggression to work off on a project. This house should fit the bill. Lots of demo to do. Did you get a decent deal?"

"Based on the size of the house and the property, I got a steal. I think maybe somebody screwed up the listing. The auction ended at midnight instead of noon. It had been on the market for a long damned time, apparently. Some past owner got it on the national historic registry, so nobody could just buy and bulldoze to make way for another McMansion."

"Sounds like the Universe is looking out for this place."

"It'd be nice if it looked out for me." She didn't realize she'd said it aloud until he took a step toward her and rested a hip against the counter.

"Maybe it is."

Deanna blinked up at him, noting his eyes were the exact shade of her favorite charcoal gray sweater and somehow just as warm. Was he... flirting with her?

Almost as soon as the thought crossed her mind, he straightened. "Faucet's fixed, for now. Show me the rest."

Cursing herself as an idiot twice over, she did as he asked. Of course, he didn't mean he could or would take care of her. No man had ever done that, and she sure as hell wasn't going to start expecting it now. The only person she could truly count on was herself. Well, and her girlfriends. But Wyatt Sullivan was a legitimate contractor with a great deal of knowledge and interest in historic homes. And he was here, so she'd take advantage of his expertise and pick his brain as far as he'd let her.

"The house is, what? About four-thousand square feet?"

"Forty-two hundred heated, according to the paperwork."

Wyatt stepped past her onto the screened-in side porch. "I'd wager this is another three hundred. For looks, I'd say eighty-six the screens, replace those posts with sturdy cedar beams, or wrap them if they're salvageable. It'd make a nice place to sit and have a beer at the end of the day. Especially if you clear out all that vegetation blocking the view to the... what is that? A lake? Pond?"

"I didn't get close enough to see how big it is. Looks might not matter at the height of summer. We don't know how bad the mosquitos will be."

"Fair point."

They moved through the rest of the first floor, checking out the half bath with a functioning, if filthy, toilet. There were more signs of started and aborted efforts at renovation in several other rooms, plus a warren of smaller ones that didn't seem to fit with what she knew of the architecture of the time period.

"I think maybe somebody hacked up some larger rooms to create these smaller ones. The original layout probably mirrored the other side of the house."

"How hard would it be to open them back up?"

"Well, you never quite know until you open up walls, but theoretically, not bad. They probably aren't load bearing, so unless they ran some pipes up through there for something upstairs, it should be easy enough."

They finished the lower floor and began moving up the stairs. Not rotten, thank God.

Wyatt's hand stroked over the banister. "Damned fine craftsmanship. They don't make them like this anymore."

A warm glow of gratification settled in her chest that he saw the potential she did. "Right? This is a staircase designed for someone to make an entrance."

He nudged her toward the window on the landing and mimed like he was framing a shot. "Great view."

Deanna's cheeks heated. Was he talking about *her?*

"You could totally build in a window seat right here to look out over the property."

She glanced over her shoulder, through the dirty panes to the rolling hills beyond. Not her. The land. Of course, it was the land.

Idiot. You've read too many romance novels with contractor heroes. This is not She Shed Casanova.

Embarrassed, she moved on up the stairs.

Her phone rang again.

"Do you need to get that?"

"She can wait."

The second floor was divided into four bedrooms, two baths, and they found a second staircase leading down the back of the house. The rooms were dark, dingy, and also appeared to have a rodent problem. One of the bedrooms had spongy floors, with clear water damage that matched the pattern of the ceiling above. More evidence of aborted renovation showed up here.

"It's like whoever had the place before just started randomly ripping things out, trying to see what problems there were," Wyatt observed.

There were many. So many that were beyond her capabilities. She could learn a lot, but not this much. And beyond a basic toolbox for maintenance, she didn't have the tools needed for any of this. That alone would eat into the money she'd be able to repurpose for the next month or two. So much of this project called for skilled labor, which meant hiring people. She didn't have the budget for that, which meant this dream she'd been entertaining wasn't attainable after all. She wrestled with that as they took the second stairway down to the first floor and came out through a door that led into the kitchen.

Wyatt turned to face her. "You've got a helluva house here, Deanna. So much potential and character." He took a step closer to her.

Her pulse picked up as she became abruptly aware of the height and breadth of him. She'd watched his show, thought she'd understood the scope of his size, but it was nothing compared to standing beside him as he looked down at her, his face alight with interest. In the moment, it felt as if they were in this together, bonded over mutual fascination with history and architecture. She caught herself about to raise a hand and step into him.

Don't be stupid.

She'd imagined the connection between them, just seeing what she wanted to see because he was a nice guy who seemed to share her vision. It wasn't real. After everything she'd been through, she was more than done with imagined connections with pretty men.

"I want to work on this house. I want to help you make it what it wants to be."

The yearning in her chest was so sharp, it felt like a knife. "You have no idea how much I want to take you up on that, but I can't."

"Do you already have a contractor?"

"I can't afford to hire anyone to restore the place. I'm financially in over my head. I wiped out my savings to buy it, and there's almost nothing left to put into even the most basic facelift. Needless to say, this wasn't at all how I wanted to do this. I have to acknowledge that I made a great, big, expensive mistake. At this point, I just want to get it in decent enough shape to sell to someone—anyone—so I can recoup my losses."

THIS ANTEBELLUM BEHEMOTH was exactly the sort of project Wyatt itched to sink his teeth into. Beneath the rough condition lay a showpiece. Restoring it was the kind of big and impressive that could get producers to sit up and take notice. They wanted more. Blackborne Hall absolutely fit the bill. He could buy it. Maybe.

"How much are you in for?"

Deanna named a figure that had his brain spinning. With the profit off the last flip, he could afford it, but he wouldn't be much better off than she was now in terms of funds to leverage toward the renovation. Not a good place to be on a flip, even if he didn't have the pressure of a mortgage payment. Then there was Scott and the cost of his care. He wasn't solely responsible, but he couldn't afford to juggle this place and other flips with an eye to profit. There was only him and Simon and the occasional volunteers. Even if he took up Levi on his offer, he didn't have the luxury of a full crew.

All that aside, this woman didn't want to sell. His question hadn't spawned hope in her expression, the way his earlier offer of help had. She'd looked like she swallowed bad sushi, as if parting with it made her physically ill.

"Why did you buy this place? I mean, apart from the wine impulse. Why did you want it or some other old home instead of a new construction that doesn't need so much work?"

Deanna remained quiet for several long moments, her gaze skimming over the room. "This house, in a lot of ways, represents my life. I guess I feel like if I can come in here and not only see the possibilities and potential but actually bring them to fruition, then there's still hope for me. I want to live in a world where character matters."

Wyatt hadn't expected such a raw and honest response, and given the bloom of color in her cheeks, she hadn't meant to give it. On the surface, Deanna James looked like a polished professional, with her wavy blonde hair, flawless makeup, and that little pencil skirt that made his hands itch to touch. But she had something to prove. That was a drive he understood down to his marrow. His chest went tight with an unexpected sense of kinship.

Her phone rang again. This time, she offered a wince of apology and answered. "Yes, Mercy Lee?"

Mercy Lee? As in Mercy Lee Bradshaw? Damn, she really was working with some famous people.

"I've been in a meeting. What can I do for you?" Her manicured fingers tapped the counter as she listened. "You insisted you needed an interview in *Songbird*. The whole spread has been arranged and the shoot with the photographer is next week."

The fingers curled into a fist, the knuckles going white, but Deanna's calm, neutral tone never wavered. "How does the fact that Taylor Swift is appearing in it this month have any bearing on your center spread next month?"

As he listened to her smoothly and confidently talk Mercy Lee off of whatever the hell ledge she was on, explaining what the interview would do for her career, it occurred to Wyatt that he could use someone like her. Someone who understood the nuance of public relations and social media and how best to use it for a specific aim.

By the time she hung up, he'd decided to do something a little bit reckless and a whole lot driven by a desire to thumb his nose at the asshat who'd basically told him, "No, you're not good enough." He was so done with anyone who believed that.

She heaved an exhausted sigh. "Sorry about that. My job interrupts a lot."

Wyatt leaned one elbow on the kitchen counter. "I have a proposal."

"I can't afford to take any less on the house."

One corner of his mouth kicked up. "I'm not trying to buy it. But I do want my hands on it. I'll do the work, with whatever help you can pitch in, pay for whatever materials you can't afford, if I can film the whole process for my show."

She blinked at him. "But... you never film renovations of other people's property."

He really liked that she'd watched enough of his show to know that. "There's a first time for everything. Here's the thing: I need a bigger project. The kind of thing that can help draw in more interest, more viewers. I want to build my YouTube following enough to leverage for a proper show, and it sounds like maybe that's an area you know something about. You could use some of those professional PR skills to help me out with that. In the end, you'll have a fully restored house you can sell for top dollar. When it sells, we split the profit. You'll have enough to not only buy, but renovate another old home if you still want, and you'll have learned the skills you need in order to actually do it."

This time she studied him during the silence, her expression a neutral mask. He wondered what was going on in that head of hers.

"Are you on Instagram? IG TV? Facebook? Anywhere you have actual interaction with your fanbase?"

Was all that required? Wyatt rubbed a hand on the back of his neck. "Um... no?"

"Bless your heart. You need me as much as I need you."

He was too excited to take offense. "So we have a deal?"

"Qualified." She held up one manicured finger. "You have to actually listen to me. I already babysit a bunch of entitled people who can't be bothered to follow directions and then blame me when they don't get the results they want."

He held up three fingers. "Scout's honor. And same goes on the listening. Renovations can be dangerous if you're not careful."

She nodded and held out a hand. "We agree to respect each other's professional capacities."

Wyatt took it, wrapping his fingers around hers, surprised at the strength of her grip. "There's just one more thing."

"What's that?"

"Part of how I've been able to do all the restoration and flipping I've done is by living in the house I'm flipping. I just sold my latest project, which is how I've got money to put into this, so I don't have a place to live at the moment. I'd need to move in here."

She bit her lip, which only served to draw his attention to the pretty pink of them. It was probably a terrible thing to notice the attractiveness of his prospective business partner.

"Here's the thing. I also have to move in for financial reasons. I can't afford to have this place and keep my apartment."

Was she going to balk? She didn't seem totally comfortable with the idea of moving in with him, and Wyatt certainly couldn't blame her. He was a stranger and a man.

"Look, that's weird for you, and I get it." He needed to find a way to convince her not to walk away from this opportunity. He needed references. "You work in country music. Do you know Kyle Keenan?"

Deanna stiffened and pulled her hand away. "I'm not introducing you."

Wyatt laughed. "Not asking you to. His bodyguard, Griff Powell, can vouch for me. Do you know him?"

"You know Griff?"

"He's a foster brother of mine."

She hesitated. "Then... wouldn't Kyle be one, too?"

"So you know something about Joan Reynolds' kids?"

"I actually stayed at The Misfit Inn right after it opened a couple of years ago. Your sisters—foster sisters?—are lovely."

"They are." Wyatt had a soft spot for Pru, Joan's eldest adopted daughter, who'd been the one to maintain the vast network of the family in their mother's absence. "Anyway, yeah, technically Kyle is also a foster brother, but we weren't raised together. I've never met him. Griff actually knows me. Talk to him. See what he says. If you're comfortable, then we'll both move in and get started on this thing."

"I'll do that. Serious question, though. Is it actually safe for us to live here? I mean, isn't stuff like asbestos and lead a concern? And there's definitely mold."

"No question we'll need to do some cleaning up. I'll get the water back on and confirm the functionality of the bathrooms. That'll be top of the list for priorities. But three of the four bedrooms are in decent shape, at least in terms of stability. And we can set up a temp kitchen and sort of lounge area in the front parlor. As to asbestos, the house is old enough that it shouldn't be an issue. Not saying there's none, but it shouldn't be the kind of thing we'd need to bring in a team for abatement, and I'll certainly check for both that and lead before we start tearing out walls and floors and stirring up the kind of dust and debris that would be a problem. I'll do a more thorough evaluation before we set up camp and figure out what needs to be immediately addressed. Does that work for you?"

After a long hesitation, her mouth turned up into a hopeful smile. "Mr. Sullivan, I believe we have a deal."

CHAPTER 6

From the front seat of Deanna's car, Bennet bounced like an over-sugared toddler. "I'm so excited to finally see the place!"

Deanna only managed a tight smile that she suspected was more of a grimace. The idea of showing the house to her friends had sweat breaking out along her spine. But she was past the point of no return. Her lease had officially been broken, and several of her closest girlfriends were presently caravanning out to Blackborne Hall with all of her worldly possessions. Not that she had all that much after her divorce.

Over the past week, she and Wyatt had worked like dogs to make the house habitable for the duration of the renovation. They'd each chosen a room, and he'd determined the functionality of the bathroom they'd be sharing. Once they got into the walls to find out whether the rest of the plumbing had ever been replaced, they'd be able to determine whether that had to be on the immediate agenda. Traps had been set to deal with the rodent issue, and he'd re-homed a raccoon that had taken up residence in the laundry room via the hole for the dryer vent—now covered. The vines growing into the dining room had been removed and the windows temporarily boarded up. Above all, they'd cleaned and aired the place out. According to Wyatt, she'd gone above and beyond on that front, given demolition was slated to start as soon as the dumpster was delivered, but damn if she was moving her things into what felt like decades of nasty. She'd accepted she was moving into a construction zone, but she still had standards. It was far better than it had been the day she'd first seen it, but it was still rough, and she worried about what her friends would say.

As they turned into the drive, Bennet clapped her hands. "We're here! We are here, right? This is the driveway?"

"Yes." The closer they drew to the house, the tighter her chest got, until they broke free of the trees. The breath exploded out of her in shock.

In the two days since she'd last been out here, Wyatt had cleared away much of the overgrowth, fully exposing the front facade of the house, revealing shades of the grand dame she'd clearly been. Sunlight glinted off the freshly cleaned windows, and the yard, such as it was, had been mowed.

"Oh, wow," Bennet breathed.

"Welcome to Blackborne Hall."

Deanna parked to one side, leaving room for Jasmine to pull her SUV with the U-Haul trailer by the front steps.

They spilled out, automatically craning their necks to try to take in the whole thing.

"This place is gigantic!" Wendy exclaimed.

Jasmine stared at the house over the tops of her sunglasses. "I can't believe you're taking all this on."

Feeling defensive of her baby, Deanna aimed for a confident tone. "It's ambitious, but I'm really excited about it. One of the previous owners replaced the roof, so that's one big expense I won't have to take on. The rest, I'll simply deal with as I go."

They all exchanged a look.

"Are you... sure you really want to live here while you reno?" Adry asked.

"I don't have much choice. Look, I know it needs work, but that was the point. I wanted a project. It's going to be beautiful when I'm finished." Even as she said it, Deanna realized she'd be making it beautiful for someone else.

A sick feeling set up in her gut. She didn't want to put in all the time and effort only to lose the place in the end. But it was the only reasonable alternative, and she hardly had a right to be upset about it. In the long run, Wyatt was giving her an amazing deal. Not that she'd mentioned the terms of that to her friends. Her new roommate was something else she worried about their reactions to.

Bennet squeezed her shoulders. "I'm sure it will be lovely."

"It's got a damned sight more personality than that palace to modern architecture Blake talked you into," Jasmine observed.

The palace he'd somehow won in the divorce.

Save it for demo day. Wyatt promised you a sledgehammer.

Wendy clapped her hands. "Okay people, let's get unloaded. Everybody grab something."

As they converged on various vehicles, Deanna went to check the door and found it locked. Where was Wyatt? She didn't see his truck. Unlocking the door, she pushed it open, wondering if there were any other surprises waiting inside.

Now that the power was on, lights illuminated more signs of rot and decay. But it didn't smell disgusting anymore. Not in here, anyway. The kitchen... Well, it needed a lot of help and was first on the list for demo day. As her friends came in, hauling boxes, she waited for their commentary on the state of the place.

"Does anybody else feel like they just walked into Mrs. Havisham's house, southern edition?" Wendy asked.

"With all that rolling land, I'm kinda feeling a Jane Austen aesthetic," Adry said. "Like one of those genteelly impoverished ladies. Can't you totally see a fainting couch in front of that big window?"

"Are we hoping for a gentleman of means to come woo Deanna?" Jasmine asked.

"I am not interested in being wooed, thank you very much."

"Maybe just a hot stableboy for a steamy affair. There should totally be one with a place like this," Jasmine mused. At Deanna's bland stare, she just shrugged. "What? You've got needs that deserve to be met from something other than your toy collection."

Cheeks on fire, Deanna was suddenly grateful for Wyatt's absence. "Can we *not* talk about that?"

"I'm getting strong post-war Tara vibes," Bennet observed.

"I think there might have been a sweet potato in the last of the food we packed up from the kitchen. If you like, I can do my best Scarlett O'Hara impression about how I shall never go hungry again," Deanna offered. "Or I can give you a quick tour of where we're putting stuff."

"I mean, if you want to be all practical about it."

Because the vast majority of the house would have work being done, everything that wasn't an absolute necessity was staying in boxes and being piled into the downstair room that needed the least work. As projects were completed, she'd shift things around to a more permanent home. She led them upstairs to the room she'd earmarked as hers, at least for now.

"Just put stuff in the corner, so there's room to assemble the bed."

Bennet carried her box into the adjoining bathroom. "Uh, Dee? I think you've got a problem."

"Is something leaking?" Paranoid, she stepped inside, only to find that Bennet had gone all the way through to the bedroom on the other side.

There was a cot with a sleeping bag in one corner and a duffel bag of clothes. A series of milk crates lined one wall and organized some other stuff.

"I think you've got a squatter," Bennet hissed.

"No, she's got a contractor." Wyatt stepped into the room.

Bennet's eyes went wide, and she blindly slapped at Deanna's arm. "Girl. You got DIWyatt to renovate your house?"

He grinned. "That is the plan, yes."

"What's going on?" Jasmine came through the bathroom, trailed by Wendy and Adry. She drew up short as she spotted Wyatt, her mouth forming into an O before melting into a wicked grin.

Before she could share whatever observation she was about to make, Deanna leapt in to make introductions. "Wyatt, these are my friends, Bennet Hartley, Jasmine Meecham, Wendy Coolidge, and Adry Patel. They're here to help me move. Y'all, this is my contractor, Wyatt Sullivan of *DIWyatt.* He's going to be filming the renovation for his show, and I'm going to be helping him with PR in exchange for his assistance."

Bennet pointed to the cot. "And that?"

"He's living here during the renovation," Deanna explained.

"So you'll be roommates," Jasmine clarified.

"And business partners," Wyatt confirmed. "Speaking of which, the dumpster should be delivered this afternoon, so we can get started on demo. I'm scheduling a volunteer workday on Saturday and Sunday. The more hands we can get on deck, the faster that part will go, and the faster we can get into guts of the restoration."

Deanna certainly liked the idea of that. "Do you have plans for lining up volunteers?"

"A bunch of my family is coming. They might bring friends." He flashed another smile. "Yours are welcome, too."

"Oh, no way am I missing this," Bennet declared.

"Come ready to get dirty."

More footsteps tromped down the hall. "Wyatt, bro, where do you want the kitchen set up?"

A younger guy with smooth, bronze skin and close-cropped black hair stuck his head through the door. Deanna pegged him around twentyish. At the sight of everyone else, he paused, then flashed a blinding white grin. "Ladies."

"Y'all, this is Simon Boyd, my right-hand man. Excuse us."

As they trooped back downstairs, Deanna found herself the center of everybody's attention. Per usual, it was Jasmine who said what they were all thinking. "You're gonna be living with your hot contractor?"

"Not like that. We're just sharing space under the same roof. It's a big house." Although it didn't feel that big when she realized they'd only be separated by one little bathroom at night. Not that she was gonna bring that up.

"Not that big," Bennet muttered, as if reading her mind.

"Can we not? Please? I'd really just like to get everything unloaded."

They got to work, emptying vehicles, making endless trips up the stairs and to the temporary storage room. By the time they were ready to start with the furniture, Simon and Wyatt had the temporary kitchen set up in the front parlor. Sawhorse counters were arranged in an L-shape. A microwave, slow cooker, and a hot plate were ranged across the top, and a series of more stacked milk crates made a sort of cubby system underneath for supplies and cookware. A dorm-sized mini-fridge sat at one end, with a plastic bin of the kind used for bussing tables perched on top.

Deanna went brows up. "This is really well thought out."

"Well, I've been doing it this way a long time, so I've more or less got the system fine-tuned. The microwave is also a convection oven, and there's a grill out back, too." At her blink of surprise, Wyatt just grinned. "Did you think I lived off of takeout all the time?"

"I mean… kinda." She'd just assumed he worked hard enough that he burned it all off. There was no sign of a gut beneath that T-shirt.

"I eat my fair share, but it's usually cheaper to cook. And I make a mean grilled pizza and burgers."

Her stomach growled at the mention of food. "Saying so without being prepared to immediately back up the claim is just mean."

"Still gotta stock the actual food, but soon. I promise."

He was going to cook for her? Blake had certainly never lifted a finger to prepare a thing. The idea of a guy who could not only cook but actually wanted to was novel enough to make her stare. Realizing she'd been doing just that, she dropped her gaze and brushed her hands off. "We'll have to discuss how we're gonna do groceries and meals and stuff."

"We'll work it out. Need some help with the furniture?"

Kicking her brain back in gear, she nodded. "Yeah. There's not too much left. I'm not quite sure we can get the bed upstairs by ourselves."

"No problem. Simon."

"Your wish is our command, my lady. But your worthy knights would appreciate payment in traditional Italian pies with extra cheese."

Wyatt hooked his arm around Simon's neck. "He's both a goofball and a bottomless pit."

"Attempting to fill the pit is the least I can do. Pizza and beer are the traditional moving day payment for a crowd."

Simon laid a hand over his heart and sketched a bow. "A noble-woman, indeed."

"This one's not legal drinking age yet."

"Dude! Nearly!"

"Two more months, little bro."

Deanna was still laughing at Simon's affront as she pulled out her phone to dial the order in.

~

WYATT STROLLED THROUGH THE HOUSE, excited as a kid on Christmas morning as he got footage of the Before. Demolition was often his favorite part of a project, ripping out the damaged, the dated, and the disgusting to reveal the canvas beneath. Sometimes it meant finding unexpected treasures, like original hardwoods or brick. Just as often, it revealed some kind of problem he wasn't expecting. He wondered what it would be today.

After the dumpster got delivered, he'd put out a call for volunteers on the family group text that included all the greater Nashville area foster siblings. Over the past couple flips, that had resulted in a solid showing of extra hands. He'd met a bunch of them at the last family reunion and had enjoyed getting to know the sibs he hadn't met during his time with Joan and hearing stories that were much like his own.

The front door opened and Simon called out, "Knock, knock!"

"Doesn't count as knocking when you're already inside." Which normally wouldn't bother him, but he had a roommate to consider on this flip. Deanna might not be comfortable with more folks just randomly walking in.

"Yeah, well, you've got incoming, and it looks like Mateo brought donuts."

The man in question stepped inside, bakery box in hand. "It's why I'm everybody's favorite brother."

"You're topping my list this morning." Wyatt lifted the lid and grabbed a chocolate glazed.

"I figure we'll work them off." Mateo handed the box off to Simon, who filched two and went to set the rest in their makeshift kitchen.

"That's for damned sure. It's a big house. A lot of work to do." Wyatt turned to take in the foyer, already imagining the wallpaper gone, though that wouldn't happen today.

"Room for two more?"

Wyatt turned to see Caleb Romero stride in, a willowy young woman behind him. In the entryway to the temporary kitchen, Simon made a choking noise, his mouth full of most of a donut. Hastily, he tried to swallow and fell into a fit of coughing.

Wyatt stifled a laugh and turned to Caleb and his step-daughter, Fiona. "Didn't expect you to be here. Isn't Emerson about ready to pop?"

Caleb's wife was very, very pregnant with their first child.

"That's exactly why we're here," Fiona explained. "She's due in a month, and Caleb's hovering is driving her nuts. She basically threw him out of the house. I'm here to make sure he stays out."

Simon swallowed and finally found his voice. "And Emerson is your...?"

"Godmother. Mom. Aunt. It's complicated."

"We kinda specialize in complicated family situations around here."

Fiona's mouth curved into a smile. "So I hear."

Wyatt could practically see the cartoon hearts popping out above Simon's head. This was gonna be interesting.

More vehicles pulled up out front. Griff and Levi came inside, trailed by Bennet and Jasmine.

"Thank y'all for coming." Wyatt made introductions.

"Where's Deanna?" Bennet asked.

"Stuck on a client call. She'll be down as soon as she shakes loose."

As everybody laid siege to the rest of the box of donuts, Wyatt briefed them. "So here's the plan. We're ripping up carpet everywhere there's carpet. Hopefully, there will be hardwoods throughout, but even if there isn't, the carpet's gotta go. In the rear section of the house, we're tearing out walls to open bigger rooms back up. I've marked all those with spray paint. In the kitchen, we'll be ripping out all the cabinets and walls. Ultimately, the brick floor will need some love, but we'll skip that for the moment. Most of these walls should be lath and plaster. If you come across any tongue and groove as you rip layers out, come find me. We want to salvage any wood we can. That includes any of the original trim. Pry bars, hammers, and sledgehammers are here. Let's talk about who's doing what."

Wyatt was in the middle of handing out assignments when Deanna thudded down the stairs. He caught a quick flash of fury on her face before she spotted the gathered volunteers and pasted on a facsimile of a smile.

"Good morning."

Despite the shorts and tank top, this was the PR professional, not the woman who'd been getting up well before the crack of dawn and putting in several more hours on the house after she got home from work. Wyatt found he preferred the unfiltered version of her. "For those of you who don't know, this is Deanna James. Blackborne Hall belongs to her."

He could still sense the simmer and bubble of her temper beneath the surface as he introduced the others. Rolling with the understanding that her client call hadn't gone well, he offered her a sledgehammer. "The lady of the house gets first swing. Where do you want to start?"

She curled her hands around the handle. "Kitchen."

"Perfect. Simon, go kill the power in the relevant sectors before we start tearing things down. Then you're on camera duty."

"You got it."

The others followed as Wyatt trailed Deanna into the kitchen. She eyed the room as if it had personally offended her. What the hell had happened on that call?

"Nothing in here is salvageable. We're tearing it down to studs." He steered her toward the water damaged wall and nodded toward the sledgehammer in her hands. "You know how to use one of these?"

"Heavy end hits the idiots in the head."

"I mean, that's one way."

"Wait, wait! I've got you, girl!" Bennet pulled a giant sharpie from somewhere and drew a stick man on the wall. Beside it, she added a stick woman. Above them, she scrawled "Blake" and "Mercy Lee," then stepped back with a flourish.

Jasmine snickered.

Before he could offer any instruction, Deanna hefted the hammer, slamming it straight into Stick Mercy Lee's face, caving in the plaster and laths beneath.

"Well, okay then." He'd known she had work ethic, but maybe those pretty, manicured hands were more capable than he'd expected. "Why don't we give you some time alone."

He redirected everyone else to other rooms, pausing to open all the windows for cross ventilation. When he came back to the kitchen, Deanna was still systematically destroying the wall. Stick Mercy Lee was already half gone. Keeping one eye on her, he began prying up countertops.

"So was it Mercy Lee on the phone this morning?"

"Of course it was." She swung the sledgehammer into Stick Mercy Lee's knee.

He'd been hearing bits and pieces of the bullshit she'd had to deal with as they'd worked together the past week. "Wasn't the interview and photoshoot for that magazine spread today?"

"Yep." Another leg caved in.

"Did she try to get out of it?"

"She tried to change the location at the last minute, when the photographer was already set up at the spot designated weeks ago. When all the staff and the reporter and a dozen other people are already on site preparing to make her look amazing. Because inconveniencing people means nothing to her." She knocked out the rest of Stick Mercy Lee.

"I'm afraid to ask if the shoot got moved."

"It did not get moved, and she will be where she's supposed to be—albeit late."

"Do I want to know how you convinced her of that?"

"Voodoo."

Wyatt couldn't tell if she was joking and decided it was safer not to ask as she started in on Stick Blake.

"What about Blake? Is he a client or the ex-husband?" He wondered which had inspired this fury of destruction.

"Ex-weasel."

"Got it." He ripped off trim from the side of the cabinets. "What'd he do to merit having the shit beaten out of him in effigy?"

With a savage glare, she growled again.

Wyatt lifted his hands in surrender. "Whatever it was, he obviously deserved it."

Deanna swung, taking out Stick Blake's arm. "I was fool enough to support the lazy son of a bitch while he pursued a music career—for *a decade*. I paid for the too lavish lifestyle he insisted he needed. I made a career entirely around learning how to make him look good. I fucking made him. And he thanks me by banging his mistress in our bed." She drove the hammer through Stick Blake's crotch. "And yet somehow, when I divorced his ass, I'm the one who got saddled with alimony and most of the debts he ran up in my name. Because it happens the judge was one of his daddy's golf buddies."

That explained a lot about her financial predicament. Wyatt couldn't fathom taking advantage of someone like that.

"Damn," Simon muttered. "Need someone to help you beat his ass for real? Because he totally deserves it."

When the hell had he wandered in?

Deanna whirled, her face going a little pale as she spotted the camera. "You can't post that."

"We won't post any footage of you without your express permission," Wyatt assured her. "Nobody will get used unless they sign a release."

"Offer still stands," Simon added.

One corner of her unpainted mouth quirked as she cleared broken laths with one gloved hand. "As gratifying as that would be, I'd be better off with a matchmaker. The only way I get free of him is if he marries someone else. Well, or pisses off someone else enough that he gets run over by a bus."

"Afraid I'm fresh out of matchmakers and buses. But we've got plenty of stuff for you to break." Wyatt yanked the counter away and dragged it to the pile on the other side of the room. "C'mon. Take a shot at this base cabinet."

"I'll take it." Choking up on the handle, she swung, crashing the sledgehammer into the end of the cabinet. Wood splintered and a satisfied grin peeked out.

"Feels good, doesn't it?"

"Yes. Yes, it does." She swung again.

Wyatt couldn't help but notice the bunch and flex of her surprisingly toned arms and the long, smooth legs exposed by her shorts. He *really* dug capable women, and Deanna James was proving to be both a quick learner and extremely competent. But beyond all that, he was finding all these brief glimpses of the woman underneath the mask as intriguing as the potential of Blackborne Hall itself. He remembered that unguarded moment here when she'd said that this house was like her life.

What would Deanna herself look like if all the bullshit in her world were stripped away and she could actually be herself? Would she even know what to do with that? And why did it feel just as important to help her with that as it did with the house?

She's a client, idiot.

Determined to redirect his attention from wondering if her skin was as soft as it looked, he reached to yank at the loosened base cabinet and found Simon with the camera pointed in his direction, tongue firmly in cheek.

CHAPTER 7

On a heartfelt groan, Deanna dropped to the front porch steps. At least that had been her intention. The reality was more like a slow folding of her creaky legs until her butt hit the stair tread. With a slow exhale, she pivoted the few necessary inches to lean against one of the front porch columns and closed her eyes, soaking up the blessed silence. After two days of furious, unrelenting hammering, prying, and sawing, the dumpster was full and their seemingly tireless volunteers were gone. Every single inch of her body ached, including a whole host of muscles she was reasonably certain had never been used in her life.

She'd never felt so satisfied.

She didn't bother opening her eyes at the sound of footsteps coming out the front door. "Just so you know, I'm sleeping out here tonight. There's not a chance in hell I can make it upstairs."

Wyatt's low chuckle rolled over her like warm molasses, eliciting an unwelcome clutch between her thighs. "This will help."

He wrapped her hand around a cold bottle. For a few moments, the feel of his touch overrode the aches and pains. Her awareness sharpened as his hands folded around her fingers, his calluses trailing over her skin as he placed something in her palm. Wary, she cracked open her eyes and stared at the little white pills.

"You wash it down with the beer."

Deanna could hear the amusement in his tone, but didn't dare look up at him. He'd be smiling, and in her current state, she wasn't at all sure she could avoid staring at his mouth. She kept her focus on the painkillers. He was taking care of her. It was a tiny thing. A simple, kind gesture. But it wasn't something she was used to from a man.

"Thank you." She tossed back the pills and washed them down with the crisp strawberry ale that tasted like heaven.

Wyatt dropped down beside her, holding up his own bottle. "To the end of demo. For now, anyway."

The musical clink of their toast was almost lost in the summer song of cicadas and frogs. Tipping her head back against the column, she stared out into the night. "It's nice to sit here and enjoy a cold drink after a hard day's work."

"Hard two days. You did good."

Uncomfortable with the praise, Deanna shrugged. "It doesn't take a tremendous amount of skill to destroy things."

"It does to keep from breaking shit you didn't mean to. You did really well pulling out that tongue and groove we found to use later. You're a fast learner, and you're not afraid to dig in and get your hands dirty." He sounded impressed by that. By her.

When was the last time that had happened anywhere but in her job?

"We'll see if you say that the further we get on this project. It will become more than apparent I don't know what I'm doing." She'd been painfully aware of it over the past week as he'd talked over the lengthy list of necessary repairs, recommendations, and renovations. Her notion that she could ever tackle such a project on her own was pure delusion. Thank God he was saving her from even more costly mistakes.

"You don't lack knowledge. It's obvious you know how to do

research and that you've done a lot of it prior to buying this place."

"A million hours of HGTV and YouTube hardly count as true education. There are miles of difference between theory and practice."

"Hey, don't knock it. Those are a hundred percent observational learning opportunities. And anyway, that's why you have me."

He didn't mean it how it sounded. Deanna knew that. But something in his tone had her looking over at him. Though she couldn't clearly see his face in the dark, she could feel the weight of his gaze. There was a pulse of—something—before he looked away, taking another swallow of his beer.

She did the same, wetting a throat gone tight with yearning. *Shut it down, James. You can only handle one mistake at a time.*

Getting involved with any man was a minefield of shit biscuits, and she'd already stepped in it with buying this house. The last thing she needed to be doing was undressing her contractor with her eyes. This wasn't about her for him. It was about getting what he needed for his show, and it was in her best interest to help him however she could with this skill for skill trade. It was time she ponied up.

"You're certainly holding up your side of the bargain. Let's talk about what I'm going to do for you."

"I'm all ears."

"I've been doing an evaluation of your current platform. In general, you've done a good job on YouTube. You understand the format and produce good quality videos—better as you've gone along—that have a lot of views. The periodic fan call-outs and thank yous in those videos are a definite good move, but there's room for improvement in engagement with those fans who are commenting on each video. The product placement for the stuff you use is also good, but you're missing out on an opportunity for affiliate income. I'd recommend a website for the show, linking to the playlist for each flip you've done, as well as a searchable DIY section."

"Isn't that all already on YouTube?"

"Yes, but you're missing out on the audience potential for everyone who doesn't already hang out there. The same with Facebook and Instagram. You've already got video content, so IG TV is a fantastic way to drive more traffic, find more viewers. TikTok might also be an avenue to explore, though I need to do some more thinking on that front. But, right now, you're largely neglecting fan engagement."

Wyatt shifted, dropping his gaze to stare at the bottle dangling between two fingers. "That sounds like a lot of stuff. I don't have a ton of time to put into answering every comment, and I don't always have reliable internet where I'm working."

Deanna recognized the same sense of overwhelm in his posture that she felt about the house, so she opted not to mention some of the feelers she'd already put out with some network contacts. She'd keep it to the basics for now. "I won't lie to you. It will be more work. That's part of how you grow a platform. But I can show you how to cross post between different social media sites, and a lot of things can be pre-scheduled. You don't have to answer every single comment, but you should go through and at least like them to indicate you've read them and are paying attention."

"How is all of this supposed to help me snare the attention of producers?"

"It shows you come with a built-in audience and that you have skill in interacting with that audience."

He hesitated. "I'm not... good with words."

Deanna frowned. Since she'd met this man, she'd never seen him be anything but a hundred percent confident and capable. There was something underlying his statement that went beyond a simple case of the don't wannas.

"You seem perfectly good with words. You're a natural host and teacher."

"That's different. That's talking."

"Talking is words."

"Not—" He cut himself off, looking out into the darkness.

"I can't help you if I don't know what you're thinking." With someone else, she might have been brusque. She seldom had patience for bullshit. But she sensed this was anything but, so she kept her tone mild.

"I'm not reluctant because I don't think you know what you're talking about. I'm just trying to play to my strengths." He didn't look at her, but she could see the fingers tighten on the beer bottle. "You want me to put up more video in other places, that's fine. But the point of all this is to create something that'll be sustainable when you're no longer there to coach me, right? I'm never going to be that guy who does a bunch of commenting and written engagement with people."

"Okay."

That got him to look at her. "Okay?"

"I'm not a dictator here. And you're right. There's no point in getting you on platforms you won't continue to use over time. You like video and talking out loud. We can work with that. But we're also going to up the ante there."

"Up the ante how?"

Thinking of the plan she'd formulated over all the sweaty labor this weekend, she smiled and tipped back the last of her beer. "I've got a few ideas."

THE BRICK FLOOR in the kitchen had to go. There were too many damaged bricks and no way to replace them with something that matched. But Wyatt was never one to waste materials, so he'd determined to salvage as much as could for some other project.

He'd been painstakingly chiseling mortar and prying up bricks for three hours when he heard the car drive up and the front door open.

"Wyatt?" Deanna's voice rang out from the foyer.

"Kitchen."

She strode in a few moments later in full professional mode, dressed in a little suit with some sky high heels that were a great way to break an ankle on a job site like this.

"Watch your step." His voice came out a little ragged, and he told himself it was just out of concern for her safety, not at the mental image of what she'd look like in nothing but those heels.

She paused at the edge of the remaining floor. "Well, you've been busy."

"Always. Didn't expect you to be home in the middle of the day."

"I carved out a little time to help Bennet get set up. Where's Simon?"

That distracted him from the shoes. "Sent him to pick up food. Help Bennet get set up for what?"

The woman herself sailed into the room. "The cameras."

Wyatt sat back on his heels, confused. "We have cameras."

"You have very specific, planned shots right now. We want to set up more cameras, so there's plenty of candid footage of the actual renovation and such. We'll also set up an interview booth of sorts, to get some of that type of footage. I want to show the guy behind the renovation as much as the work itself."

"I don't understand. You want to interview me on camera?"

"Not in a formalized show with a host kind of way, but like those little call out segments you see in a lot of shows where it just looks like the people on there are answering questions. One of us will give you a prompt, and you'll just talk candidly about whatever that is."

"Okay." He drew the word out, trying to wrap his brain around what she was suggesting. "Why?"

"A good construction reality show tells a story. Yes, viewers tune in for the transformation, but it's as much about the people as the work. Since you aren't typically working with clients, the people in this case are you and the volunteers and other craftsmen you work with. In order to get what you want from producers, you have to sell yourself as much as your work. I happen to have a lot of experience with that."

Because of Blake. She didn't say it but the thought hung between them, emphasized by the faint tick in her jaw. Wyatt remembered what she'd said during demo. *I fucking made him.* He'd looked Blake Lucas up the other night and had to concede she was right. The guy certainly hadn't made any inroads with his derivative, dude bro music, and Wyatt didn't for a minute buy that aw shucks, good ol' boy facade. But it seemed plenty of people were. Kudos to Deanna for her skill.

Wyatt understood he was incredibly lucky to have someone like her working on his behalf, but he recognized the situation might bring up some issues for her personally. He hadn't gotten where he was by ignoring potential foundation problems.

"Is that going to be a problem for you?"

"What?"

"There's some similarity to the situation with your ex. I don't want you to feel uncomfortable." And he sure as hell didn't want to be compared to that jackass.

Surprise cracked that neutral expression she wore. "It's not the same. This is a business arrangement. One I'm getting the better end of because you're saving my ass on this renovation."

Business. The word might as well have been a shield shoving him back from those unguarded moments they'd had. And maybe he needed the reminder that she wasn't remotely interested in anything other than getting out from under this albatross of a house. He didn't have the bandwidth for anything else either, even if he did find her appealing on multiple levels.

"Fair point. I just wanted to put it out there in case you felt… weird or something."

Her lips twitched. "I can assure you, in my line of work, this doesn't even come close to meriting weird."

Wyatt lifted a hand in concession, and she continued.

"Now, in addition to the interview booth, we're setting up a series of time-lapse cameras. They're motion activated, so we won't just have empty footage in every room they're set up in. We only have three, so we'll be moving them around as renovation progresses. Bennet's going to take all of that and edit the footage into something more formal than the cell phone and GoPro footage you've been using."

Wyatt glanced at Bennet where she tested a camera mount. "Not that I don't appreciate the help but are you…" He searched for a word that wouldn't come off offensive.

"Qualified?" Deanna suggested. "Yes. I'd wager she has years more experience with video editing than you do. She cut her teeth at Channel 5 and is part of the most sought after team of wedding videographers in the metro area."

Bennet made kissing noises in Deanna's direction.

Wyatt wasn't exactly sure what any of that had to do with a renovation show, but he wouldn't turn away the gift of help. Whatever time he didn't have to spend on video himself could be turned to the house. "That's amazing. But why would you help me?"

Satisfied with the camera position, Bennet secured it. "Because you aren't the only one who wants to break into this business. I want to produce, and this will help give me some credits in a way that does not involve wasting years of my life getting coffee for a bunch of misogynistic asshats or splicing together the perfect wedding video for nauseatingly happy couples." She beamed at him. "We're going to make beautiful TV together."

Her grin was infectious.

"I definitely love the sound of that. I've been doing this more or less on my own for a long time."

"I think you should be proud of what you've bootstrapped and figured out by yourself. We're just going to elevate it," Deanna promised.

"I'll be honest, this is a lot more than I expected when I suggested this deal." That Deanna was bringing so much to the table both humbled and excited him.

"You're taking a hell of a financial risk to do this. I'm determined to make sure you don't regret it."

"I need to dial in the focus on this camera. Come, be my guinea pig, Wyatt."

He dusted off his hands and strode over to Bennet. "Where do you want me?"

"Right… there. Yes, perfect. I'm going to do some test footage. Deanna, hit him with an interview question."

"Okay, remember we're going to be cutting out the prompt itself, so phrase your answer in such a way that it's clear what the question was."

"Got it."

"Tell us how you got into all this. Flipping houses. Restoration. Why do you love it?"

She had no way of knowing what a loaded question that was. No way was he sharing the painful details related to school and family. But he could talk about Scott.

"I was always into building things, working with my hands. My brother and I built a treehouse the summer I was twelve. I think that's where it started. He was the reason I got into flips in the first place. I'd been working construction in one form or other since I was sixteen. I'd been thinking about getting my contractor's license but waffling on it." In truth, he hadn't been sure he could pass the written test. "But my brother bought this total disaster of a house that had been condemned by the city. Didn't matter what kind of deal he got. I thought he was nuts. If there was something that could be wrong, it was."

Remembering his first tour of the place, Wyatt smiled. "My foot went straight through the subfloor about three steps past the front door. I told him he'd thrown his money away. But he told me he could see the potential in the house the same way he could see potential in me. So he basically dared me to take it on, turn it into something beautiful. And I did. I found my calling because my brother had more faith in me than I had in myself and put his money where his mouth was."

Because he was watching Deanna instead of the camera, he caught the naked yearning in her eyes. She wanted someone to believe in her. He understood that on a deep and visceral level. Every time she dismissed her dream or her capabilities outside her job, a part of him wanted to reach out and reassure her. But that fell into the realm of the personal, and as she'd said, this was a business arrangement. She was just a job.

If they were going to survive this renovation, it was best he remember that.

CHAPTER 8

"—Mr. Haywood was actively trash talking our product on social media."

Horrified, Deanna shifted into damage control even as she pulled up the relevant Twitter feed on her phone. "I am so beyond sorry, Tamra. This is obviously not what you were going for when you provided Eric with your product for promotion."

As she skimmed the offending tweets, she held in a stream of profanity. Did the idiot not understand how product placement worked?

"What are you going to do about it?"

Shove a boot up his ass to start.

"I absolutely understand that you're upset. I'll speak to him. Have the tweets removed immediately."

A bead of sweat trickled down her spine, as much from anxiety over this latest PR disaster as from the fact that the power was off while they worked on replacing outdated wiring.

"That's not going to help with the retweets or the impact he's already had. This is bad for our brand."

"Yes. I absolutely agree." Brain spinning, she tried to find a solution that wouldn't result in her being the one reamed out for someone else's unacceptable behavior. "I have other clients with bigger platforms. I should be able to find someone more... appropriate to promote your brand. Would that be agreeable to you?"

"How much bigger?" Tamra's voice had turned speculative.

"Kyle Keenan." Even as his name left her lips, Deanna winced. She hated to volunteer him without talking to him first, but desperate times. Kyle was the only big client on her roster who didn't habitually do stupid shit. He was happily in love and floating on cloud nine. He'd do her a solid. Probably.

"Oh, that would be fantastic!"

"Let me make a few calls and see what I can do. I assure you, this will not happen again."

"Keep us updated." Tamra hung up without saying goodbye.

"Okay then." Shaking her head, Deanna immediately sent Kyle a text explaining the situation. She needed to get this dealt with so she could get back to helping Wyatt with the rewiring. Ripping out approximately eighty years of electrical technology was the big project for the week that needed to be completed before they could push forward with anything else.

When Kyle's answer of **Happy to** came back, she breathed a sigh of relief. Eric Haywood would still need taking to task, but this solution would satisfy the Tamra's people. Probably.

She was still congratulating herself on a bullet dodged when a knock sounded on the door. Were they expecting another delivery of supplies? Had Wyatt called for more volunteers? Maybe it was the electrician who'd be putting in the new breaker box. She hadn't thought he was coming before next week.

Shoving her phone into the back pocket of her shorts, she opened the door... and froze. "Mom! Dad!"

For the briefest moment, she wondered if she slammed the door and hid, would they forget they'd seen her? Which was ridiculous. They were here, and her questionable grace period was up. Time to face the music.

Her hand clenched on the knob because she knew. She

knew how this conversation was going to go, and she dreaded it. It was why she hadn't told them about any of this. Pulling up her metaphorical big girl panties, she fixed her face into what she hoped resembled a pleasant smile. "What are y'all doing here?"

"Perhaps a better question is why you up and *moved* without feeling the need to tell us." The censure in her mother's tone had Deanna's shoulders inching toward her ears.

How the hell had they found out? More, how had they actually found her out here?

"I had an opportunity, and I jumped at it. As it happened rather quickly, I haven't had a chance to update you." *And I didn't want to.*

Without waiting for an invitation, they shoved inside. She couldn't keep them out without shutting the door in their faces, so she stepped back, conscious of what they were walking into.

"Oh, Deanna. How could you do something like this?" Her mother's face twisted in shock and disappointment as she took in the walls that had been stripped of wallpaper and the periodic holes in the plaster and lath that they'd made to deal with the wiring. "How could you throw your money away on this money pit? You know you should be putting your time into your job and securing your future."

What? Because her job was so tenuous? She fucking rocked at what she did, however thankless it was. There'd been talk of making her a partner in the firm in another year or so.

Her father took in the stack of reclaimed lumber waiting to have nails removed in the room opposite the front parlor and added his voice to the pile on. "Honey, you can't afford to be wasting frivolous energy and effort on a flight of fancy."

Hell would freeze over before she admitted to either of them that she'd drunkenly bought this house in an auction. But she'd committed to following through, so she squared her shoulders and lifted her chin. "I'm a grown adult. I get that this is something y'all don't understand, but it's going to be an excellent investment."

Her father heaved a long-suffering sigh. "Deanna, this kind of thing is reckless. It's hard work. With a house this old, there will always, always be problems that show up, and you don't have the money to sink into buying a house, let alone the cost of the materials and labor for renovations."

He had no idea exactly how true that was, and he'd have a coronary if he knew the arrangement she'd agreed to in order to get things taken care of.

"It's hard work," her mom added. "The kind of work you have to have professionals for."

Right. Because they couldn't imagine her capable of anything more than painting a wall. Resentment rose up to choke her, even as the weight of their criticism and concerns strained the fragile hope she'd built that everything would be alright.

"She has a professional."

At the sound of Wyatt's voice, Deanna closed her eyes for a moment, wishing she could sink through the floor. Heat crawled up her neck that he'd overheard any of this dressing down, even as she was grateful for the interruption.

"Who are you?" Suspicion dripped from her father's voice.

"Wyatt Sullivan. Deanna's contractor. And you would be?" He ranged himself beside her, his posture deceptively easy, but his jaw was granite beneath the unshaven scruff. He edged forward, as if he could shield her from their criticisms.

For a moment, she wanted to hide behind him, let him take the brunt of this onslaught. She was so taken aback by the urge, it took her a moment to remember to make introductions. "These are my parents. Phillip and Valerie James."

Wyatt nodded. "Ah, well, it's commendable you'd be concerned about your daughter's wellbeing, but let me assure you, she's uncovered a jewel here. It looks rough now, but the house is structurally sound and has so much potential."

Phillip frowned. "Potential or not, it's expensive."

"Not as bad as you might imagine. We're salvaging and reusing as much material as possible. And Deanna is doing a lot of the work herself."

Valerie pressed a hand to her chest. "But surely that isn't that much. She can't have that much time if she's doing her job properly."

Right. Because they thought she was an imbecile who couldn't do anything right or manage her own life.

"She's working exceptionally hard. Why don't we give you a tour?"

A tour? No. She wanted them gone.

But Wyatt was already leading them toward the back of the house, where they'd opened up walls and re-cased openings.

Needing a minute, Deanna didn't follow, but she could hear Wyatt explaining what they'd done, what they'd planned. Could hear, too, her parents as they asked questions, their voices less accusatory with him.

Of course, they'd be more accepting of all this from him. He was a man and a professional. Naturally, they'd give more weight to his opinion. Resentment bubbled up, hot and toxic. Not at Wyatt. God knew she appreciated the assist. But at her parents for being like this.

She'd made one monumental mistake in marrying Blake, and because of it, they thought she was foolish and incapable in everything. In the wake of her divorce, they'd turned to treating her as if she were still a foolish teenager. As if it were her fault that she'd gotten screwed in the settlement. As if the only answer was to spend the rest of her life living small and never taking risks.

She didn't want that. She'd never wanted that. But just being around them made her doubt herself and her ability to carry out this lunatic plan.

"—going to be gorgeous when we're through." Wyatt led her

parents back to the foyer. He didn't make any move to show them the upstairs.

For the best. No way in hell would they respond well to the fact that he was living here with her.

"Well, I, for one, feel better that someone qualified is overseeing the project," Valerie said.

Phillip nodded. "Our girl has a tendency to leap without thinking."

Deanna squeezed her phone so tight, she wondered the screen didn't crack. Not trusting herself to speak, she just held back as Wyatt deftly reassured them both and nudged them toward the door.

Her mother stopped, wrapping her in a hug. "I wish you'd told us. I hope everything turns out... okay."

She had so little confidence in Deanna that she couldn't even hope it turned out well? Demoralized, depressed, Deanna could only lift one arm in a mechanical squeeze as they said their goodbyes and finally, blessedly, walked out the door.

THE TEMPER SNAPPING in Wyatt's blood made it hard to shut the door instead of slamming it. Watching Deanna's parents dismiss and infantilize her was bad enough, but seeing how that so clearly hurt her, how they diminished her in almost every way with their well-intentioned and wholly misplaced concerns hit way too close to home and had rage bubbling up, ready to spew. He knew exactly what it felt like to be on the receiving end of that brand of parenting.

He wanted to hit something. And turning back, seeing her slumped shoulders and downcast gaze, he wanted to hold her. None of that was appropriate, but he couldn't just go back to work when she looked so damned... defeated.

Crossing his arms, he leaned back against the door with a far more casual attitude than he felt. "I'm the youngest in my family. My parents adopted me when I was twelve. They already had one son who was theirs by blood. Scott was sixteen, and our parents adored him. He was the golden boy, who could do no wrong. That could've made him an asshole, but it didn't, and I kinda worshipped him, too."

Deanna was watching him now, her expression guarded.

"Anyway, my parents are high achieving people. College professors. They have astronomical expectations. Scott met them as easy as breathing. I... did not. Everything about school was a struggle. Just graduating high school felt like scaling a mountain. With Scott's help, I did more than just scrape by. But Sullivans are high achievers, right? So college was expected." He flashed a humorless smile as he thought about the hell that came along with that.

"I lasted a year before I couldn't take it anymore. My parents were pissed. Asked what the hell I was going to do with my life without an education. They never asked why I quit or what I wanted. That never mattered to them. I was just the disappointment. The family fuck up. My girlfriend at the time piled on, too. Saying I would never amount to anything as a college dropout. My brother is the only one who never made me feel that way."

Straightening from the door, he took a step toward her. "All that to say, I get it. I get what it is to be judged by standards that don't fit you. To be seen through a lens that warps everything you are and everything you do into something wrong. To feel shame and doubt for not meeting expectations you don't even want."

Those hazel eyes were riveted to his now, and he couldn't stop himself from moving closer, wanting so much to touch her. "They're entitled to their opinions. That doesn't make them right."

She swallowed. "They aren't entirely wrong, either. I drunk bought a house. That kind of impulsiveness is seriously problematic."

"There's a big difference between making a drunk mistake on

something you didn't even want, and the alcohol lowering your inhibitions enough to do the thing you've been admittedly thinking and dreaming about for years. The way I see it, the drunk just got the fear out of your way."

Her bitter laugh echoed in the foyer. "I wish it had stayed gone."

"Let me ask you something, Deanna. Have they ever approved of anything you've done? Or is every conversation a chance to remind you of your mistakes?"

He was close enough now he felt the breath she expelled.

"Have you been tapping my phone?"

"Don't have to. They're afraid for you. That much is obvious. Anything that's more than walking the straight and narrow, that's more than living small and safe, is going to feel like a risk to them, and that means you could get hurt again. They'd rather see you stay in a safe little box than get hurt. And that means they're going to be disappointed no matter what because you don't fit that box. Continuing to try will just crush your soul. So you might as well take the risk."

As Wyatt watched her pupils blow wide, he realized he wasn't just talking about the house. He wanted to touch her. To slide his hands into all that silky hair and take her mouth until they'd both forgotten her parents' visit.

Deanna's breath went short and shallow, her chin tipping up just a fraction. "You're an incredibly astute man."

He was astute enough to realize she wouldn't push him away if he gave into desire and kissed her. The idea of it had his fingers curling, itching to reach for her. But he had just enough presence of mind to remember that all of this was a terrible idea. They worked together. Lived together. She needed him professionally, and neither of them could afford to fuck that up.

With a herculean effort, he took a step back. "I just don't want to see you kicking yourself. You're here. You're doing the work. That's what matters."

She blinked and cleared her throat. "Thank you. It means a lot to me that you believe in me. In what we're doing here."

"It means a lot to me that you don't think my dream is crazy either." Feeling strangely vulnerable and needing to do something to banish the lingering tension, he headed for the back door. "Come on, I want to show you something."

Deanna followed him out of the house, across the weedy lawn to the old barn.

"I was doing some exploring while you were at work the other day."

"I can't believe I haven't been out here yet."

"You've been focused on getting the house to the point of reasonably livable. Nothing wrong with that. But I think you'll be glad to see what I've found."

"What did you find?"

Putting his shoulder into it, he wrestled open the door. "A honey hole." Dragging it as wide as he could, he stepped inside. "At some point, I guess whenever somebody renovated before, they hauled all kinds of old stuff from the house out here to store. The door was hella stuck, so I don't think anybody's been out here in years."

Her steps were soft on the dirt floor. Dust motes danced in the sunlight that streamed through the door, gilding that golden hair. Damn, she was beautiful.

She reached a hand out, trailing it over an old carved mantle as if it were the finest velvet. Reverent. He watched as she picked her way through the stacks of wood and old trunks, eyes skimming over antiques in various conditions. With a gasp, she leapt forward, hands outstretched to touch the piece he'd known she'd fall in love with.

"Wyatt. This buffet." And when she looked back at him, he saw it. The light in her eyes her parents had extinguished.

He joined her, stroking a hand over the dusty wood. "Solid

mahogany. The finish has seen better days, but it can probably be salvaged."

"We have to save it. It would be gorgeous. In the dining room. Or maybe the kitchen."

"Plenty of time to decide. And to go through the rest of this stuff to see what else you want to use. There's a big pile of old lumber I want to plane and see what we have. I'm thinking we might be able to make custom butcher block countertops for the kitchen."

"That would be amazing. And I love the idea of using stuff that was already here, already a part of the house's history." Delighted, she looked around at the rows and stacks of other treasures. "I need to make an inventory."

"That'll be a good rainy day project. For now, we need to get back to that wiring so we can get the AC back on. I think if we give a solid push this afternoon, we can probably finish up tomorrow morning. And that means we can start talking walls."

"Now you're speaking my language. Let's do it."

Satisfied he'd banished the shadows from her eyes, he led the way back to the house.

CHAPTER 9

*L*ightning flashed beyond the sheets tacked up over Deanna's bedroom windows. Thunder grumbled as wind and rain lashed the house, making it groan like something out of an old school horror flick. She couldn't sleep.

Despite Wyatt's prior assessment that the roof was perfectly sound and had been replaced sometime in the past fifteen years, this was the first true summer thunderstorm since they'd moved in, and she was paranoid about leaks. She'd had an up-close-and-personal view of exactly how much damage water could do in short order. When she'd been a kid, the water heater in her parents' house—the one some genius had put in the attic—blew up, flooding the entire lower floor of the house. Ceilings, walls, and floors had been ruined. Given the current state of deconstruction, there was less to ruin in Blackborne Hall, but they still couldn't afford more setbacks.

As she flopped over again, punching the pillow, she had to admit that it wasn't the thought of a leak keeping her awake. It was that almost kiss from last weekend.

She was way, *way* out of the game, but she knew she hadn't read that wrong. He'd wanted to kiss her, and she'd wanted to let him. They'd had a Moment, damn it, as they'd bonded over unnecessary parental judgment. He'd opened up about himself in a way she hadn't expected. A way that had made her feel seen and supported.

Then he'd pulled back.

It was the smart move. She'd already established it would be a mistake to get involved, and she'd definitely met her quota of those. She ought to be relieved. Instead, she was hot and restless and so very aware he was sleeping just on the other side of that bathroom. Not for the first time, she considered doing something to relieve the ache. But she knew firsthand how thin these walls were, and what if he wasn't asleep?

Oh, yeah, sorry. Your truly decent behavior has made its way into my fantasy bank, along with you in a tool belt.

Nope. Not a conversation she wanted to risk. Too many potential sources of mortification.

Giving up on sleep, she switched on the bedside light. Distraction. She needed distraction. Instead of grabbing her laptop and falling into work, checking the stats on the campaign she'd designed to increase Wyatt's following, she brought her sketchpad back to bed. Over the past several days, as they finished the wiring and plumbing for the new kitchen layout and the en suite master bath upstairs, her brain had been working overtime on how she could use the treasures out in the barn—the only thing interesting enough to rival her unwilling fantasies about the man who'd showed them to her.

Setting pencil to paper, she filled up page after page with design concepts, room arrangements, and upcycling projects. Quick, loose sketches that captured the impression she wanted for each room. Of course, these projects required space and tools and time. Most were outside her current skill set, so she'd need Wyatt's help. If they rearranged out there, it would be fairly simple to turn part of the barn into a workshop. A permanent installation of his tools would be more efficient than the mobile setup he was operating with now and would be more practical for future projects.

She caught herself halfway through a sketch of a workbench.

What the hell was she doing? Neither of them would be here long term. They were finishing this house, selling it, and moving on. That was the deal. Nothing had changed, no matter how much she'd fallen in love with the house and in serious like with her contractor.

Disgusted, Deanna tossed the notebook aside. She'd grab a bottle of water from the mini fridge and try to go back to sleep. Aware of the risk of stepping on something in the construction zone, she slipped on shoes and headed downstairs. They left a small light on in their temporary kitchen, but the faint glow did little to light her way. The continued flashes of lightning cast creepy shadows that made her grateful she wasn't alone in the house. She wasn't particularly prone to self-induced scaring, but this place certainly had a less than welcoming atmosphere in its current state.

Soon. Soon we'll be putting back walls and you won't be imagining homicidal ghosts hiding in every shadow. No more Supernatural *reruns until then, though.*

The thought was a comfort as she twisted the cap off a fresh bottle of water and guzzled down half.

Something thumped.

Heart skipping a beat, she edged back toward the stairs, looking up for Wyatt. But he wasn't there, and it had sounded like the noise was somewhere on the first floor.

Don't be a fraidy cat. Just go see what the noise is.

Ignoring the voice in the back of her mind saying *this is how the horror movie starts*, she set the water aside and grabbed up a length of two-by-four. The sound came again. Probably a tree branch thumping against the house in the wind, but it didn't hurt to be prepared. Moving slowly, she crept through the house, ears straining. At another thump, she stepped into what had been a study but currently served as storage for all her packed boxes. Why the hell hadn't she thought to grab a flashlight?

A closer strike of lightning illuminated the space, revealing nothing unusual. Not that she could see much past the neatly stacked boxes of her stuff. But as the crash of resultant thunder faded, and she turned to go back upstairs, an eerie, keening cry sounded from *inside* the wall.

Deanna screamed, dropping the two-by-four as she stumbled back and ran.

A door crashed upstairs. "Deanna!"

"Wyatt!"

She collided with him on the landing in the dark. His arms wrapped around her and he pivoted, putting himself between her and danger. Or maybe just stopping them both from hurtling down the stairs headfirst. Either way, she hung on, pressing into the heat of his broad, muscled chest.

"What is it? What's wrong?"

She shook so hard she could barely speak. "G... g... ghost."

He pulled back, his capable, callused hands wrapping around her upper arms and giving her goosebumps. "What?"

"S... something s... screamed from inside the w... w... wall." Deanna knew she was one step above gibbering, but she couldn't seem to stop shaking.

Wyatt tightened his hold. "Where?"

"S... st... study."

"I'll go check it out." He started to release her, but she clung to him.

"Don't leave me alone."

She appreciated that he didn't tell her she was hysterical and that ghosts weren't real.

"Okay." His hand closed around hers, a reassuring connection in the dark. "Stay close."

She practically huddled against his back like part of the Scooby Gang as they crept back downstairs. He hit the light switch at the base of the stairs. The sudden glare blinded her. As her vision cleared, she took in what she hadn't quite realized when she'd been in his arms. He was shirtless and barefoot, wearing nothing but a pair of low-slung basketball shorts. She'd screamed, and he'd come running just like this. If not for the fact that she was more than half scared to death, she'd likely be swooning at that because, holy shit, he was beautifully made, his body a playground of dips and valleys made by the swells of his work-hardened muscles.

By the time they made it to the study, he'd set every light that remained to blazing. The spill of it cast long shadows from the stacked boxes. Deanna braced herself for the noise again as they went inside, but she couldn't hear anything over the pounding of her own heart and the wind whistling around the house. She didn't see anything either when Wyatt finally made it to the light switch on the far side of the room.

Could she have freaked herself out over nothing more than the sound of the storm?

"Which wall?"

Deanna pointed.

Squeezing her hand once, Wyatt stepped away, eyes skating over the surface of the exterior wall. "I haven't spent much time in here since you moved in. The room was structurally sound, so there hasn't been much cause yet, other than taking out that unnecessary dividing wall."

There was nothing to see, and in the light, Deanna began to feel a little foolish. "I don't know what I heard. Maybe I just psyched myself out."

"Maybe." But he didn't sound judgy as he began at one end and knocked along it.

Something scratched back.

He stumbled back a couple of steps. "Jesus." Moving closer, he knocked again and got another answering scratch. "You're not crazy. There's something in the wall. An animal maybe?"

"That sounds way too big to be a rodent." She didn't much want to consider what else it might be.

Following the length of the wall, he tap tap tapped, until he reached a section that had a deeper sound than the rest. "It's hollow."

"Hollow? How?"

"This side of the house is still covered up with vegetation and stuff. Could be it extends further than we realized."

"To what end?"

The smile he turned on her was full of little boy excitement. "It's a really old house. Maybe there's a secret passage."

The idea of that would probably be more appealing when it didn't feel like she was living out a story that began with *It was a dark and stormy night* and ended with a face-to-face encounter with the undead. Still, she got up the nerve to cross to the wall and run her fingers over it herself. The thing in the wall whimpered. Rats didn't whimper. Did raccoons?

Wyatt determined where the deepest echo was coming from, and they both continued to examine every inch around it.

"I think there's a seam here. See, the wallpaper masks it." He outlined a space that would've made up a small door.

Riding on the memory of all the Nancy Drew and Hardy Boys books she'd devoured as a kid, Deanna examined the carved detail of the molding. It was a floral pattern. Tudor roses. Very unusual for the time period of the house. She began to press and prod each bump. Something shifted faintly beneath her finger. Leaning in, she put her weight behind it, feeling the center of the rose sink deeper into the trim. Something clicked and a chunk of the wall popped open a fraction of an inch.

"Holy shit," Wyatt breathed.

He wedged his fingers in the gap and tugged. With a scraping noise, the door swung open.

The thing inside the wall bolted out, a flash of white. Deanna's scream cut off as it hurtled directly into her, knocking her flat on her ass. Throwing up her arms in defense, she cringed away… and felt a warm, wet tongue.

What the…?

As Wyatt began to laugh, she cracked open her eyes and came nose to nose with a skinny, filthy, wriggling dog.

"What on earth?" She sat up, fending off kisses from the animal who was now wagging and whining. "How the hell did you get into the wall?"

Wyatt stuck his head in the hole. "There are stairs going down. We'll need flashlights to check it out, but I think for now, we should close it back up and deal with our guest."

The dog sprawled across Deanna's lap, rolling belly up. With a sign of resignation, she wrinkled her nose at the smell of wet fur and mud—and rubbed his tummy, anyway.

"Well, at least you're a friendly ghost."

"IF YOU CAN DO without me for a bit, I want to go out to the barn to figure out which pieces I need to start refinishing."

Wyatt smiled at Deanna's barely repressed excitement. He loved seeing her enthusiasm and couldn't wait to see what she came up with out of their honey hole finds. "Go ahead. You've been burning the candle at both ends between work and the house the past couple of weeks."

"Come get me if you need me." She tapped her thigh, and the dog immediately rose, tail wagging ninety to nothing. "C'mon, boy. Let's go do some digging."

As Deanna and her canine shadow headed outside, Wyatt became aware of Levi's stare. "What?"

"I can't believe you kept the dog."

"I'm not sure there was much choice. You've seen her with him. After a bath and a meal that first night, he curled right on up at the end of Deanna's bed, and she was a goner." And yeah, okay, maybe he was a little bit, too.

"The fans certainly love him," Simon conceded. "Everybody coos all over him on Instagram, and that episode we did about how you found him has been the biggest hit yet. People really like animals."

"Also secret passages. Even if they do only lead to a root cellar we didn't know we had." Wyatt also privately thought that they liked the glimpses of Deanna, too. He certainly did. Not just the memory of that little tank top and sleep shorts she'd been wearing the night of the storm, but over the last couple of weeks, she'd started to soften and bloom, really leaning into the project now that they were to the point of reassembling rooms.

But he wasn't about to talk about that with his brothers, so he kept the conversation on the dog. "I mean, you have to admit, he's pretty damned cute."

"What is he? Part Husky?" Levi asked.

"We think. And maybe Great Pyrenees. He's got those double dew claws on his back feet."

"No collar?"

"Nope. And his ribs are showing, so we don't think he belongs to anybody." Nobody had responded to their efforts to find an owner. Not that they'd tried too hard. "Either way, Casper's definitely Deanna's dog now. He's got the collar, dog bed, and clean bill of health from the vet to prove it."

Simon arched a brow. "Deanna's dog, huh?"

"What's that supposed to mean?"

"Nothin'. I just think it's funny how you two started out business partners, but now y'all are all cozied up living together and co-parenting a pet."

"We are not cozied up. We have separate rooms, thank you very much." More was the pity. "And it only makes sense I help take care of Casper while she's at work."

Simon and Levi exchanged a look.

"Uh huh," Levi muttered. "So the fact that you've been smiling more the past month is just coincidence?"

Wyatt was starting to regret that they'd reached a stage where he could use other folks as help for labor. "Oh, shove it, both of you. It's not like that between us." *And maybe if I keep repeating it, I'll agree with myself.*

He was having a harder and harder time keeping himself emotionally distant and business only.

She was still on his mind when he and his brothers broke for the day. The sun rode low on the horizon as he trekked across the yard. Casper lay just inside the open door of the barn. His tail thumped in greeting, and Wyatt bent to scratch behind his ears, grinning when one leg kicked in ecstasy. He didn't see Deanna, but given that Casper seldom strayed too far from her side, she had to be in here somewhere.

Stepping around the dog, he noticed a notebook open on the buffet she'd been lusting after. Curious, he paged through. The whole thing was full of designs and floor plans. He recognized several pieces at the core of her sketches, but he hadn't imagined they could be so transformed. The possibilities excited him. Her vision was unique and creative, and so utterly her in a way he couldn't quite define.

"Oh, hey. Did you need me?"

Wyatt looked up to see her emerging from a stall further down. "No. The guys and I just broke for the day. Thought I'd come see what you'd gotten into." He tapped the sketchbook. "These are fantastic. Why aren't you doing this professionally?"

An odd mix of pleasure and embarrassment colored her cheeks. "I don't have any sort of training. I just know what I like. That does not a professional make."

Wyatt didn't like hearing her dismiss her talent like that. It meant something that she could do this, could *see* this. But God knew he understood imposter syndrome. That was probably more of her family talking. Flipping through the book, he pointed to one of the designs. "Tell me about this."

Everything about her lit up.

"So there's this old dresser back here in one of the stalls. It's got a few issues and has seen better days, but I think it would make the best kitchen island. Come see."

As he followed her to the back of the barn, Wyatt surreptitiously slid out his phone and hit record, angling it just enough to capture her animated face as she showed off the piece and described the project. He wanted to be able to show this to her later as proof that she did actually know what she was talking about when she didn't get in her own way.

"These top drawers wouldn't be practical, but they could be removed and that whole section repurposed for open storage for large serving pieces or some cool baskets. I'd take off the top and replace it with some of the barn wood we found to make a wider, more appropriate countertop, with enough overhang for barstools. Obviously, there would need to be something to support that overhang. I haven't figured out what that might be yet. Anyway, I'd cover this back section here with some of the salvaged beadboard from the house, update the hardware with something more rustic, and refinish the whole thing so it looks appropriately aged. Some combination of milk paints, probably. I think it would look fantastic."

Her love of the possibilities was infectious. As she spoke, Wyatt found himself wanting to do something for her. It wouldn't be that hard. He could take the time away from the main project while she was at work this week. The slight delay would be worth it to see the look on her face when some of her vision was brought to life. And maybe it would go some way toward proving to her that training wasn't everything.

"That'll be awesome."

Self-conscious again, she bit her lip. "You think?"

"I know." Ending the recording, he tapped the phone against

his leg, brain already spinning with an idea. "C'mon. Let's knock off for the day and start supper. I've got some kebabs to throw in the grill."

"Let me just grab my stuff."

As she did, he made a snap decision and sent the recording to Bennet.

Wyatt: *I think we should use this in a future episode.*

It would test his theory about whether fans really were into her perspective. And just maybe it would give her the confidence she needed to consider a change.

CHAPTER 10

*E*xhaustion dragged at Deanna as she finally turned into the winding drive to Blackborne Hall. All she really wanted to do was fall face first into bed and sleep for fifteen hours. Instead, she was going to change out of her business attire and put in a couple of hours on the house, partly because she was determined to uphold the sweat equity part of her agreement with Wyatt, but also because renovation gave her a sense of actually accomplishing something in a way that dealing with her clients did not. She needed that sense of control more than the sleep.

The warm glow of lights in the windows lifted some of her sour mood. She parked and got out, pausing for a minute with one hand on the car to try to find some energy for whatever work needed doing. Maybe just removing nails from some of the reclaimed lumber.

The front door opened, and Casper bolted straight across the yard to greet her with cheerful yips and licks and that happy, happy tail. Crouching down to greet the dog, she felt more of the crap mood evaporate. Had anyone ever been this thrilled to see her get home from work?

Glancing up, she caught sight of Wyatt on the front porch, his mouth curved in amusement as he watched them. The instant punch of home and yearning stole her breath for a moment. The crash of reality came just as fast. Sure, they'd been playing house for more than a month, but Blackborne Hall wasn't her real home, and Wyatt was just a temporary roommate, not a partner who wanted to share her life. She needed to remember that. But he had become a friend over these past weeks. After the day she'd had, she could use one of those.

Straightening, she headed toward the house. "Sorry I'm late. Work was a shit show. I'll get changed."

"It's fine. Slow down. Have you eaten?"

"There was half a salad at some point. That counts, right?"

"Hardly. Come and sit. I'll fix you a plate. The work can wait."

Deanna's step faltered as she followed him inside. He was going to make her dinner? Maybe she looked as bad as she felt. No help for it now. And what did it matter? They were business partners. Roommates. She'd just be grateful for the consideration.

Because it was easier than arguing, she trailed him into what she thought of as the lounge. The front parlor housed most of her living room furniture, along with the temporary kitchen. She sank into the welcoming embrace of the sofa. Casper leapt up beside her, immediately curling his skinny, sixty-five pounds into a ball at her hip and assuming the position for pets. Deanna sank her fingers into his fur and lamented all the years she'd given in to Blake's resistance to having a dog. Just one more thing he'd robbed her of. But at least this she could make up for.

Wyatt moved around the kitchen, piling food in a bowl and popping it in the microwave. "So why was today a shit show? Did Mercy Lee pull more diva-tude?"

"For once, no. I've been working on a campaign for another client for a few months. The label gave me the themes of the upcoming album, and I ran with it. Everything was designed, scheduled, and ready to go. It launches day after tomorrow. This morning they contacted me to say that everything had changed and, oh, did I mind redoing everything with twenty-four hours' notice?"

"Shit. Does that kind of thing happen often?"

"More often than it should. Not like people can't change their minds on things, but they often don't notify us, and then suddenly their inability to plan becomes my crisis. I *hate* the wasted effort."

"Don't blame you." The microwave dinged, and he brought over her food. "Here. Eat."

She took the plate, inhaling the rich, tomatoey scent. "You made spaghetti and meatballs in here?"

"It's freezer meatballs and jarred sauce, so not gourmet, but it's stupid easy in the Instant Pot."

"It's perfect. Thanks." She twirled the pasta on her fork. The moment the flavor hit her tongue, she realized she was ravenous.

Wyatt came back a couple minutes later and offered her a red Solo cup half full of wine. "Here, you need this."

She absolutely did. "Should I be having alcohol if I'm going to prospectively be handling power tools later?"

"No power tools tonight. You've been killing yourself, effectively working two full-time jobs for the past several weeks. We can afford for you to take the night off."

The idea of it almost had her bursting into tears of gratitude. She was *so* damned tired. With a nod, she accepted the cup and sipped, waiting for her throat to ease so she could dig back into her dinner.

Wyatt settled on the other side of Casper, scratching behind his ears. "Can I ask you something?"

Still eating, she hummed an affirmative.

"Your job is stressful and seems generally unfulfilling. Why don't you go do something else?"

It was a question she'd asked herself a hundred times, so she took her time answering, waiting until she'd polished off the last bite and set the bowl on the coffee table. "It's not that simple. I'm basically held hostage because of the alimony I'm expected to pay

Blake. I don't get to just easily change jobs. And aside from that, what the hell else would I do? This is what I'm qualified for."

It was far too late to change careers. She'd made peace with that a long time ago. Mostly. Figuring out her career stuff would have to wait until she was free of Blake. There was simply no bandwidth to put toward that right now.

Abruptly, Wyatt stood up. "I want to show you something."

Not waiting for her assent, he grabbed her hand and tugged her up. The feel of his callused fingers wrapped around hers sent a bolt of heat up her arm. There was something electric about him. A vibrating excitement that translated through his touch as he led her back toward the actual kitchen.

"I've had a project I've been working on this week. A surprise for you."

He stepped aside, and Deanna gasped.

In the center of the room was an island. *Her* island. He'd captured her design perfectly. Right down to the antiqued finish and unique reclaimed hardware. He'd added his own touch in the supports for the overhang of the counter. A pair of iron brackets she recognized as the decorative bottoms from some exterior light sconces. Emotion clogged her throat as she stepped forward and laid her hands on the barn wood countertop. It was real. Her idea brought to life by his talented hands.

"I can't believe you did this."

"You knew it would look stupendous in here. You were right."

The satisfaction of that was sweet. It overrode all the sense of wasted time and effort from the rest of her day. She could see in her mind's eye how the rest of the room would come together and knew it would be gorgeous. He'd done this gloriously lovely thing, just for her. And in the end, she'd have to walk away from it. From him. Because all of this was temporary.

Tears spilled over, scorching her cheeks. Appalled, she pressed her lips together to try to stem the tide, but she didn't have the energy to hold it back any longer.

"Hey, hey. What's this? Come here." Wyatt didn't wait for a response, just pulled her in with those strong, capable arms.

That just made her cry harder because she so wanted to lean into him, to lean *on* him in every way because he felt so damned good wrapped around her.

"I'm sorry. I should have made you a part of the build. Of course you'd want to be involved. It was your design. I just wanted to surprise you."

"No, that's not... This is so wonderful. It's exactly how I saw it. I just..." She hiccupped and admitted the truth she'd been carrying around for weeks. "I don't want to sell the house."

Wyatt lifted a hand to her cheek, brushing away the tears, his eyes searching her face.

Desperate to get herself under control, she swallowed. "I know it's not what we agreed to. I'm not backing out of our deal. I just... The house is going to be amazing. It feels like my dream is finally within reach, and I only get to keep it for a little while. I know that. I agreed to that. I know I have to give it up. It's just—"

His palm cupped her cheek, and he lowered his brow to hers. "Don't."

Right. He was a guy. He didn't want to deal with tears and hysterics. "I'm sorry. You didn't sign on for this."

She started to pull away, but he only tightened his arms. "Deanna." Her name on his lips was rough, but his touch was so very gentle as his fingers slid into her hair.

His mouth came down on hers with a sigh that could be nothing but surrender. For a long, humming moment, Deanna was too stunned to do anything but hold on to the fistfuls of his T-shirt. Then the body that had been slowly reawakening around him for the past month simply melted. All the stress, all the worry, all the protestations drained out of her, until all she could think, all she could feel, was Wyatt and the play of his lips against hers. It was as simple and as devastating as that.

He eased back, pressing his brow to hers again, so they still shared the same air. "Don't sell the house."

Her brain had been liquified, so she could only manage, "What... why?"

"Because you get it. Because this work, this house, lights you up inside. Because I need to give this to you."

Scrambling to make her neurons fire, she pulled back just far enough to look up at him. The intensity in his expression had her stomach flipping. "Why would you do that?"

His mouth quirked in that charming grin. "If you have to ask, I clearly need to work on my technique." One big hand skimmed down her spine. "I'm crazy about you. And I knew from day one that you didn't want to sell. I can't ask you to give up a part of your soul."

God, this man and his big, impractical, well-intentioned heart. "Wyatt, I—" She hardly knew which part of this to respond to first. "It means more to me than I can express that you'd be willing to do that for me. But I don't see any other way to make this work. I can't afford to pay you back in any reasonable span of time without selling. We don't have any other options. That's how we got into this in the first place."

Frustration twisted his features. "Deanna, honey, you have to stop with the preconceived notions of what's possible. Look at this." He whipped out his phone and started swiping at the screen. "A few days ago, you said that you didn't have any sort of training, that you just know what you like, and that doesn't make you a professional. But look at these reactions."

He handed over the phone so she could see. It was the *DIWyatt* Instagram feed. More importantly, it was *her work* being highlighted.

"You posted my sketches? My designs?"

"Yeah. I know I should've asked first, but you'd have said no. Look what people are saying."

They'd been shared over four thousand times, and the

comments… People were going nuts, wanting instructional posts. Others wanted to know where they could buy something like this.

Stupefied, Deanna stared. "They… like it."

"They love it, and they want to see more." He took her by the elbows, pulling her in again so she was flush against that muscled chest. "You wrote yourself off before you even gave yourself a chance. You're qualified to do more than PR. This proves it. And maybe this is a harder road. But it's the road that'll make you happy in the long run. The road that'll feed your soul. So let's give the house, the show, a real chance. We'll figure the rest out as we go. Okay?"

The prospect of keeping the house, of getting to live out her dream, was too good to pass up, even if she didn't have the first clue how to make all this profitable.

"Okay." But that wasn't the only thing that had come up tonight. "About that other thing."

"What other thing?"

She bit her lip. "The crazy about me thing."

Wyatt sobered. "It's not a deal breaker. None of this is conditional. I don't want you to feel pressured or like this is an exchange."

Sweet, considerate man.

Deanna pressed a finger to his lips. "Thank you for all of that." She stroked a hand along the scruff of his jaw, loving the rough feel of it against her fingers. "But it only seems fair to admit that I'm pretty crazy about you, too."

His broad chest rose and fell as he pressed his brow to hers. "Thank God."

"Never seen you smile this much, while putting in floors. I wonder what could be the source of that good mood." Simon's tongue-in-cheek tone made it very clear he knew the cause.

Wyatt couldn't even be annoyed with him. His mouth seemed to be stuck in a permanent grin, despite the ache in his knees and the myriad of details he and Deanna hadn't yet figured out.

He shot a row of nails into the reclaimed heart pine flooring they'd elected to use in the kitchen and reached for the next board. "Whatever, man. Life is good. The kitchen's well on its way to coming together."

"And you and your roommate have gotten... close."

Yeah, his little brother clearly thought that was a euphemism.

In fact, he and Deanna were taking things slow. He was fine with that, figuring this time with her was shoring up the foundation of friendship they'd already built. Given her history and their unusual circumstance, he was willing to do whatever it took to make sure she felt comfortable.

Levi, apparently an equal opportunity ball buster, fixed Simon with a look. "Uh huh. And what about the heart eyes you were making at Fiona Gaffney during demo?"

Simon suddenly got very busy checking the fit of the next piece of flooring. "So, um, I've got a birthday coming up this weekend."

"I know we've been pushing hard, but I don't plan to make you work on your birthday."

"I appreciate that, but that's not actually where I was going with this. Pru and the girls are throwing me a birthday party, having kind of a mini-reunion. I know you weren't actually *at* Joan's when I was, but I wondered if you'd come."

Levi gave him a friendly thump on the arm. "Wish I could, little bro. I've got an out-of-town job interview."

"Way to bury the lead on that one, dude. You haven't even told us about the one you left." At Levi's bland stare, Simon rolled his eyes. "I know, I know. If you told us, you'd have to kill us."

It was the reason Simon had settled on for why Levi was so closed mouthed. After working with the guy for a few months, Wyatt wasn't sure it was entirely off base.

"What about you, Wyatt?"

"I mean, technically, we're supposed to be working on the house, but Deanna's been busting her ass for two months, on top of her normal job. She could use a bit of a break, even if it's just an overnight. And who doesn't like cake? There will be cake, right?"

"Not just any cake. Joan's four-layer caramel cake. Pru learned how to make it just like her."

Wyatt's stomach growled in memory. Before he could reply, Casper shot from his spot in the corner with a volley of barking, bulleting straight to the front door. When it opened a minute later, his telltale happy whine told Wyatt Deanna was home. Early today. His heart did a jig. Because he wanted to leap up and go kiss her, he settled the next board in place and nailed it. He could play it cool in front of their audience.

"Did you know the camera was there?" Deanna's carefully controlled tone had Wyatt's automatic smile fading, his instincts blaring an alarm, even before she stepped into the room.

Danger. Danger, Will Robinson.

"What?"

"In here, the night you showed me the island."

The night he'd kissed her.

Oh shit.

Setting aside the flooring nailer, he steered her out of the room, away from his brothers and the camera he did remember. "You're saying we were filmed?"

Without a word, she handed over her phone. There was no sound, but the two of them were clearly visible in the frame. Her tears. His attempt to comfort her. The kiss. It was a raw an unfiltered encounter. One they'd both thought was private. But just the existence of the footage wouldn't have her this upset. And she was upset, no matter how controlled she appeared to be. Which meant that somehow the footage had gone beyond her control.

"What was done with this?"

She crossed her arms, her mouth set in a grim line. "It's all over social media as part of the teaser for the next episode."

He hadn't made the teaser. Bennet had. Most of the production editing had shifted to her. But why the hell would she have used this? "Why? Who's going to care?"

Deanna snorted without an ounce of humor. "A lot of people, apparently."

Taking the phone back, she swiped to something else and held it out again.

Wyatt blinked at the screen, his brain refusing to process. "What am I looking at?"

"The latest subscriber count on your YouTube channel."

His mouth fell open. It had quadrupled in the last two days. "You're saying this is because of this video?"

Jaw tight, she nodded, finally giving in to Casper's insistent head-butting against her leg and scrubbing behind his ears. "It's the thing that changed."

And suddenly Wyatt understood. This wasn't about the violation of their privacy. At least, not entirely. If he didn't handle this properly, their nascent relationship would go up in smoke.

"I did move the camera earlier because we were going to be starting on the kitchen and needed the time lapse footage. But I didn't set you up. I didn't even remember it was there, let alone that it was on." He chanced a step toward her, relieved when she didn't move back. "I wouldn't do that to you. To us. We're too new, and even if we weren't, I'm not out to profit off this thing between us. That's not who I am." And if she couldn't believe that, then it was better he find out now than get in any deeper.

The ice melted from her eyes, along with the carefully blank mask from her face. "It's not. I know it's not. I'm just not used to that."

Yet again, he wished he could plow a fist into Blake Lucas's face. Instead, he pulled Deanna in. "I get it. You needed to ask. To be sure. But I'm not him."

"No. You definitely aren't." She burrowed in and leaned for a moment, her head pressed against his chest. It felt like a victory. This woman didn't share the load, didn't show weakness or vulnerability.

Pressing a kiss to her brow, he tucked her close, loving how she fit just beneath his chin, even in heels. "I'm sorry our private moment is out there for public consumption. I suppose that's a danger of filming where we live. Forgetting the cameras are there or that we might be mic'd."

"Our carelessness isn't the problem. There's only one other person who'd have access to post this, and I need to go murder her now."

Wyatt didn't let her get far when she pulled away. "In the name of keeping you out of jail, maybe call instead of showing up in person?"

"Fair enough."

She made the call from the lounge, one hand curled in his, the other sunk into Casper's fur.

Bennet answered after two rings, her cheerful voice ringing out over speakerphone. "Deanna, girl, y'all have gone viral!"

The hand in his tightened reflexively as Deanna sucked in a slow breath. "Exactly what gave you the right to post a very private, very personal moment as part of the show?"

Bennet didn't even hesitate. "You recruited me to help elevate the production value of the show. That calls for story. Anybody with eyes this season can see that you two are the story."

"What are you talking about?"

"It's all over the footage the way y'all look at each other, especially when you think the other isn't looking. Fans have been asking will you or won't you for weeks."

Deanna's tone went sharp. "What? Where?"

"In the fan forums."

"We have fan forums?" That was news to him.

Deanna nodded. "Yeah. I set them up early on, but I've been so busy I haven't checked in with them. They were a later phase project for when I had a little extra bandwidth."

"Don't worry. I've got you, boo. And hey, Wyatt! Way to finally make a move!"

"Uh…" What could he say to that? "Thanks?"

Deanna pinched the bridge of her nose, clearly struggling with what to say. "Bennet—"

"Listen, I know you're pissed that I pulled that whole asking forgiveness rather than permission, but sorry, not sorry. It's raising the profile of the show and adding what was missing. People love a good romance. Especially in home improvement. If you play your cards right, you could be the next *Fixer Upper* or *Home Town.*"

"That isn't the show we're selling," Deanna bit out.

The idea struck Wyatt. He'd been doing this on his own for a long time, and it hadn't been quite enough. The producer at CMT had said there was no hook, no interest in the premise of him alone. But the thought of continuing to do this sort of work with Deanna by his side as a partner held more than a little appeal. He'd had more fun on this renovation than any other he'd ever tackled, and that was predominantly thanks to her.

"Maybe it should be."

Deanna stared at him as if he'd sprouted a second head. "What?"

"I mean… maybe Bennet has a point."

The woman in question took advantage of her friend's distraction. "Sounds like you two have stuff to talk about. Ta!"

The line went dead, and Wyatt was left staring at the woman who might be the answer to the future he'd always wanted.

IN THE SILENCE, Deanna's heart sank. He'd literally just reassured her he wasn't out to profit off the thing between them. Was the prospect of how much impact it could have really enough to change his mind that fast? Had she let herself be fooled by a pretty face and pretty words? Again?

Needing to move, she shoved up from the sofa and began to pace.

"I can see your brain going to a not great place. Just hear me out." Wyatt lifted his hands in that expressive way he had, clearly intending to soothe. "Whether we like it or not, this is out there. People are into it. This is the growth and exposure we wanted. Maybe not the way we wanted, but it's still information about the prospective audience. They aren't interested enough in just me. Even before this, the posts and segments getting the most engagement since we started on the Hall are the ones with you. Bennet will say that's because people are hoping for a romance, and maybe that's true of some of them. But I have a different theory."

"Enlighten me." Deanna knew her tone was dry enough to border on bitchy, but she couldn't seem to stop it.

"I think people want more about the design. The inspiration. I don't completely ignore it, but that's not my thing. I've been more focused on the doing of things and showing people the how it's done. It's not balanced. They want the how behind the design, too. You give that missing piece. The vision. And viewers are responding to it. You should use that momentum to really take on the design work as a job."

Wait... what? "I should what now?"

"You love design, and you're great at it. This is your chance to really see if you can make a go of it."

Deanna stared at him, taking in his earnest face. "You want me to take advantage of all this for *me*?"

He vibrated with excitement again, as he had the night he'd presented her with the island. "Yeah. It takes time to start this kind of thing from scratch, but if you can piggyback on what I've already established, it could take literal years off the process."

A cynical part of her, the part of her that Blake had burned, pointed out that the corollary to all this was that Wyatt enjoyed more success for himself. But she didn't think that had entered his mind. Nothing he'd said was about what he could get out of this. He hadn't even said "we." From the get-go, he'd been supportive of the idea of her pursuing design, pushing her to have faith in her own abilities because he believed in her.

"C'mon," he prodded. "You've been in PR for a lot of years. Haven't you at least considered how you'd launch something like this? Haven't you let yourself dream?"

There'd been so little room for her dreams in all the years with Blake. All that time she'd let herself believe that his dreams, his goals, were the most important thing. But even then, there'd been a kernel.

"I mean... yes. Never in this format. A blog. Instagram. Pinterest. But I never *really* believed I'd have an opportunity to *do* it. It was just hypothetical."

Wyatt crossed over, curling his hands around hers. "Believe it. This is your shot. If you want it."

The prospect of that filled her with a mix of excitement and terror as all those hard taught lessons of caution warred with want. "You've been working toward this for years. Why would you be willing to share that?"

The question seemed to baffle him. "Why wouldn't I? You getting something out of this takes nothing away from me."

God, was he really that selfless? Maybe he didn't truly understand what he was offering.

"Going in this direction, making us a package deal, means that's what producers would be expecting. They might not be willing to look at you on your own."

"I think that's already been proven."

"No, I mean... If we did this together, and you made me a part of the show, then something happened down the line where we went our separate ways, you might not get another shot."

"As in, we have some awful break up and decide we hate each other? I don't see that happening."

His casual confidence was terrifying. How could he be thinking long term? *Was* he thinking long term?

"We... this... thing between us is new. We don't know where it will lead or if it will lead anywhere. You shouldn't risk your future on someone you can't be sure of." She'd done that and look where it had gotten her.

"I am certain of one thing—there is no certainty in life. There are no guarantees. Living—really living—is about taking risks. Sometimes they pan out, sometimes they don't. What matters to me is making the effort because the things most people regret at the end of their lives are the things they didn't do." He stepped into her, lacing his hands at the small of her back and stroking her spine with his thumbs. "The way I see it is that regardless of what happens between us personally, we stand a better shot together professionally than we do apart. It's a calculated risk that I'm more than willing to take because I believe in you and in what we can do together. Do you?"

What would it be like to do this with him so wholly on her side? Did she want what he was offering? A part in his show? A springboard into the possibility of a career doing the thing she was passionate about?

The answer was yes. It would be so easy to give in and take the leap with him. His gift was making things seem not only possible but doable. But saying yes meant she had to trust him, and that was a whole other thing.

"Do you have any idea how much it scares me to say yes to this?"

"I'd wager a lot. That means you're still being sensible. Nothing wrong with that. But, consider this—you are amazing at your job in PR. If you quit and tried this and it didn't work, you could find another job in PR. But when will you ever have the boost of all this social proof to elevate your efforts toward what you really want to do?"

Probably never again.

If she waited for a more ideal time, she might wait forever. If she put it off until she was somehow, miraculously free of Blake, wasn't that the same as continuing to put him first, as she had for all those years of their marriage? She'd vowed never to do that again. Never to give him any more control over her life than she'd been forced into by the divorce decree. Didn't she deserve to take a chance on herself for once?

"Okay."

"Okay? Really? You'll do it?"

She felt the need to qualify. "I mean, I'm not just going to quit, but I'm willing to try this. To put myself out there with the design thing. Because you're right. I'm never going to get another chance like this."

Wyatt beamed, scooping her off her feet to whirl in a circle. "Hot damn! You won't regret it."

She hoped like hell he was right.

"Now that that's settled, how would you feel about a quick trip to the mountains?"

CHAPTER 11

The Misfit Inn. Tongue-in-cheek name for the former foster home that had, over twenty-five years, seen countless kids brought to better circumstances under the love and care of Joan Reynolds. Now an actual inn and spa run by Joan's daughters, the three-story Victorian still had the same welcoming feel to Wyatt as he climbed the steps. A lot of that had to do with the woman beaming at him from the open front door.

"You made it!" Pru Reynolds Bohannon opened her arms wide, pulling him in for a hug.

She'd done the same thing when he'd shown up as a scared kid all those years ago, a self-appointed one-girl welcoming committee, making him feel wanted. She'd been a chip off of Joan's block, even then.

Wyatt folded her in, feeling something restless in him settle at the embrace of his found family. "Hey, sis."

"So glad you're both here. The birthday boy beat you by a couple of hours. He's been telling us all about the house!" Pru stepped back and turned an impish smile on Deanna that suggested she'd been hearing about more than Blackborne Hall. "So good to see you again."

Again?

Deanna gestured to the renovated barn adjacent to the inn. "The spa has come a long way since I was here last."

Oh right. She'd said she'd stayed here shortly after the inn actually opened.

"You have no idea. Full staff and menu of services now. We've still got a few open slots on the roster, if you want to book a massage while you're here."

Deanna pressed a hand to her heart. "Dear God, I might weep with gratitude. With all the renovations, I've basically just gotten used to something being sore all the time."

I could help with that. The words hung at the tip of Wyatt's tongue. He'd do a lot to get his hands on Deanna. But he'd promised himself he'd go at her pace, no matter what. She had the bigger trust issues.

"We'll be sure to get you booked in. Flynn, you want to carry their luggage on up?"

"Dude, we could've gotten our own bags," Wyatt protested.

Pru's husband laughed. "Part of the service."

As he strode past them into the house, Wyatt noticed Deanna's cheeks flushing deep red. What was that about? Filing it away to ask about later, he followed them inside.

Pru led the way upstairs. "I put you in your old room. I thought you might appreciate the nostalgia. But that was before I knew Deanna was coming. You can totally push the twin beds together, and we can get some king-size bedding."

Because, of course, they assumed he and Deanna were sleeping together. He heard her step falter. Right. He needed to find a way to make this situation less awkward.

Deanna spoke up from behind him. "The twins are fine. We don't want to put you out. As I recall from my last visit, they're incredibly comfortable."

Up on the third floor, they walked down a short hall that was considerably brighter than it had been twenty-odd years ago. Pru opened the last door on the right. "Here we go."

Flynn preceded her inside, setting the bags he carried at the foot of one of the beds. "Bath's through that door. Extra towels in the cupboard there."

Wyatt cast his gaze over the room, which was done up in a coordinated color scheme of misty greens with crisp, white accents. "It's a lot different than it was when I was a kid."

His sister laughed. "You will not find an ongoing poker game hiding under the bed."

"More's the pity. I feel like I could totally take on the birthday boy for an extra slice of that caramel cake."

"Don't bet on it. Simon will surprise you. And if you try to take more than your fair share of his birthday cake, we might have a throw-down."

He grinned. "I'll be sure to behave myself so as not to sully the good name of your establishment with a wrestling match."

"Oh psh. If you think Athena's boys haven't had multiple already, you're mistaken. We're a little fancier than we used to be, but it's still home."

It was something he'd been seeking for years since he left this place. Something he'd found himself building with Deanna at Blackborne Hall. But that was new and untested territory, not something he could count on. The Misfit Inn would always be home to Joan's former misfits.

As if she sensed the direction of his thoughts, Pru stroked a hand down his arm. "Mom would be glad to see you happy."

Was it that obvious?

At his self-conscious smile, she stepped back. "I'll just leave y'all to get settled. Come on down to the lounge when you're ready. I feel certain Simon's gotten into the game closet and been nagging Athena for snacks."

"He's a bottomless pit."

"You know she loves them like that. See you in a bit!" She shut the door, leaving them alone.

"Your sister is charming."

"She is. I'm guessing you're thinking her husband is, too." He smirked to let her know he was teasing. "What was that blush about? Is it the Irish accent?"

Deanna bit her lip, not quite meeting his eyes. "So... when I was here before, it was for my Thank God I'm Divorced party. I came out with all my girlfriends to celebrate for the weekend. There was a *lot* of champagne, and I might have hit on your brother-in-law. Although, to be fair, he wasn't your brother-in-law at the time."

"Uh huh. And was Bennet on this trip?"

"She was."

"That explains the alcohol consumption."

"I mean, the whole Thank God I'm Divorced Party was her idea."

"Of course it was."

"One of my other friends actually moved here not too long after that. I was hoping to get a chance to see her before we head back home."

"I'm sure we can make time for that." Still grinning, Wyatt opened the closet door, his fingers reaching for what he only barely remembered. But the initials were still carved into the door frame. He traced the letters. WY. Wyatt Young. The name he'd been born with.

The teasing smile faded, dragged down by memory.

"Wyatt?" The concern in her tone told him she'd caught the shift in his mood.

He could put her off, but if he wanted this woman as part of his life, he had to share more of the past that had made him. "I was nine when I came here. My birth parents were... Well, I never knew who my father was. My mother had a drug problem and a habit of forgetting I existed. Social services took me away three different times before she ODed."

"Oh, my God. Wyatt, that had to be so hard on you."

He jerked a shoulder, keeping his back to her, so he didn't have to see the inevitable pity for what he'd come from. "Coming here was a relief. Or it was once I figured out I wasn't gonna get kicked out and there'd always be plenty of food to eat. I loved being one of Joan's kids."

"You said you were adopted when you were twelve?"

"Yeah. Another big change. New city. New name." For better or worse, the Sullivans had been a huge part of his life.

"But you stayed in touch?"

"No. Not for a long time. Not more than birthday and Christmas cards from Joan."

Turning, he could see her trying to work out what he wasn't saying and waited to see if she'd ask.

"Is it strange for you to come back here when you were adopted so long ago?"

Not the tack he'd expected. "Yes. And no. Joan was a special woman. She had this magic about her that made all of us feel like we were family. Even those of us who were adopted into another one. The last few years, I've been reconnecting with that, with everyone I grew up with and the others who went through here."

"Why? Curiosity?"

He shut the door and sank down on the bed. Far plusher than the one he'd slept on all those years ago. "Partly. But it was more that my adopted family wasn't perfect. When you're a foster kid, you hope for that forever home. That forever family to make you theirs. My brother was amazing, but my parents... I always felt like they were disappointed in me."

She sat on the bed across from him, one hand curling around the post of the footboard. "You said school was really difficult."

Wyatt grunted, not missing her hesitation. "What?"

"I was just wondering if you ever got evaluated for learning disabilities."

He closed his eyes and tried not to wince. He hadn't told her for a reason, not wanting to see her regard for him tainted by pity or disappointment. "What makes you ask?"

"Because I think you might be dyslexic."

His stomach sank. "You knew?"

"I figured it out early on. You don't text, hate most social media, and dictate notes to yourself. I put two and two together and adapted the plan. It hasn't held you back at all. You're so gifted on camera, we've skewed all your content to video, and I've tackled the blogging. Which has worked beautifully, if I do say so myself."

She'd seen and figured out in a couple of months what his parents hadn't recognized in years. More, she'd adapted to it so that he wouldn't be put into a situation where he'd struggle. Wyatt opened his eyes and stared. There was no sign of pity, no glimmer of disgust or disappointment. Her gaze was full of warm affection, exactly as it always was.

Something in him loosened at that unquestioning acceptance.

"I wasn't assessed until after I dropped out of college."

"Didn't it make a difference with your parents? To have a reason for why you struggled?"

"I never told them."

She blinked. "Why?"

"Right after I found out, my dad died. It devastated our family, and my shit just didn't seem worth bringing up at that point. It didn't really impact the business I'd chosen for myself."

"But why not tell your mom? I mean, I get why not then, but later."

That was the last thing he wanted to talk about. "We had a falling out several years ago." It was a sterile word for one of the most painful experiences of his life. But he'd brought enough darkness from his past into this sunny room. "We've been estranged ever since. Scott's the only part of the Sullivan family that I still claim. That's why I've been reconnecting with my foster family."

Deanna crossed to sit beside him on the bed, skimming a gentle hand over his cheek, into his hair. "Thank you for sharing this with me."

Lulled by the touch, Wyatt leaned into it, into her, until he could cover her mouth with his. The kiss was another layer of comfort he needed, balm to a wound she didn't even fully know existed.

Easing back, she rested her brow against his. "I don't know about you, but I'm in desperate need of some of this caramel cake I keep hearing about."

Yeah, he could use some more sweetness in his life. "Then let's go fight the birthday boy for it."

WYATT SUPPOSED it was inevitable that there'd be drinking in honor of Simon turning twenty-one. The birthday boy was being smart about it and staying in, so no harm no foul there. But Wyatt hadn't anticipated that Ari would keep covertly refilling Deanna's wine glass. When he'd caught her leaning over the back of the couch, tipping more Cabernet into the glass, she just winked at him and offered a thumbs up, like she was doing him a solid getting his girlfriend tipsy. If Deanna had planned to have more than a glass or two, that would've been one thing. But Wyatt knew how sensitive she was about drinking to excess, and he didn't want her put in any awkward or compromising positions. Especially as she got more affectionate the more wine she drank, and they were sharing a room with only a few feet of space between their beds.

He loved having her cuddled up against him on the sofa, loved listening to her laugh, seeing her at ease with his family. And if she hadn't been drinking, he'd have loved nothing more than to follow up on the promise she made with the hand that kept inching higher on his thigh. But damn it, she had. And they needed to get to bed, anyway. To *sleep*. God, he hoped he could sleep. They'd still have work to do once they got back home tomorrow.

"Little brother, I wish you a very happy birthday, and a very short hangover. We need to turn in."

Simon beamed the bleary grin of the happy drunk. "More cake!"

"If you have more cake, you're going to hurl," Athena announced. "I'm not cleaning that up. Here. Have a glass of water, pal."

As his sister, the chef, worked on slightly sobering up the birthday boy, Wyatt pulled Deanna to her feet. She swayed into him. Yep. Tipsy at the very least. Damn it.

Wrapping an arm firmly around her, Wyatt wished everyone goodnight and led Deanna upstairs to their room. The feel of her pressed all up against him the entire way had him rethinking the whole pushing the beds together thing. She was the one who shut the door behind them, leaning back against it in a provocative pose that made him want to pin her there and devour her mouth. His hands itched to streak over her, stripping off that gauzy shirt and those form-fitting jeans to touch and take. He wondered what it would take to make her scream.

Not here. Not now.

Scrabbling for some control, he cleared his throat. "You want the bathroom first?"

Was that disappointment in those hazel eyes? Probably just wishful thinking on his part.

"Sure." She shoved away from the door and took her bag into the bathroom.

Wyatt scrubbed both hands over his face. *Get a fucking grip, Sullivan.*

But as he heard zippers and the whisper of fabric, he couldn't stop his mind from imagining her undressing behind that door, baring those long, slim thighs he so desperately wanted wrapped around him. By the time the water came on, he was fighting to keep the blood in his brain.

Should he change while she was in there? Or wait until she came back out? Why was this a hard decision?

He'd change. It's not like it was a big deal.

Decided, he tugged off his shirt, just as the bathroom door opened.

Deanna stepped out in a cami top and sleep shorts. The full outline of her breasts was visible beneath the soft fabric, and the pert tips of her nipples drew his gaze like a magnet. He lost the fight with his arousal and felt himself go hard. He'd been trying so damned hard not to think of her exactly like this since he'd seen her the night they found Casper. Knowing she'd been wearing just these little scraps of fabric in her bed, on the other side of that jack-and-jill bathroom, had been torture. Knowing she'd be wearing them tonight, barely more than an arm span away, just might kill him.

"See something you like?"

Appalled he'd been staring, he jerked his gaze up. "Sorry."

Her lips curved into a feline smile. "You don't have to apologize. I'm enjoying the view, too." Closing the distance between them, she took the shirt he'd bunched in his hands and tossed it aside.

He shivered as she laid her palms on him, running them up his chest and over his pecs and shoulders.

Jesus God.

"I do appreciate what the job does for your body," she purred.

"Um... saves on gym fees." Why did he sound like a prepubescent boy?

Her fingers threaded into the hair at his nape as she rose to her toes. "Wyatt?"

"Yeah?" he croaked.

"Kiss me."

Just a taste...

Surrendering to the heat bubbling in his blood, he hauled her against him, taking her mouth as he wanted. She opened in an instant, melting against him in a surrender that made him want to bear her down to the nearest mattress. His hands slid beneath the hem of her top, soaking in the soft, silky feel of her skin. Christ, she felt so damned good circling her hips against the hardness behind his fly.

Just a taste...

Drunk on the flavor of her and half blind with lust, he hitched her up and backed her toward the door. Those legs he'd dreamed about locked around him. This wasn't enough. Not nearly enough. But he could give them both this little taste.

Her head fell back with a delicious gasp as he rocked into her. Every breath, every whimper seemed to shoot straight to his cock as he drove her up, delighting in watching her let go of all the rules, all the poise, all the control in pursuit of her pleasure. As her body tensed, he took her mouth again, drinking in her cry as she shattered.

He wanted to make this woman come apart over and over again. But this was all they could have tonight.

Less than steady, he let her slide down his body until her feet hit the floor.

Her lips lifted to his throat, trailing kisses up to his jaw. "That was a hell of a warm-up act." Her hands went to his belt.

On a groan of pure regret, he stopped her. "Deanna."

"What?"

"Baby, you've been drinking."

"I'm not drunk, Wyatt." Her eyes did, in fact, look perfectly clear as she stared up at him, cheeks still flushed from her orgasm.

But he couldn't risk it. "You're impaired. And much as I want to—like really really want to—we can't."

Her brows drew together. "Why? Is it being in your family's house?"

"No. I'd have hardly done what we just did if that was a concern." Cursing himself and wondering if this would put him in line for sainthood, he put a little space between them. His dick ached in protest. "You hate making mistakes. You still have issues with the fact that you drunk-bought the house. This is too important for you not to be stone cold sober. So, much as I want you, want this. Much as I may hate myself in this moment—which I assure you is a whole hell of a lot—it's better than you having regrets and hating me in the morning."

She dropped her hands with a sigh. "It's hard to argue with that."

"I'm sorry. Truly, I am." Being canonized as Saint Blue Balls would be worth it, right?

"Me too." Her disappointed smile had a mischievous edge. "So no pushing the beds together?"

And finding having the temptation of that body wind up under or over his sometime in the night when what remained of his control was gone? "Woman, are you trying to kill me?"

Huffing a laugh, she skirted around him and slid into one of the beds. "Good night, Wyatt."

As he blew out a breath and headed into the bathroom himself for a cold shower, he reflected that at least it had been for one of them.

"Sooo, tell me about the hot contractor." Ivy's green eyes glimmered as she sank back into one of the comfortable chairs scattered on all sides of the wrap-around porch and folded both hands over her very pregnant belly.

"Not even a hi, how are you?" Deanna asked with mock offense.

"You said you're leaving in a couple of hours. I'm just being efficient. The 'how are you' is inevitably bound up with him if that kiss was anything to go by."

Deanna settled back in her own chair with a steaming cup of coffee, delighted for the chance to visit with one of her oldest friends, even if it meant something of an inquisition. "Saw that, did you?"

Ivy grinned. "Boy, did I. Spill it, woman. You swore off men for life after Blake."

"Well, to be fair, at the time, I believed 'men' was synonymous with 'assholes.' Wyatt's not like that." He was, she was coming to understand, a breed of his own.

"You two have chemistry with a capital C."

"Is it that obvious? Bennet said it was, but you know her. She's always looking for the couple to ship." Ivy didn't tend to operate with romance-tinted glasses, so she was a more objective opinion.

"Oh, girl, it totally was." The new voice sliding into their conversation belonged to Pru's teenaged daughter, Ari. Pourer of the wine last night that had made Wyatt put on the brakes. "Fiona and I have been wishing and hoping for *weeks*. Ivy, I brought you some of that peppermint tea."

Yeah she'd screwed the pooch with that one.

As the girl handed over the mug, Deanna tried to trace the family tree for how Ari was connected to Fiona Gaffney. A sort of cousin since her mother Emerson was married to Caleb, who was one of Joan's boys? She remembered he'd been at demo day.

"The payoff was really damned satisfying," Ivy agreed. "Bless Bennet for posting the footage."

"I'm sitting right here," Deanna reminded them.

Unrepentant, Ivy just grinned. "Sorry, not sorry. Anyway, it was probably more obvious to me because I know you , but... yeah. I called it weeks ago. I kept wanting to text you to ask what was going on behind the scenes, but I didn't want to make you balk."

There was no sense denying that she might have. As a trained profiler, Ivy Blake Wilkes always saw more than people wanted her to. Thank God she mostly only used her powers for the best-selling thrillers she wrote.

"Wyatt's great!" Ari defended. "Why would you have balked?"

At Deanna's bland stare, she blew out a very teenaged huff. "Fine. Not my conversation." Reluctance dragged her feet as she walked away.

Deanna waited until she heard the door slap shut. "Well, the whole thing was a surprise to me."

Ivy looked askance in her direction. "Was it? Or was the fact that it wasn't all in your head the surprise?" She could always be trusted to dig into the heart of the matter, picking out those subtle shades of difference that changed everything.

"Maybe both." Deanna tapped restless fingers against the mug in her hands. "I didn't expect to be here again."

"You look happy."

"I am happy." The words sank into her with the resonance of truth. "I *am* happy."

"And that scares you down to the bone, doesn't it?"

Of course Ivy would know that. She'd been there for so much of the misery with Blake. "Wyatt is a good man. No one would do what he's done for me without being a good man. I just... I'm terrified to trust anything again. Things are really new and complicated. We live together. We're business partners. The stakes are really high. If things go somehow bad or wrong between us, then it screws everything up for both of us. He needs the house and everything we're doing to it as fodder for his show. He needs my PR skills to elevate that to something he can truly leverage for a network contract. I need his skills to actually finish the house. And... well, he wants me to pursue design for real. To use the platform of the show to really give it a go. Which is terrifying in its own right because I want it so damned bad, and there's all this extra pressure because what if I tank it for him?"

"That is definitely a lot."

"Neither of us can afford for anything to go wrong."

"That may be, but I think you're also afraid for everything to go right. Because what would that mean for you?"

Deanna bought time by sipping at the truly excellent coffee. "Opening my heart to truly trust again. Letting him close enough that he could break me."

"Scary stuff."

The mild words made her bristle. "I feel like I have the right to be scared. I was burned pretty damned badly."

"Nobody's disputing that. You have a right to whatever fear and pain you're still toting around over that asshole. But I'd also point out that Wyatt is a patient guy. That's obvious in the kind of work that he does. He doesn't rush. He takes his time and does things the right way. I'd expect he'd deal with people much the same way."

"You're not wrong." He'd pushed her in pursuing the design thing, but never regarding their relationship. Case in point, last night's one-sided orgasm. She'd been more than ready to go to bed with him, but he'd been noble, damn it. How could she fault him for that?

"I feel like there's a 'but' hanging around in there somehow."

"He's letting me set the pace with our relationship."

"And what pace is that exactly?"

Glacial. "We've been taking things slow. There are a bunch of very practical reasons for that. I rushed into things with Blake, and it was a titanic mistake."

"Buuuuut."

Deanna glanced around, making sure neither Wyatt nor any of his myriad of foster siblings were within earshot. "There's a part of me that wants to leap in feet first, because holy hell, the man is hot, and it's been a *loooong* time." And if he could give her an orgasm like that with her clothes *on*, what could he do with all of them off?

Ivy laughed. "Hey, I dragged Harrison to bed within about twenty-four hours, so I'm the last person to criticize. If you want him, make that clear."

"I think I will." She sipped more coffee. "And how is your adoring and very sexy husband?"

Her friend grinned that smug, happily married grin that used to feel like a slap. "He's very good. Scared to death about this baby, so he's devoured about seventeen different baby and parenting books trying to prepare."

"The fact that the former Army Ranger is scared of *this* continues to amuse me."

As they continued to chat about the upcoming baby, Deanna found she no longer felt the prick of envy at her friend's happiness. And that said as much as anything because she felt like maybe she'd finally gotten it right in her own life. With Wyatt. With the house. And that was a scary and wonderful place to be.

But maybe, just maybe, she could put all that aside and let herself enjoy the ride.

CHAPTER 12

"Okay, easy. Easy. A little to the left. Watch your fingers." Wyatt's muscles bunched as he, Levi, and Simon wrestled with the last of the kitchen countertops.

Simon and Levi released their hold, and Wyatt shoved the counter into place on the newly installed cabinets.

"Perfect fit, as always." Simon held his knuckles up.

Wyatt gave him a fist bump and stepped back to take in the full effect. This was his very favorite part of the process. When a room truly began to take shape, and he could see the way to the finish line, but they weren't quite there yet.

"I think I'm going to cry." Deanna pressed a hand to her mouth, and those gorgeous hazel eyes did look a little glassy.

Wyatt tugged her back against him, resting his chin on her shoulder. "There's no crying in renovation. At least not when nothing's a disaster."

"Ooo, man." Simon whistled. "Don't you say that. It's tempting the gods."

"Happy tears. Ecstatic tears. Wyatt, the cabinets are exquisite. And these custom butcher block countertops from all the reclaimed wood are so special." She reached out to run a hand lovingly over the surface.

Wyatt wondered what it would take to get her to do that to him again. They'd been business as usual, wrapped up in the renovation since they got back from Eden's Ridge. Still, seeing her obvious pleasure in his work was its own reward. "It'll be awhile before we get to staining the floors, and we still need to pick out appliances, but it's coming together. To actually look like a kitchen."

"Maybe we should rethink that. I know there are a lot of practical reasons to wait on refinishing the floors until we can do everything at once, but for the purposes of the show, it might make more sense to go ahead and finish them out, so we can give them the payoff of a finished room."

"Is that because you actually think that would please viewers more or because you're desperate for a real, functioning kitchen?"

"I mean… it can be both. The only thing I want as much as a kitchen is a finished master bath with a massive soaker tub and a steam shower, and we haven't even started on that beyond the rough-in of the plumbing."

Wyatt laughed. "We'll talk about it."

"The woman has a point," Levi conceded. "Disaster to big reveal is the more typical pattern on home improvement shows."

"We aren't typical. We do a lot more of the actual how to, and viewers like that. Take that tutorial Deanna did on stripping and refinishing the pressed tin ceiling tiles in here. People loved that."

"True. Stats on that post and episode are looking great." She tipped her head back against his shoulder to take in the finished ceiling. "They came out so well."

Wyatt couldn't resist pressing a kiss to her brow. "We do good work, Miss James."

"Yes, we most certainly do."

When she didn't protest or pull away, he counted it a win. They'd both more or less resigned themselves to the fact that

Bennet would play up the romance, but Deanna was still reluctant to allow PDA on camera on purpose. The shit-eating grin Simon kept aiming their way probably didn't help matters.

He pressed a hand to his heart. "Aww. Love in the time of renovations."

When Deanna slipped away, Wyatt glared at him. "Your commentary is not required."

"Keep pushing, Simon, and I'll have Bennet add in a secondary subplot romance," Deanna warned.

"With who?"

"Absolutely nobody missed you making eyes at Fiona Gaffney."

Simon sputtered, shooting panicked glances at the camera in the corner. It was time-lapse, so didn't capture audio at all, but apparently he was too flustered to remember that. "Bennet, you can't put that in there. I don't consent. There's no release."

"Pretty sure it's covered under the general release you signed at the start of the season. I'm sure we could arrange another workday." Smirking at his discomfiture, Deanna grabbed her camera and waved him out of the shot so she could get pictures of the new counters.

Satisfied his little brother had been shut down, Wyatt circled back to their earlier conversation. "Carson said he had a run on tin ceiling tiles after you posted your tutorial."

"Yeah?" Deanna paused, camera in hand. "Have you ever considered approaching him for sponsorship?"

"Thought about it. Never have. He gave me my start. Asking for anything else feels… weird."

"That man adores you. You use tons of his materials, and your platform would be a potential boon to his business."

"We'll add it to the list for discussion." It was getting longer by the minute. Might as well continue the trend. "I also was thinking it might be worth doing a limited-run special on the deconstruction and salvage process."

She brightened, and he could see the wheels turning in her

head with some new idea. "Oh, that has possibilities. I wonder if we could negotiate a trade for materials?"

Before Wyatt could reply, Casper shot out of the room, loudly announcing that someone had arrived.

Deanna set the camera aside. "Are we expecting anyone?"

"At seven o'clock on a Thursday night? No."

"Did somebody order take out?" Levi asked.

Simon's response to that was a massive growl of his stomach. "No, but we totally should. I'm starved."

"You're always starved."

The doorbell rang.

Wyatt made it to the door first, tugging a barking Casper back by the collar. "Settle down, pal. You have served your duty as alarm system."

Deanna opened the door. "Patrick!"

Who the hell was Patrick? Wyatt thought about letting Casper loose on the suit standing on their front porch. He looked slick and polished, and the gaze he tracked over Deanna said he knew her better than Wyatt liked and wanted to get to know her better still.

She stepped back. "Please, come in."

The suit stepped inside, eyes moving to take in the foyer and landing on Wyatt.

"Patrick, this is Wyatt Sullivan, my business partner and the talent behind *DIWyatt*. Wyatt, this is my friend Patrick McCall. He's an associate producer with the True Country Network."

"A producer?" Well, Wyatt figured he could shape up enough to shake the man's hand.

"I contacted Patrick a couple of months ago to see if there'd be any interest from TCN in your show." She folded her arms, one brow lifted in censure. "I rather thought you'd blown me off."

"Sorry about that. You know how things get. But I did finally catch up on what you sent me and what you've put out so far. Gotta say, I really liked what I saw."

"I told you, you would."

"So you did. I didn't realize to begin with that you were looking to be a part of the whole thing, Deanna. That changes everything."

So he'd seen the kiss. Probably. Wyatt felt an unreasonable satisfaction that he'd effectively marked his territory.

"It does?"

"I'll just get right to the point. You two have something special going. As you know, TCN has been working to expand its market share by branching into slice-of-life reality shows that fit the aesthetic of our network. We think you could be our network's *Home Town* or *Fixer Upper,* and we want to prove that CMT passed up a good thing."

This was what he wanted. What he'd been working toward. Wyatt resisted the urge to whoop. He'd thought he'd made it before and been ultimately shot down. But an assistant producer had to be higher up the totem pole than Curt Welling, right?

"That's very flattering, Patrick. What's the catch? If you were ready to make some kind of offer, you'd have called us up to the network offices rather than showing up out here after work."

"Well, not everybody at the network is on board yet. We have a big party coming up. All the big wig decision makers will be in attendance. I want to have the party here. It would be your chance to really wow them with the finished product and show your chemistry in person."

A party. They wanted to host a party. It seemed a weird way to go about things, but he could work with that. "When is the party?"

"Labor Day."

That was a month away. Blood roared in Wyatt's ears as the list of all the remaining work to be done scrolled through his brain. They had a timeline. A tight one to start. This was… this was…

"We'll do it." Deanna's confident voice echoed through the foyer.

Wait. What? No.

They needed to discuss this. He was the renovation expert. The one who knew what went into all of this and how long it would take. She'd said she'd bow to his expertise. But Wyatt couldn't seem to make himself speak, and Patrick was already shaking her hand, then his and walking out the door.

The moment Patrick's car cranked up, Deanna threw her arms around Wyatt's shoulders. "This is *it!* This is our shot. I've met a bunch of these producers. These are people who can and will make a legitimate decision."

"What the hell did you just commit us to? Do you remember our timeline? The one that doesn't have us finishing with things for two whole *months* after this party?"

"Hold up. Slow down. We can revise the timeline."

"Revise the timeline. How?"

"For a party, we only need to get the lower level public areas done. We can shift around all the upstairs work until after that. It'll still be tight, but we can recruit some more warm bodies to help." She framed his face in her hands. "We can do this, Wyatt. *You* can do this. I believe in you."

Her words settled over him, settled *into* him, calming the rising panic. No one had believed in him like this since Scott. He hadn't realized how much he'd needed that from someone else.

Curling his hands around her hips, he dropped his brow to hers. "Okay. Okay, if you think we can do this, we'll find a way to make it happen."

"Sounds like we need to make a plan to tackle everything." Simon's voice sounded from down the hall. Of course, he'd been eavesdropping on that entire exchange. "If you're done with this touching moment, can we order food so we can get started on that?"

Deanna laughed softly. "The man has a point."

"I call Chinese."

"I'll call it in."

~

I HEREBY RESIGN from my position, effective immediately.

Deanna stared at her computer screen, pouring over every word of the letter she'd drafted, as if that was going to give her clarity on this situation. She wanted to quit. That was nothing new. But now she felt a pressure to actually do it.

Wyatt was freaking out over the deadline she'd committed them to. If they were going to meet it, they needed all hands on deck. He believed enough in her to make her a part of what he'd built with *DIWyatt*, so he deserved her full investment.

But the prospect of actually pulling this trigger, leaving the security of a guaranteed paycheck and health insurance, of potentially burning bridges with this precipitous exit, absolutely terrified her. There was no turning back if she did this. No safety net. Her parents would flip their lids. And God knew how Blake would react. She had a month, maybe two at the most, that she could swing alimony at the rate specified in the divorce decree and then...

The whole thing was a gamble. She'd gambled before and lost big. Wyatt was so much of a better man than Blake. If this didn't pay off, it wouldn't be because he was lazy or using her. He was all in.

She wanted to be.

And yet.

Her office phone rang.

"Deanna James. How can I help you?"

"Deanna, it's Lacey. Mr. Neal would like to see you in his office to discuss a new client."

Another one?

She couldn't afford to take on another client. Her existing load already took about sixty hours a week, and she hadn't gotten more than six hours of sleep a night since she'd bought Blackborne Hall.

Closing her eyes, she took a soft breath. "I'm on my way."

Before she left her office, she printed off the letter and signed it. She wouldn't give it to her boss right now, but the possibility of it felt like a talisman against allowing herself to be pushed around, so she slid it into the leather folio she took to meetings.

On the elevator ride up, she dreamed of a day when this would be a straightforward decision. When there'd be no one she had to think of but herself. When she'd actually be free to just live her life the way she wanted. She hadn't dared to even imagine that before Wyatt. Not really. He'd opened up her world and helped her step back out into it. She'd needed that. But it meant that the status quo chafed now in a way she hadn't acknowledged before.

At the desk outside Mr. Neal's office, Lacey looked nervous. Great. That suggested a high maintenance client. Like they needed another one of those with Mercy Lee on their roster.

Wanting to put the woman at ease, Deanna flashed her a smile and strode inside.

"And here she is. Our best account executive."

Damned straight, she was the best. Her superiors acknowledged it seldom enough that she took a moment to bask in the glow of acknowledgment. But that warmth faded as she caught sight of Gavin Waters, her least favorite agent, rising from one of the chairs in front of Mr. Neal's desk.

"Deanna. Good to see you again."

A sense of dread lodged in her gut like a chunk of concrete. Without responding, she slowly pivoted to take in the rest of the spacious, top floor office. Standing in front of the window, looking like an ad for some wanna-be-a-country-boy cologne, stood Blake.

Remain calm and professional.

"What's going on?" She addressed the question to her boss.

Richard Neal beamed. "Gavin's client just inked a deal with Quicksilver Entertainment. They want to hire our firm, and they want to work with you."

Gavin's client. As if Richard wasn't perfectly well aware that Blake was her ex-husband.

This could not be happening.

Knowing her smile was probably one step above a snarl, she kept her attention on Richard. "I'm flattered by the request, but I already have a full client load. I'm afraid I can't possibly take on anyone else."

Richard dropped into the chair behind his desk and steepled his fingers in a way she'd watched him do countless times over the years. It was his king issuing a proclamation position. "I'm not being clear. They want our firm and only you. This is not negotiable."

She gave up even the pretense of a smile. "You're aware of the conflict of interest here?"

He shrugged that off. "It's been, what? Two years? You're a consummate professional. It won't be a problem." His tone was so certain, as if there wasn't a doubt in his mind that she'd fall in line.

And why shouldn't he expect that? She always had, hadn't she?

The unmitigated gall of these people astounded her. It was bad enough she'd had to work a job for years where she regularly chanced running into her ex-husband. But to be expected to actually work with him? To be at his beck and call? It would be like being married again.

There wasn't enough money on earth to induce her to put up with that.

With one sweeping gaze of the men in the room, she returned her focus to Richard as she opened her folio. "As hell has not frozen over, that will not be happening. I quit. Effective immediately."

She dropped the letter on his desk, taking pleasure in the expression of profound shock on his face before she sauntered out.

Lacey had obviously been eavesdropping. Her jaw hung practically to the floor as Deanna exited the office.

"Good for you," she hissed.

Deanna just nodded and made straight for the elevator. Now that it was done, she needed to get the hell out before reality sank in.

"You can't just quit."

She repressed a sigh. Of course, Blake had come after her. Not bothering to look in his direction, she pivoted and headed for the stairs. "I believe I just did. You don't control me anymore."

"Are you fucking him?"

"Excuse me?"

"The carpenter. Are you fucking him?"

Seriously? Even her ex-husband had heard about her involvement with Wyatt? What kind of publicity magic had that kiss video had?

"Who I take to my bed stopped being your business a long time ago. Not that fidelity was a concept that apparently ever meant a damned thing to you." She yanked open the door to the stairwell.

But Blake couldn't just leave well enough alone. He followed her inside. "You still owe me alimony."

"We both know that's bullshit. You just signed with one of the biggest labels in Nashville."

"That doesn't change anything."

"Oh, but it should. And I'm finally going to do what I should have done in the first place and contest the divorce decree based on the conflict of interest of the judge. I'll see you in court."

And feeling lighter than she had in years, she left her ex-husband gaping after her and went to gather her personal effects.

CHAPTER 13

"This totally isn't on the new schedule until after the party."

Wyatt didn't even spare Simon a glance from his crouched position. "I am aware." He was the one who'd lost sleep the past week and change to pull it off.

"I still can't believe you managed to keep it a secret. Doesn't Deanna go through the house daily to check for changes?"

"Yeah. I've kept her busy downstairs with all the other prep. She's not expecting changes anywhere else, and we're both so tired by the time we're done with work for the night, there's no energy left for anything else."

"That's just sad, man."

Wyatt rolled his eyes. "Get your mind out of the gutter." He was spending plenty of time fantasizing about it himself. He didn't need any help on that front.

Last fastening tightened, Wyatt pushed in the modified drawer and stood. They both took in the finished room, the product of their hard, sneaky labor. Deanna was going to love it. At least, Wyatt hoped she did.

"Well, if she doesn't jump your bones for this, your relationship is doomed."

"That's not why I did it." He'd wanted to thank her for her faith and hard work. Because of her, he was closer to his dream than he'd ever been. Even if the reaching for it might lead to his first ever legitimate panic attack.

Casper rose from his spot on the floor and peered out the window, his tail swishing like a metronome, his nose leaving prints on the glass. On a yip, he tore out of the room and raced for the stairs.

"Shit, she's home early. Go, go, go. She can't see this yet." He had a plan for presenting this surprise and it didn't include tools and drywall dust being everywhere.

They shut the door and bolted downstairs after the dog. Wyatt had a bottle of water in his hand when Deanna came through the door.

"Hey! I wasn't expecting you for a couple more hours yet."

Coming into the lounge, she dropped her purse, and he got a good look at her face. Her eyes were wide, her expression a little shocky. Going on alert, he set the water aside and moved to her, curling his hands around her elbows. "Are you okay?"

"I… don't know."

"What happened?" Had she gotten bad news?

"I just turned in my letter of resignation, effective immediately."

The flood of relief and excitement had him scooping her into a hug. "Oh, my God. That's huge! How do you feel?"

"Um… Somewhere between giddy and terrified. But I'm finally free. Of that at least."

"That's freaking fantastic." Simon held up a fist for a bump. "Congratulations."

In a daze, Deanna returned it.

"That's amazing. Seriously. I'm so proud of you. What made you pull the trigger?" He hadn't really believed she'd be able to make herself take the risk. Maybe she was finally really making progress on exorcising her parents' voices from her head.

She slid her arms around his shoulders. "If we're going to make this deadline, I need to be all in. And my boss tried to force Blake on me as a client."

"He did what?" Wyatt knew his voice was one step above a growl. But how the hell could anyone expect her to work with that good-for-nothing shit biscuit.

"Quitting on the spot and handing over the letter of resignation I'd been carrying was a pretty fantastic mic drop moment." She grinned, her fingers curling in the hair at his nape. It was the first sign of her coming back to herself since she'd walked through the door.

She'd really, truly done it. There'd be consequences but in this moment, nothing else was more important than acknowledging the enormity of her action.

"This calls for a celebration."

"Does that mean I get input on our project for the night?"

"It means we're knocking off for the night early and going out on an actual date."

Her brows drew together. "Are you sure? There's so much to do."

"Other than Simon's birthday weekend, you haven't had a break since we started on the Hall. We can take one night to toast to this."

She angled her head in concession. "Alcohol of some kind seems like it might help head off the impending—holy shit, what have I done?—freak out. I want to change clothes. If I never see another pair of stilettos or pencil skirt again, it'll be too soon."

Wyatt kept hold of her. "Full disclosure: I kinda like the shoes and the skirts. So maybe keep a few?"

She laughed. "Noted. But nothing formal tonight."

"Fair enough. Go change. I'll be right behind you to shower."

A flash of unmistakable heat flickered in her eyes. Maybe she felt like celebrating some other way? Wyatt's pulse kicked up several notches as Deanna brushed her lips over his. He didn't think he was misreading the promise he tasted as she stepped back.

The moment she was up the stairs, he turned to Simon. "I need a favor. Changing won't take her long. I need you to distract her until I'm out of the shower so she doesn't see what we've been up to."

Simon smirked. "Looked like you could distract her yourself *in* the shower."

As appealing an idea as that was, he didn't intend their first time to be a fast, hot coupling while his brother was roaming the house. "Please, man."

"Fine. I've got your back."

"And after we leave, could you please go finish the last cleanup? I want to surprise her when we get back."

"In the name of doing you a solid, I can do that, too."

"Thanks, bro."

Deanna was not waiting in the bathroom, and she didn't come in during his whirlwind shower. He found her outside with Simon, peering up at the second floor galley. She'd traded the businesswear for jeans and a little light sweater set. It was very girl next door, yet another side of her he hadn't seen before.

"—need to see if we can tackle some of the outside as well. Fresh paint and shutters. Maybe some landscaping. But none of that makes sense if we have to rebuild or massively repair the gallery." Deanna turned to him. "What do you think?"

Wyatt felt another hitch in his chest at the idea of adding anything else to the to do list, so he fell back on the party line. "We'll discuss it. Later. Tonight is not about work." Taking her elbow, he steered her toward the truck.

"Have fun, you two! I'll lock up."

At the head of the driveway, Wyatt turned to her. "What are

you feeling? We could go all the way into Nashville proper, hit up Lower Broadway for some music and dancing."

"Ugh, God no. I'd like to stay far from the country music scene. You know what I'm really craving? A gourmet burger."

"I know just the place."

The Pharmacy was a Nashville institution. As ever, the beer garden was packed, but that was the price you paid for one of the best burgers in town. They kept up an easy, running conversation while they waited, both steering clear of work. As they were finally seated at one of the outdoor tables beneath the trees and string lights, Wyatt was very conscious this was the first actual date they'd been on. Hell, it was the first date he'd been on period in… He couldn't remember when.

Deanna settled with her menu. "What are you thinking?"

"About how long it's been since I went out on an actual date. I really can't remember."

"That's easy for me. This is my first date since my divorce."

"Really? I'd think you'd have had plenty of offers."

She shrugged. "Oh, it's not my first opportunity. It's just the first one I've accepted. After Blake I was not, as you might imagine, feeling particularly kindly toward your half of the species."

She'd had her trust shattered. Wyatt understood what it meant that she'd gotten involved with him. He took her hand. "Well, I'm glad I'm the lucky guy who got the yes."

Those glossy pink lips quirked, and her eyes crinkled with amusement. "Technically, you didn't ask. You told. I just happened to be on board with spending some non-work-related time with you. We've been doing this relationship thing kind of backwards."

He stroked his thumb over the pulse point of her wrist, feeling it jump. "Maybe, but it seems like it's working out pretty well all around."

"True enough."

"Oh my God, you're DIWyatt!"

They both jolted at the voice, yanking apart like guilty teenagers.

The forty-something woman clasped her hands together in excitement. "I'm so sorry to interrupt. I just love your show."

Wyatt found his host's smile. "Glad to hear it."

"I've been following along with the renovation on Blackborne Hall, and it's just awesome! I can't wait to see the kitchen finished!"

In his periphery, Wyatt saw Deanna's smug smile. Her campaigns to expand the audience were working. Not that he hadn't been recognized in public before, but it was a rare thing.

"Thanks. It's a hell of a house."

A server materialized, clearly ready to take their order.

"Oh, I'll get out of the way. But could I possibly get a picture?"

A picture? Like he was somebody? That was new. Acting as if he got this kind of request all the time, Wyatt dialed up the smile. "Of course."

"I can take it." Deanna held out her hand for the woman's phone.

"Oh no! You have to be in it. It wouldn't be the same without you."

Delighted she'd been recognized and appreciated, Wyatt watched Deanna sit back in shock as the woman turned to the server instead. "Would you mind?"

"Sure. Gotta document the Wyanna sighting."

"Right? You know the show, too?"

"Of course."

Deanna leaned toward them. "I'm sorry. Wyanna?"

The server grinned. "Didn't y'all know you have a hashtag?"

"I… did not." Clearly flummoxed, she looked at Wyatt.

He shrugged. Bennet had said people were into the idea of them. This just seemed to prove it. It was kinda weird, but if it expanded their audience base, wasn't that the point?

"Please?" the woman begged.

"Um, sure."

The fan crouched down between them both and mugged for the camera.

"Say keys!"

"So what did you think about our first official public outing?"

From the passenger seat, Deanna rolled her head toward Wyatt. "The date or being recognized?"

"Mmm, both."

"Five stars to choice of restaurant. That was the best burger I've had in years, and the atmosphere was perfect. As for the rest... it was so surreal. I'm used to being in the background with my work. I never expected to be recognized." An oversight on her part. By taking a more active role in the show, she automatically became more visible. But somehow she hadn't expected all her hard work at expanding the *DIWyatt* audience to already be bleeding over to her. Apparently Bennet wasn't the only one out there with a gooshy, romantic heart. Deanna wasn't exactly sure how she felt about it.

Wyatt turned into the drive for Blackborne Hall. "The first time I got recognized in public because of my show was the biggest thrill. I almost asked the guy if I could get a picture with him to prove it."

"Prove what?"

"That what I was doing was legitimate. That I was reaching people."

That I mattered.

He didn't say it, but Deanna heard the subtext. Given what he'd told her about his adopted family, that had to underscore everything he did. For all his confidence in his abilities, he needed that external validation. Had she given him enough of that herself?

"Is it still a thrill?"

"I'm not sure it will ever get old." He shifted the truck into park. "Is that something you're going to be okay with? The increased recognition?"

"I don't know. It's not something I've ever sought. But it feels kind of like a sign from the universe that I made the right call, you know?"

"I absolutely do. I think it's evidence that we're on the right track." He skimmed his fingers over her cheek, and Deanna turned into the touch, basking in the little zings across her skin. "I already said it once, but I'm really proud of you. I know quitting goes against all those internalized messages from your parents. It's the hard thing."

She curled her hand around his wrist, holding him to her just a few moments longer. "It's not nearly as hard knowing you're in this with me." It was so different from what life had been like with Blake, where everything they did was in service to his questionable career and his pursuit of adoration. In an effort to be supportive, she'd lost herself. Deanna didn't think Wyatt would let her do that with him. He'd made it very clear he wanted her to succeed at what she wanted on her own terms. That kind of support was something she could get drunk on.

"I'll be with you every step of the way. C'mon. Let's go let Casper out."

They went inside, laughing their way through Casper's ecstatic greeting. The domesticity of letting him out and securing the house for the night added an icing of contentment to an already fantastic night. Coming home with Wyatt felt good. Too good.

The idea of it gave her pause. There was no longer a built-in expiration date, no more threat of losing the house. But a part of her still didn't want to fully trust in the longevity of this. Of them. She didn't know if she had it in her to fully give herself over to another relationship. But she was too happy to worry right now, so she shoved the thought away to think about later.

At the base of the stairs, Wyatt took her hand and drew it to his lips for a lingering kiss that made her heart thud. "We should do this date thing more often."

"It was a good night." A night she wasn't ready to end. The look in his eyes said he'd be amenable to that. But Deanna knew she'd have to make the move. He wouldn't push her, wouldn't rush. That wasn't his way. If she wanted him in her bed, she had to speak up. Preferably before Casper finished his dinner and installed himself at the end of the bed, as he considered his due.

"I want to show you something."

Jarred from her thoughts by his statement and the undercurrent of nervous excitement suddenly pumping off him in waves, she could only nod and follow him upstairs.

"I've been living like this—the middle of a job site—for years. I'm used to some pretty rough conditions. You weren't. But you jumped in feet first, without complaint. You've lived rough for months, tolerating all the practical reasons why it made sense to do things to the whole house in phases rather than one room at a time. So I did a thing."

He opened the door to what they'd decided would ultimately be a master suite somewhere well down the line.

"Holy shit." Deanna stepped inside.

He'd taken out the wall between this room and the next, opening it up to a much larger space. The old water damage was a thing of the past. New walls had been erected, making way for a massive walk-in closet and what was presumably the bathroom they'd discussed. The drywall wasn't finished yet, but it was damned close. He'd gifted her a blank canvas, ready and waiting for color and texture—all the things she loved best.

"This is amazing." Her mind spun, imagining the sort of furniture and finishes she wanted in here. Dreaming of a comfortable, lavish retreat from all the chaos of renovation.

"Oh, this isn't what I wanted to show you. It was just a necessary part of the rest." Wyatt pulled her past stacks of lumber and more drywall to the closed door beyond. *"This* is what I wanted to show you."

She saw the tub first, a massive soaker in a gleaming copper. It sat on the exact vintage patterned tile she'd lusted after at Restoration Station. On the opposite wall, a vanity had been made of the antique buffet from the barn. He'd refinished it to a polished mahogany sheen, exactly as she'd wanted. A toilet had been tucked in a little alcove beyond, with a pocket door just waiting to be slid shut. And with a dawning sense of wonder, she caught sight of the shower reflected in the antique mirrors over the vanity. It was massive, somehow combining vintage lines and shapes with modern, spa-like elegance.

A potent tangle of gratitude, awe, and lust bloomed in her chest as she soaked in the space. Like the kitchen island, he'd plucked it straight from the pages of her design sketchbook. A dream come to life.

"I knew you hadn't quite settled on a wall color yet, so I stuck with a basic cream. Something that would suit on its own if you liked it, but work as a primer coat if you didn't. And I know you'll want to pick out the rug and linens yourself, so I didn't—"

Deanna launched herself at him, yanking his mouth to hers in a desperate, delirious kiss. His stubbled cheeks were rough beneath her palms, and the body he wrapped tight around hers was hard. She wanted it. Wanted him with all his big-hearted, thoughtful gestures. She needed to know if that generous nature extended to bed. Or the shower.

And tonight she intended to find out.

THROUGH ALL THESE months with Deanna, Wyatt had caught glimpses of deep wells of feeling, always quickly shut away and controlled. He'd wondered what she would be like if she finally let go. As her fevered joy flowed over him, he thought he'd happily drown in it. He'd inspired this, and he intended to ride the wave as far as she was willing to take it.

"Does the shower work?" she gasped.

"All plumbed up." Not that he'd done more than test the water. He'd figured she'd want dibs on the first real shower.

"I need to be inside it with you inside me."

"Fuuuuuck," he groaned.

"Yes." She kissed him again, her fingers dragging at his clothes as she stumbled across the room. "I had one beer. I am sober as a judge."

"Thank God."

More than on board, he shoved that prim little cardigan off her shoulders and tugged at the sleeveless sweater beneath, breaking the kiss to pull it over her head. Her bra was exactly the sort of lacy confection he'd expected. Classy and sexy, like the woman herself. Her skin was silk beneath his work-roughened fingers as he worked loose the clasp and drew the fabric away.

He cursed again with reverence as he took in her breasts. Those high, round globes rose and fell with her unsteady breaths, her nipples pearled and rosy and begging for his mouth. A flush worked its way up her chest and throat, climbing into her cheeks. Wyatt dragged his gaze to hers, making sure she was still alright with this.

Lifting her chin, Deanna reached for his hands, bringing them up to cover her breasts. Definitely still on board. He shifted his grip, circling her nipples with his thumbs and watching her eyes fall to half mast on a groan that went straight to his already iron hard cock.

"I've been dreaming about your hands on me."

"Have you now?"

"Mmm."

"Where?"

Those eyes glittered up at him, the gold flecks seeming to glow with her arousal. "Everywhere. It's been terrible for my sleep, knowing you were on the other side of that bathroom door."

He'd had plenty of sleepless nights himself for the same reason. "Did you want me to come to you in your bed?"

"Sometimes. I also feel really guilty about that stupid cot."

Wyatt laughed. "I'm used to it. Not that I don't appreciate an actual bed when I'm in one. Sleeping is definitely not what I've imagined when I've thought of yours."

"We'll get there. Shower first."

Officially the best date ever. "Happy to oblige."

He paused to turn on the water and tug off his shirt before coming back to take the hands she'd dreamed about on a tour, down her torso, to her belt.

"You're beautiful."

"So are you." Her fingers skated down his abs as she rose to her toes to kiss him again.

By the time they'd stripped off the rest of their clothes, the shower had filled with steam. With an expression of pure, unadulterated lust, Deanna opened the door and tugged him inside beneath the waterfall spray. She tipped her head back, wetting her hair and groaning with pleasure as the water drummed down on them both. "Just so you know, I'm moving into this shower. This is now my place. I'm never leaving."

With a rumbling laugh, he drew her against him, loving the wet slide of her flesh against his. "Then allow me to give you your first shower warming gift."

Spinning her so that her back was to his front, he palmed one breast and slid his free hand down the slope of her belly, slipping his fingers between the golden curls between her legs to find her drenched. She let out an inarticulate sound, somewhere between a gasp and a moan as he found her clit and circled. Her head fell back against his chest, her arm rising to hook behind his neck.

"More," she demanded.

"Yes, ma'am."

Wyatt slid a finger inside her, curling it until her hips chased the motion. She began to rock, rubbing her ass against his erection until he was tempted to bend her over and drive inside. Sometime maybe, but not now. Not when this was likely her first time in two years. Clinging to his control, he added a second finger. Tight. She was so tight. He needed her loose and languid, so he trailed his lips down the column of her throat, listening for every hitch of her breath, every groan of pleasure as he played her body.

She skated over the edge on an almost silent shudder, her walls clamping around his fingers, her nails biting into his nape. When she went limp, he pressed a kiss to her shoulder and eased her down on the bench.

"Okay?"

Head lolling, she peered up at him through the steam. "I'd forgotten man-made orgasms could be that good."

"Oh, darlin', we're just beginning. Hold whatcha got."

Slipping out of the shower, he dove for his pants, fumbling for his wallet and the condom he'd stashed there. Ripping it open, he rolled it on and stepped back into the steam.

"Did you have plans for me tonight?" It was amusement rather than censure in her tone.

"No expectations. Hopes. That you're surpassing, by the way."

"Happy to oblige," she murmured, throwing his words back at him as she rose. "Sit."

Because it put her breasts right at mouth level, he complied, curling his hands around her hips and pulling her close enough to suck one budded nipple. Deanna's fingers threaded into his hair.

"Mmm, much as I'm enjoying this, there's the small matter of you having destroyed the structural integrity of my knees."

"Hearing you say structural integrity is weirdly hot. Come here."

He helped steady her as she straddled him, settling those slim, muscled thighs on either side of his hips. He'd imagined this as he'd installed this bench. Thought of her braced over him, her eyes hot and hungry on his as she took him in.

Reality was so much better than his fantasy.

She sank down, down, down. A slow, ineffable slide, until he was buried inside her as deep as it was possible to go. Leaning forward, she pressed her brow to his as her body adjusted to his girth.

"Okay?"

"So, okay," she gasped. "Why weren't we doing this weeks ago?"

"Because the shower wasn't ready?"

"Should've built it first."

He was laughing as she began to move, a shallow rise and fall. Though he held her hips, he let her set the pace and rhythm, taking what she wanted. They watched each other as steam billowed and pleasure built anew. When her thighs began to tremble, he gripped her tighter, adding his own short, sharp thrusts, until she lost her grip on that magnificent control and shattered around him, pulling him over the edge.

He locked his arms around her, holding her close as their bodies continued to quake and the water rained down.

"I vote we end every day exactly like this."

"Sold." Wyatt liked this. Not just the sex—although, holy hell, that was stupendous. But her. Living with her, being with her. She was a partner. He'd never wanted one, never realized he'd needed one. But he wanted her. He wanted this house and the life they were building in it.

The part of him basking in a post orgasmic glow wanted to put the whole thing out there. To say the thing, make the plans, and ride this roller coaster. But it was too soon. Deanna's trust was a fragile thing, as was her confidence in what they were doing. She'd come a long way from that first day of panic at Restoration Station, but there was still so much to do, so much to prove. She needed more time. And there was another, deeper part of him that wondered if, at the end of the day, at the end of the project, he would be enough for her.

Oblivious to the direction of his thoughts, Deanna sighed, dropping her brow to his. "Thank you."

Shaking off the worry, Wyatt mustered enough energy for a smile. "For the orgasms or the shower?"

Her laugh made her inner muscles clamp around him again. "I mean, both. But not just that." She straightened, sifting her fingers through his hair.

Wyatt leaned into the touch.

"For all of it. For helping me save this house. For giving me the confidence to pursue the thing that I love. For giving me a *way* to pursue it. No one's ever believed in me like that."

He understood that belief was a powerful thing. His foster mother had instilled that in him before the Sullivans had adopted him. His brother had reinforced it all these years, even as his parents had undermined it.

Because the water was cooling, he reached past her to shut it off. "You make it easy. I'm just calling it like I see it. You're a powerhouse. And I'm thrilled to see you finally turning all those talents to yourself for a change. You deserve to follow *your* dreams instead of someone else's."

The smile she beamed absolutely lit him up inside.

"I really like this whole supportive boyfriend thing."

"Is that what we're calling this?"

"Well, live-in lover and business partner feels like too much of a mouthful, so…"

"Boyfriend it is. Even though it totally makes me feel about seventeen."

Her smile turned impish. "How about you carry me to bed, and I can remind you of how very adult we can be?"

"I am here for it."

And he was for the rest of the night.

CHAPTER 14

"We don't know how old this siding is, so power washing is too big a risk. It could further damage the wood. So that means we're going to do this the old-fashioned way with scrapers. Since there is probably lead in the paint in a house this age, safety first." Deanna slid her mask into place and demonstrated the proper technique for both the collected volunteers and the camera being trained on her by Simon.

"The goal is to remove any loose paint. As you go, make a note of any damage: dry rot, wet rot, any warped boards. We'll have to replace it before we can move forward." They'd get more footage of examples as the day wore on and splice them into the montage. "Everybody clear?"

"Aye, Captain!" Wendy offered a smart salute with her scraper.

"Fantastic. Wyatt and the guys are replacing the joists supporting the second-floor gallery today, so steer clear of the front of the house. Otherwise, let's take advantage of this gorgeous weather and get some work done!"

A cheer went up, and Simon gave a thumbs up to indicate he'd stopped recording. "I'll be back later to get some progress footage."

Once he'd gone, Deanna gave a round of hugs to her girl-friends. "Seriously. Thank y'all for coming out to help today. We need all the help we can get to knock these renovations out in time."

Bennet blew her a kiss. "We've got you, girl."

They all donned their masks and moved to the nearest wall to scrape.

Wendy attacked her stretch of siding with vigor. "Gotta say, it's really cool to see you doing all of this. I mean, I knew you were into HGTV and stuff, but it's a totally different thing knowing you actually *know* stuff. I never imagined you'd end up on a show yourself."

Deanna laughed and climbed up one of the ladders. "Neither did I. Turns out Wyatt has a lot more faith in me than I had in myself. He's really good for me."

"A refreshing change from the limp-dicked weasel. You deserve a good guy. Extra bonus points that this one is good, sweet, *and* hot. It's not exactly a hardship splicing together video each week." Bennet waggled her eyebrows.

Jasmine propped an arm against a lower rung of the ladder and peered up. "We've been taking bets on whether this glow you have going on is because you finally wised up and dragged that tall drink of water into your bed."

Deanna was grateful for the mask hiding her face. "I've got plenty to glow about. I'm doing work that I love. I'm dating an interesting, attractive man who shares my interests. And I'm finally free of the albatross of a job I hated. I keep waiting for the panic to set in, but I feel so much lighter being able to dump all that stuff off my mental plate. I deleted all the social media alerts related to all my clients, and I can actually leave my phone in another room without worrying I'll miss something. Nobody's calling me with their latest disaster or changing their mind at the last second or just never saying thank you for saving their ass. I feel so much *relief*. Quitting my job was the best thing I could have done." She paused, unable to hold back a feline smile. "But yeah, the multiple orgasms definitely don't hurt."

Her friends whooped.

"Now you're just bragging," Wendy complained.

Deanna could only shrug. "What can I say? I prefer having him in my bed than in the room next door." Above and beyond the fact that he was a generous and inventive lover, she enjoyed starting and ending her day with him, talking in the dark about her dreams. Their dreams. It was an intimacy she'd never shared with Blake, one she'd become addicted to.

Wendy shifted over to a new section of siding. "It's about time you were with someone who put you first."

"As he should," Bennet agreed. "Just don't forget which rooms we have cameras set up in."

"Yeah, we won't be making that mistake again." They were very, *very* careful.

"Again!" Adry squeaked.

"After the kiss. Geez. We're not going around christening every room in the house. It's still a construction site." Not that she hadn't thought about it. She had some particular fantasies involving that island he'd built for her.

Jasmine snorted. "Well, freedom and regular orgasms look good on you."

"Oh, my."

The words startled Deanna so much she nearly toppled straight off the ladder. Dropping the scraper, she grabbed the rung in front and held on, heart hammering. Once she was certain she had her footing, she slowly turned her head.

Sure enough, her mother stood just a few feet away, one hand pressed to her throat, eyes wide.

Great. Just freaking great.

Had she overheard the part about Deanna quitting her job? Probably not. She wasn't shrieking in panic. So it was just the stuff about Wyatt. Not a whole lot better.

Drawing on all her poise and pretending Valerie hadn't just gotten a front-row seat to her girlfriends' discussion of her sex life, Deanna climbed down the ladder. "Mom. I wasn't expecting you."

"You're living with him? Sleeping with him?"

I am a grown ass adult who can make her own decisions. I do not need my parents' approval.

She squared her shoulders. "That's not really your business."

"So it's fine for you to parade your relationship on the show for all and sundry to see, but you won't tell your mother?"

Deanna blinked. "You've been watching the show?"

Valerie looked hurt. "Of course I've been watching the show. I want to support you."

For a long moment, she could only stare at her mother. She'd dreamed of her parents actually supporting her decisions for *years*. But with all their judgment and anxieties over mistakes she'd made in the past, she'd never imagined they'd really be on her side. Had she been wrong about that?

Valerie continued. "And really, I would have thought you'd tell us something so important as you finally dating again." The hesitation before "dating" made it clear she didn't approve of everything that entailed, either.

And risk you judging him, too? No, thank you.

But Deanna didn't want to fight. She tugged off her mask. "It's still new. And we've both been really busy working hard on the house. Why don't you come inside and see the progress?"

She didn't think the subject change would work, but she needed to get Valerie away from everyone else before she embarrassed her any more. She steered her mom around the back of the house, toward the side door leading into the kitchen.

When Valerie got her first look at the rehabbed kitchen, the expression of stunned delight was more gratifying than chocolate. "Oh, this is lovely."

"We've got the appliances on order, and the floors and backsplash will be some of the last things we tackle, but it's coming along."

Hesitant, her mother moved into the room, laying a hand on the island. "You designed this?"

"She sure did. Your daughter has a hell of an eye." Wyatt strode in, flashing his host smile. "Good to see you again, Mrs. James."

"This is really good work."

He circled the island and slid an arm around Deanna's waist, creating a united front. "We're an excellent team."

She wanted to kiss him again, her mother be damned.

"I understand that's personal as well as professional."

Wyatt didn't even blink at the implied judgment. "We have a lot in common. You've raised a brave, creative, resourceful woman. I consider myself very lucky."

Valerie blinked in surprise, as if she wasn't quite sure he was talking about her daughter. Deanna tried not to take it personally.

"I was just about to give Mom the progress tour."

"Oh, absolutely. We've gotten so much done since you were last here."

He came with them, keeping Deanna's hand in his as they walked, but he let her do the talking. As they moved through, room by room, with their canine escort, and her mother saw that Blackborne Hall no longer resembled an antebellum flop house, Deanna began to feel a little more hopeful and a whole lot stronger having Wyatt's support and backup. They were doing good work. Legitimate work. And her mom was actually acknowledging it without picking things apart. She should have Wyatt around for every conversation.

"I can hardly believe it's the same house."

"All it needed was vision and someone who loved it enough to save it. Deanna has both. It's a privilege to get to work with that kind of passion."

"You should come to dinner. We want to get to know you better."

Deanna froze. No. No, they couldn't go to dinner. She couldn't do an entire *meal* with both of her parents. Not even with Wyatt by her side. As she wracked her brain, trying to come up with a way to get out of it, he squeezed her hand.

"We'd be happy to."

Valerie nodded, clearly satisfied, and Deanna realized that this had been the entire point of the visit. To corner him into a politely scripted occasion for interrogation. Something she dimly recognized as panic crawled up her spine.

"Sunday," her mom declared.

"Sunday?" Deanna squeaked. They couldn't do Sunday. It was a mass work day. The house would be crawling with volunteers.

Wyatt squeezed her hand. "I'm afraid it'll have to be awhile later. We're at a pivotal point in our timeline, and we've got a houseful of people coming to help out for a workday tomorrow. But I promise we'll come as soon as we're at a reasonable place to pause."

"See that you do. We won't take no for an answer."

Of course they wouldn't.

The moment her mother was gone, Deanna rounded on him. "What the hell are you thinking?"

"I'm thinking that they're concerned and want to get to know the man in your life. And as that man, I should get to know them and reassure them that I am not, in fact, the misogynistic user they're worried about. This seems like a good way to do it."

"But they're… them. You've met them. It's liable to be awful." She just wanted to lose herself in her house, in the restoration, and forget about everything outside her property line.

He reeled her in, dropping a kiss to her brow. "Power of positive thinking, baby. It'll be fine. We're in this together, okay? Besides, we're on such a tight deadline for the party, there's not a chance in hell we can go until after, and by then we'll hopefully have the show in the bag. What can they say if we show up with *that* news?"

Knowing her parents, they'd find something. But the idea of it buoyed her spirits. "From your mouth to God's ear. In the meantime, we have work to do."

~

"I CAN'T BELIEVE we're almost to the point of furnishing the downstairs. Or at least starting." Deanna bounced in the front seat of Wyatt's truck, looking worlds lighter than she had the past few weeks. "Maybe I should give you my wallet so I don't have the means to impulse buy everything that catches my fancy."

Wyatt grinned at her enthusiasm. "What makes you think I'd stop you?" He kinda wanted to see her taking the antiques dealers at the flea market by storm. She struck him as a take-no-prisoners negotiator.

"One of us has to be the responsible one here. And we're talking furniture. I don't think you understand what a weak-willed hussy I can be."

He laughed. "I like this side of you. It's fun."

"It's dangerous, is what it is." She whipped out her phone, tapping buttons. "The flea market will probably take us a big chunk of the day, but if we get done in time, there are a few places north of the city I'd like to check out."

"We can do that. But we've got a stop to make first."

"Oh? Did we need to pick up supplies or something?"

"No. I promised my brother I'd bring you by to meet him." He'd been putting it off and neglecting his visits in the name of pushing through on the house.

"Oh! I didn't realize he lived in town. As much as you've talked about him, I'm surprised he hasn't he come out to see the house."

Wyatt tensed at the perfectly innocent statement. She didn't know. Of course she didn't. He hadn't been able to bring himself to share this part of his life. But if they were building a future together—and God willing, they were—she needed to see behind the curtain, as it were.

"He can't."

"It doesn't seem like you to play temperamental artist and hide the project away until it's done."

He kept his gaze firmly on the road. "No. I mean, he physically can't. He lives in a residential facility for people with traumatic brain injuries."

"Oh." She didn't voice either of the obvious questions. Not what happened? Not why didn't you tell me? But Wyatt felt them both.

"He was an attorney. A brilliant one. A total workaholic, which I was always razzing him about. It was pretty pot-kettle because I was working my ass off on flips. But anyway, I convinced him to take a brothers-only vacation. We decided to go rafting up in West Virginia. Somewhere we could both really unplug. They'd had a really wet spring, and the rapids were bigger than usual. He got thrown out and ended up slammed against the rocks with the full weight of the raft on top of him." The memory of the roar of water and the helpless terror and rage of knowing his brother was underneath had Wyatt's hands tightening on the wheel.

"Jesus."

"It was bad." Such an understatement. But he didn't want to revisit the aftermath of pulling him out of that river. "They said it was a miracle he survived at all, and he wasn't the same after. No more lawyer. No more career." Wyatt had worked his way around to intellectually accepting it hadn't been anyone's fault, but he still felt the weight of *if only.*

Deanna's hand curled around his arm. "I'm so sorry. How long ago was this?"

"Three years. He's come a long way with lots of therapies, regained most of his speech, but he still can't live on his own. I come to see him as often as I can." It wasn't enough. Nothing ever would be. But he'd keep coming. Keep doing whatever he could to support the man who'd done everything for him.

The hand she stroked along his arm soothed his disquiet. "This is why you're working so hard on the show."

He chanced a glance at her. "Huh?"

"Scott can't make it big anymore, so you feel like you have to in order to prove his faith in you isn't misplaced."

If Wyatt hadn't been driving, he'd have stared. How did she know? "What?"

"I mean, you love what you do, but it's more heart than ambition driving you. I know the difference. And that's what makes you stand out from everyone else who wants to do what you're doing. It's what I want people who watch the show to see."

Her insight was dead on, and it left him feeling exposed and vulnerable. It was one thing to show off his skills and designs. It was something else entirely to show himself, and he wasn't entirely sure how he felt about it. So he said nothing, driving through the gates at Fairland Village and leading her into the main complex of the building, greeting the staff he knew by name.

"Seems you have quite the fan club here," Deanna observed.

"The staff has been a great support."

Following directions from the front desk clerk, they found Scott in the gym, sweating it out on the recumbent bike and glaring at his occupational therapist. At the sight of Wyatt, he brightened. "My favorite brother. Save me from this sadist!"

"You'll do no such thing." Alton braced himself on the handlebars and fixed Scott with an intense drill sergeant stare. "You can pedal and talk. It's good practice at multitasking. You'll hit twenty minutes before you get a break."

Wyatt didn't miss the crackle between them and hid a smile. "Scott, there's someone I want you to meet." He tugged Deanna forward.

"'Bout damn time. Been hiding her away."

"More like working our asses off. This is Deanna James. Deanna, my brother Scott."

Scott divided a look between them. "Where's my milkshake?"

Before Wyatt could reply, Deanna arched one delicate brow. "Did I forget the entrance fee?"

Scott's twisted grin pulled the skin around one eye taut, giving him a piratical air. "Damned straight."

"I didn't forget. It's 8:30 in the morning, man. They aren't open yet."

"Bad planning on your part."

"My fault," Deanna said. "I dragged him out early. We're shopping for furniture today."

"Tell me." Scott issued the order in the same tone he'd once used in cross examinations.

So she did, outlining their progress on the house and the plans she had for the downstairs rooms. Wyatt and Alton exchanged a look as Scott blew past the twenty-minute mark and kept going, his attention riveted on Deanna. He wasn't having to pedal with one hundred percent focus. That was more progress.

"We're keeping the footage limited and piecemeal right now because we don't want to ruin the big reveal before the TCN's network party."

Scott's gaze finally swung back to Wyatt. "Network?"

"That's why I haven't been by here as much lately. We're amping up the timetable to host the thing."

Scott slapped the handlebars and crowed. "Hot damn. This one's gonna happen. I can feel it."

As they continued to talk, easy as old friends, Wyatt felt some last bastion of defense against her simply crumble. He was unquestionably, without a doubt, in love with this woman.

In the end, she was the one who had to be reminded of the shopping and work still to be done.

"Get to it, then. I'm still fighting the good fight here."

"You do that. It was so wonderful to meet you, Scott. And I

hope you'll come out to see the house sometime." The invitation was issued with warmth and sincerity. She couldn't know the prospective bomb she'd just dropped.

But his brother didn't explode. Didn't baldly point out his limitations. He didn't say anything at all as he finally stopped pedaling and took the water bottle from Alton.

"He plans to be able to take a full tour of both floors of the house by the time the whole thing is finished," Alton announced.

Scott only grunted in acknowledgment, but it was the first time he'd willingly made a plan to do something outside the facility since he'd moved in.

Wyatt's throat went tight. "I'd love that, man. "

His brother's eyes gleamed with a determination Wyatt hadn't seen since before the accident. "It's gonna happen. You'll see."

"Can't wait."

CHAPTER 15

"*I* can't imagine anyone being a bigger hit with my brother."

Tired and relaxed after a happy, successful day, Deanna tipped her head back against the seat and shifted to smile at Wyatt. "I can see why you adore him. He's great. And it seems like he's working really hard on his recovery."

"He's had a big attitude change since he started working with Alton. He's letting himself hope again, which is huge and something I didn't think I'd ever see."

She had more than an inkling of why that might be the case and wondered if Wyatt had noticed. "Seems like they have a pretty tight bond."

"I think at least half the reason Scott's busting his ass is so he won't be a patient anymore and there are no ethical concerns with them pursuing a relationship."

Delighted, Deanna blew out a breath. "Okay, whew. So I didn't imagine that chemistry."

Wyatt's chuckle rumbled in the cab. "You're getting as bad as Bennet. Anyway, I don't know if anything will come of it, but I hope so. I'd like a chance to know the man who's bringing my brother back to life."

Given what he'd told her this morning about the accident, she could only imagine what having Scott regaining some independence and some measure of his old life would mean for Wyatt. He hadn't admitted it, but she could sense the lingering guilt he carried. Knew that there was some piece he was still holding back.

"We should plan a dinner party for when he comes to tour the house. That visit seems like a big goal post for him, so we should make a big occasion of it. Not in a whole congrats on your recovery kind of way—because that would be kind of ableist—but in a welcome to our home kind of way. A celebration of family."

As soon as the words were out, Deanna wished them back. What was she doing making statements about home and family? They hadn't discussed those things, hadn't discussed their future beyond this house. God knew she'd had plenty of lessons about the danger of making assumptions, and she didn't want to undermine their nascent relationship by pushing too far, too fast.

Wyatt reached across the center console to lace his fingers with hers. "Scott would love that. More to the point, so would I. I like the idea of making a home with you."

She looked down at their twined hands. "Me too." And it scared her shitless.

Needing to lighten the mood, she glanced out the truck's back window at their accumulated treasures. "Of course, we have to finish and furnish first."

"This load is a good start. It'll at least get us a dining room table."

"Once you've made the top."

"Once I've made the top," he agreed. "Let's stop and let Casper out, then go drop this stuff in the barn. We can hunt through the honey hole and see what looks good to go with that base."

He parked in front of the house, and they both slid out.

Deanna met him in front of the truck, automatically leaning in with a contented sigh when he wrapped an arm around her. In the lowering autumn sun, they studied the fruits of their labor. The fresh coat of crisp, white paint made the exterior pop. The newly repaired gallery above was just waiting for a pair of rocking chairs and a cool morning with a steaming mug of coffee. They still needed shutters, the brick of the chimneys needed repointing, and the landscaping was nonexistent. Inside, yet more painting awaited, along with all those floors to refinish. But their goal was in sight, and not a moment too soon. The party was just over a week away.

"She's coming back to glory," Deanna murmured.

"Because of you. Because you had a vision and got drunk enough to act on it."

"Maybe we can leave that part of the story out when we tell people?"

He steered her toward the front steps. "I like that part of the story."

"I like the part where it led me to you."

Wyatt went rigid, and she wondered if she'd overstepped. "What the hell?"

The sharp tone had her shoulders hunching up to her ears as he jerked away and raced up the steps.

The wet steps.

"Fuck!"

Wyatt fumbled the key into the lock, and she saw what he'd seen. Water ran out from beneath the front door in a steady stream.

Her blood chilled. "No."

Throwing open the door, Wyatt pushed past a dancing, soaking wet Casper and raced into the house. With every soggy step through the puddles that covered their precious, salvaged oak floors, Deanna's chest tightened.

The moment he spotted the water spewing from a pipe in the ceiling, Wyatt spewed more profanity and ran for the new shut-off valve he'd installed shortly after moving in.

Deanna's gaze fixed on the ceiling. On the pipe that would have been dealt with weeks ago, if she'd listened to Wyatt and let him take care of everything in the order he'd wanted instead of pressing him to put it off, so they could get the downstairs done on time for this party.

The water stopped spurting, and in the sudden silence, she could hear the steady drip, drip as the last of what was in the pipe drained out onto the floor. In stupefied horror, she lowered her gaze to take in the ruined sheetrock of the walls and the floors that were already buckling from water damage.

Her fault. This was all her fault.

"Get your phone! Call Simon. Have him activate the family group text for a 911. We need every able body, every shop vac, every fan we can get."

But Deanna couldn't move. She could only stare at the ruination of their dreams.

On another curse, Wyatt wrestled a shop vac into the room and shoved it into her hands. "Suck up whatever you can." When she only blinked at him, he curled his hands around her shoulders and shook once. "Deanna, snap out of it! We have work to do."

Galvanized out of her stupor, she nodded and turned on the shop vac as he raced out of the room. She sucked up water until the vacuum was full, hauling it to the back door and dumping before returning to do it all over. Again and again, she filled the tank. Eventually, more people showed up. Simon. Mateo. Caleb. Levi. Others she didn't recognize. More shop vacs began running. Box fans were set up all over the house. What felt like an entire store's worth of towels materialized from somewhere to mop up yet more water. The house was an ant bed of activity, as everyone scrambled to save it.

But as she moved from room to room, Deanna saw the curling

edges of the historic hardwoods. Utterly destroyed. Given the volume of water they removed, the pipe had likely burst much earlier in the day. Because the house wasn't entirely level, water hadn't spread into every single room. But it had entered most, including the nearly finished kitchen, with its reclaimed heart pine floors. Back in the study, water wicked up the sides of every box of her stored belongings, destroying who knew what in the process.

So much waste. Wasted materials. Wasted work. Wasted money.

All her fault.

She didn't know when the tears started. No one stopped to comment or comfort. They were too busy frantically trying to turn back the clock. Evidently, she was the only one to recognize the futility of their actions. But she went through the motions of trying to help because she couldn't do anything else. Facing the reality of what came next was beyond her capabilities at the moment. Facing Wyatt felt nigh on impossible. What could be worse than seeing the disappointment and outrage he had to be feeling?

"Oh my God!"

"Deanna, what the hell happened?"

She squeezed her eyes shut, curling her hands into fists. *Why? Why did I tempt the universe by asking what could be worse?*

On a bracing breath, she turned. "Mom. Dad. We had a little problem."

"I THINK we've got up all the standing water," Simon reported.

"Good, that's good." The response was automatic because Wyatt recognized that his little brother needed some reassurance that they'd done everything that could be done to salvage the situation. "Why don't you help Mateo load all those wet towels up to haul back to the gym?"

"Sure thing." Simon paused to squeeze his shoulder before continuing on through the house to find the others.

The moment he was out of sight, Wyatt released the careful hold on his expression, letting the frustration and the fury free for just a little while.

This shit was beyond bad. Even with all the people who'd answered his call for help, it was weeks of labor undone and so many thousands of dollars of materials wasted because he ignored his instincts and didn't put his foot down on the order things should be done.

He knew he should have dealt with all the plumbing before tackling any of the prettifying. He knew he should have checked it all, made certain it was up to code and would hold up under the additional pressure on the system from the new fixtures and appliances being installed. Experience dictated that if there could be surprises, there would be. Usually of the negative variety. But he let himself believe the plumbing would hold, that it would be fine. That the chance to impress the network was worth the risk of putting it off.

They wouldn't be impressed now.

And it was all his fault. He was the expert. It was on him to say no. To be the voice of reason. There was a lesson about hubris in all of this, but he didn't have the time to consider it. He just had to keep doing the next right thing. That meant renting some equipment and getting down on his knees to pray like he'd never prayed before.

As he began another pass to check the progress, he realized that Deanna's parents had arrived. Just fucking perfect. The icing on this shit cake. He could hear the tones of anger, even over the drone of all the fans and shop vacs. Veering in their direction, Wyatt braced himself for a rescue.

"How the hell could you quit your job for this… this… travesty?" Phillip demanded.

Even from well down the hall, Wyatt could see Deanna's shoulders hitch, as if her father had struck her. He couldn't hear her reply, but it prompted her mom to lay in next.

"—told you this would happen. With these old houses, it's always going to be something. And now where are you? In the middle of all this drama, just to make more ratings for his show?"

What the hell?

"Excuse me?" Deanna gasped.

"He's just using you. Exactly like Blake. You're pouring all this time and energy into somebody else's career. Somebody else's dream. You're losing yourself again. When are you going to learn?" Her father sounded disgusted.

Wyatt waited for Deanna to defend him. To explain how he was nothing like that asshole. How he was bankrolling this renovation. How this was their home, and he'd never sink so low as to put it at risk for ratings. How the show was *their* dream now. But she said nothing. She simply stood there, head bowed, as if waiting for another kick. Something about that defeated posture stung. As if she were just accepting their judgement as law, writing everything off without lifting a finger to protest.

Looked like he was going to have to take care of this himself, too.

Barging right into the middle of their little cluster, he fixed her parents with a glare. "Listen, you can feel however you feel, but right now, we have work to do. So you can either pitch in or get out of the way."

Rude? Absolutely. But they'd insulted him in his own home, and if they weren't part of the solution, they were contributing to the problem.

Phillip's nostrils flared, but he took Valerie's elbow and steered her out of the house. As soon as the door shut behind them, Wyatt turned to Deanna. Her face was ravaged by tears. The sight of them made his gut twist, but he couldn't deal with that right now, either. There'd be time for comfort on the other side of this nightmare.

The next right thing.

"We need to rent industrial fans and dehumidifiers. As many as we can get, as fast as we can." The floors were bad, but if they could dry them out properly, some might be salvageable. The warp might settle down. He'd seen it happen.

She lifted her head, exhaustion written in every line of her body. "We're going to have to cancel the party."

Her announcement interrupted the list in his head like a record scratch. "What?"

"I'm just being the voice of reason here. We don't have the time and resources to pull this off. The network will need to make other arrangements, and that takes time. We can't afford to destroy whatever goodwill we have by canceling at the very last second or—worse—have them show up to a disaster."

He was breaking his back to fix this, pulling out all the stops, and this was her response? This hurt so much worse than her lack of defense against her parents' accusations. She was giving up. On the dream. On him. "After all this, you don't have faith in me?"

She shook her head. "This has nothing to do with you. I'm just being realistic. The whole thing was a big mistake."

The temper already at a simmer hit a rolling boil. "Oh, of course. The old standby of parroting your parents. God forbid you stick to what you actually believe. No matter what I've done to build you up, you always go back to their opinions, their messages."

Her brows drew together. "Wait, build me up? I'm not one of your projects, Wyatt."

He took a step closer, going toe to toe with her. "Aren't you?"

"No!" And finally he saw something other than defeat in her eyes. Insult and anger warred, making the gray flecks in her hazel eyes stand out in stark relief. It was better than the dejection, better than the nothing of her reaction. Even if it was too little, too late.

"Well, I'm not one of your mistakes."

Without another word, he spun on his heel and stalked out. He had phone calls to make.

CHAPTER 16

"Have you slept at all?"

With profound gratitude, Deanna accepted the steaming cup of coffee Bennet held out and sank back into one of the cushy chairs in her friend's apartment. Casper stretched out beside her with a sigh that encompassed all her weariness. "Not really. Wyatt didn't come home last night."

She'd spent all night wondering, worrying, paranoid he'd pack up all his things and go in a fit of temper, even though she knew deep down he'd never abandon the job unfinished. But she had no such confidence about him not abandoning her. Not when she'd inadvertently hurt him in his most tender wound.

Bennet curled up with her own mug. "Did y'all have a fight?"

Did a conversation so short even count as a fight? Did it matter? She jerked her shoulders and admitted the truth she'd wrestled with all night. "I think he's done with me. And I don't blame him. I made him a promise there's no way I can deliver now. I failed him. More than that, I failed myself. I swore I wasn't going to make another huge mistake, and what do I do? It's just like my parents warned me. Except this time, it's not just me who has to deal with the consequences of my foolishness."

Bennet frowned. "I feel like you're leaving out a lot of the middle of this story. Start from the beginning."

So she did. Deanna took her through the whole thing, from getting home to find the flood, all the way through the fight and Wyatt walking out. "I thought he'd come back after we'd both cooled off and we'd talk about it. But he never did."

"As first fights go, this one's kind of a doozy. A lot's on the line that matters to you both. How did Patrick take the news when you canceled?"

"I haven't called him."

"Why not?"

Deanna gripped the mug, soaking up every last scrap of warmth from the ceramic into her palms. "Because I can't stop seeing the look on Wyatt's face when I gave up. And because, foolish though it may be, I don't really *want* to give up."

Bennet's shrewd gaze pinned her in place. "On the show? The party? Or Wyatt?"

"All the above. But mostly him. I don't want to let him down. He's had so much of that in his life, and I don't want to be another person he can't count on. Does that make me crazy?"

"Why would that make you crazy, honey?"

"My parents think he's using me like Blake."

"What?" Her shriek had Casper leaping to his feet, looking for threats.

Deanna stroked a hand along his back until he settled again. "They all but flat out said that he'd set this whole thing up himself to create more drama for the show."

"Wyatt would never do that."

"I know. But just… all of it. They think I'm giving up everything I want for a guy, like I did with Blake. And, I mean, I've made a lot of changes since Wyatt came into my life. I don't think it's the same, but I didn't think what I did with Blake was wrong when I was in it, either. I told myself I was being supportive because I loved him. Am I wrong?"

Bennet considered. "You disappeared in your marriage. I don't see you doing that with Wyatt. But let's question the premise: Do you want what he's offering? Do you want the show? The career in design? The whole thing? Or is that just something you've gotten into in the name of supporting his thing?"

"I wanted all of it before him. Well, not the show. But the rest of it. He just built me up enough to go after it."

"I think that's your answer. Blake never built you up. He never did anything to support you. It was only ever about him. Wyatt's gone out of his way to make you visible, to make sure you're seen and that your talents are appreciated. He's been as much into helping you come to shine as in his own success. That doesn't sound like a man who's using you."

She'd been so insulted by the idea that she was one of his projects, as if he thought she was something broken. But he put so much love and care into the things he tended and restored. Would it be such a bad thing? It was just reflective of his support. Not a put down. At least, not when he wasn't pissed off and upset himself. That wasn't the kind of man he was.

"I want to do this for him because I'm a supportive partner. Because I think that's what a partner is. My problem with Blake wasn't that I supported him to the extreme, but because he didn't support me back. I didn't have a partner with him. I do with Wyatt. Or, at least, I did." She swallowed down the lump in her throat at the idea that she'd screwed that up. "I don't want to lose him, Bennet. And I'm afraid the things I said in the moment will be a deal breaker for him."

"You're in love with him."

Miserable, Deanna nodded. "I didn't ask to be."

Laughing, Bennet bent forward and laid a hand over hers. "We've known each other a lot of years, so I feel like I'm in a good position to say this. You are usually great at taking most things as they come. You handle emergencies all the time. But when things get really huge and overwhelming, you have a tendency to retreat.

You have to shut the door on the noise so you can sift through all that information and make a plan. That's all you were doing. What you're still doing. That's not giving up, and it's not screwing up. Wyatt just hasn't known you long enough to know that about you."

Deanna realized it was true. She'd done it when she suspected Blake of cheating, taking longer to pull the trigger on the divorce than others might have. She'd done it with work regularly, holing up to get her thoughts straight when she had to pivot without enough time. Hell, she'd tried to do it when she bought Blackborne Hall. Her parents had just found out about it before she'd figured out the right move. And yeah, amid all her worry, she'd been thinking about how to salvage this situation.

"I've been wracking my brain, trying to find a way to make it work. We can replace the damaged drywall and get the painting done, but the floors still need to be replaced. They're almost a total loss. We don't have the budget or the manpower to do that in time for the party."

"Y'all have been thinking outside the box on materials from the get go. Surely there's a source somewhere."

Something began to percolate in the back of Deanna's mind. "Maybe... But even if we managed to get the damaged floors ripped out and new ones installed, there's no way they can be finished in time for the party. It takes days for the stain and poly to cure."

"Set the acquisition of them aside for a minute. Does finished for the party have to mean perfect and ready to sell? Is it possible to do something unconventional that would make it beautiful for the party and the let y'all finish for real later?"

Her mind immediately spit out possibilities for how it could be done. "I mean... it would take an army."

Bennet reached for her laptop and typed something in before turning the screen. Deanna stared at the subscriber count for the *DIWyatt* YouTube channel for a long moment as her mind finally began to formulate a plan. The whole thing was a Hail Mary of epic proportions, but maybe that go big or go home attitude was merited right now.

"Do you have a camera here?"

"Of course."

"Set it up. I need to make a call."

By the time she'd finished, Bennet had gone brows up. "You *do* need an army."

"Then let's use what we've built to get me one."

Deanna positioned herself in front of one of the few blank walls in Bennet's living room. She didn't check her hair or makeup. This was all about raw and real.

When Bennet gave the signal, she began to speak.

"Hey *DIWyatt* fans, we need your help."

DESPITE THE EARLY HOUR, the gym was hopping. Wyatt recognized a couple of regulars working on the heavy bags as he stepped inside. He considered taking the time to whale on one himself, but he hadn't bothered to pack a bag before his precipitous exit last night, and somehow, over the past few months at Blackborne Hall, he'd actually moved in, so there wasn't a bag of spare anything in his truck.

From behind the front desk, Mateo looked up, a deep groove dug between his brows, the phone pressed to his ear. "Not cool, Odette. Very not cool. You're leaving me up shit creek here."

Apparently, his morning wasn't going great either.

He grunted at whatever his office manager said in reply, a muscle in his jaw jumping. "Yeah. Yeah. I gotta go." Without another word, he hung up the phone with the slow, deliberate motion that told Wyatt he wanted to hit something.

"What's going on with Odette?"

"She quit. With no notice. Apparently, it became of paramount importance that she follow her bliss across country to train with some hippy dippy health guru in Sedona."

Wyatt winced. "Ouch."

Mateo pinched the bridge of his nose and blew out a breath, finally focusing fully on Wyatt. "I'd ask if you slept okay, but you look like shit."

He felt it, too. He'd spent more time than not staring at the ceiling, and the very idea of all the work he needed to do had all his limbs dragging. "Thanks for letting me crash last night."

"No problem." If he had an opinion about the fact that Wyatt hadn't wanted to go home, he kept it to himself. "What's next?

"Gotta pick up dehumidifiers and industrial fans as soon as the rental place opens. Beyond that, I have no idea. I know all the necessary steps to fix it, but I don't know if there's a point. Deanna wants to cancel everything."

Mateo folded his arms across his chest. "Does she want to, or does she just think that's the only choice?'

There was no erasing the picture of her resignation from his brain. There'd been no effort at problem solving, no brainstorming, no nothing. Just calling it quits and cutting their losses. Wyatt was working hard not to think about that quite yet. "She thinks it's done. There's not enough money or people or time."

"What about you? Do you see a way?"

To fix the damage? That was his jam. To get it all done right and in time for the party to impress the suits? Well, he hadn't bothered putting much brain time to that since she'd already said they were canceling. "Man, I don't know. I just feel like the only way through is forward. Whether the party happens or not, the shit's gotta be fixed. I'm just putting one foot in front of the other."

"You aren't the only contractor in the family. Maybe Porter and some of his crew could shake loose to lend a hand. Call Pru. Activate the full Misfit Inn phone tree."

If anybody could pinpoint who was in a position to help, it was

Pru. In the absence of their mother, she was the one who'd led the charge on keeping the broader family ties alive for all the fosters who'd gone through Joan's care over the years. They were legion.

The idea of having more skilled labor was appealing. And yet. "It doesn't feel reasonable to ask them to drive four hours from Eden's Ridge." Even now, he was so programmed not to be a bother to anyone. Be helpful. Don't need help. That was part of why he'd always preferred working alone.

Mateo jerked his shoulders. "If they can't come, they won't. Doesn't hurt to ask. Joan would be pissed if she thought you were operating from that place of feeling like you're a burden. You know how she felt about that."

"Yeah." And it had taken a fair chunk of his adult life to remember it after the struggles in his adoptive family.

"Think about it. Either way, I've got my hands full right now. With Odette gone, I'm having to juggle phones and classes and every damned thing, and I've got to figure out what the hell I'm going to do to replace her."

"Good luck with that, bro. And thanks again for all your help."

"Anytime, man."

Because the rental place wasn't open yet, Wyatt headed to visit Scott. It wasn't one of his normal days, but his brother never turned down the company, and Wyatt could use a little injection of belief that he wasn't crazy. The campus was just getting moving when he arrived. Waved through by the front desk attendant, he headed for the residential wing.

Scott was at his little dinette table, sipping at a cup of coffee in a lidded mug, when Wyatt knocked on the door. "Hey! I wasn't expecting you again so soon."

"Sorry. Everything has sort of gone to shit, and I needed your perspective."

He hesitated.

"Do you have a PT or therapy session soon? I can come back later."

"No, no. It's fine. You know I'll help if I can. What's going on?"

Wyatt dropped into a chair across from his brother. "The house flooded yesterday."

"What?" Scott asked the question with the appropriate expression of horror.

He spilled the whole thing out, all the way through his walking out. "After everything we've done, everything we've been through, how can she just give up? How can she call us a mistake?"

He hadn't meant to ask that last question, but it was out there now. And damn it, that was the part that stuck in his craw the most. The part that had kept him up the most of the night. When had she become more important than the house? The show?

Scott's eyes sharpened. "Objection. Request for clarification. Did she call your relationship a mistake or the situation with the house?"

Of course, he'd drop back on semantics. Once a lawyer, always a lawyer, traumatic brain injury or not. "A rejection of one is a rejection of both. It's all one and the same with us."

"That's spurious logic."

Wyatt went ramrod straight at the sound of his mother's voice. How long had she been there? *Where* had she been that he hadn't noticed her presence?

She moved into his line of sight—from the bathroom, he realized—and he was shocked at her change in appearance. Always a tall, sturdy woman with an imposing presence that filled a lecture hall as surely as her booming alto, her frame had winnowed down to almost gaunt, and the skin seemed stretched taut over bone. Lines of strain bracketed her mouth and eyes, as if grief had been permanently etched into her face. It was so like how she'd looked after his father had died, after Scott's accident. But worse, somehow. Deeper. Older.

Despite himself, Wyatt felt the stirrings of worry and had to remind himself that this was the same woman who'd stood over

Scott's hospital bed when he lay in a coma and said the unforgivable.

It should have been you.

Three years. He'd managed to stay away from her for three years. He'd thought the time and distance would dull the pain, but he still felt the slice of her words as if they were new.

It should have been you.

And she presumed to lecture him about his logic? Fuck no.

Wyatt stood to leave.

"Don't!" The order barked out before she squeezed her eyes closed and softened her tone. "Please. Just listen."

Conscious that there were others in the residential wing, he kept his voice low and controlled. "There's nothing you have to say that I want to hear."

"Maybe not, but you need to hear it."

His hands curled and uncurled at his sides, but he didn't move.

Marjorie linked hers together, an uncharacteristic show of agitation. "I've watched the show."

Wait. What?

"I know that Deanna is a special woman. The kind of woman who comes along once in a lifetime. The kind of woman you deserve. You can't throw that away because she might have misspoken."

Wyatt blinked. Who was this woman and what had she done with his mother?

"Once, when I was grieving and lost and out of my mind, I said a terrible thing. A thing I know I can never take back. And every single day, I wanted to say how wrong I was, how sorry, and knowing that would never ever be enough. So I did nothing, letting it fester, wasting years, until the only thing left was regret." Tears gathered in her eyes and spilled down those sharp cheeks, but her voice stayed steady. "For whatever it's worth, I love you, Wyatt, and I don't want that life for you. So find a way to talk to her and make it right. Don't let your pride, or the old wounds that I inflicted, be the thing that destroys what you have with her."

Dumbfounded, he could only stare.

Message delivered, Marjorie nodded. "I'll be back later. You two need this time together." Without another word, she picked up her purse from the table by the door and slipped out of the room.

Wyatt stared after her for a long minute, his brain struggling to process what had just happened and coming up empty. "What the actual fuck was that?"

Scott set his mug down with a thunk. "An olive branch. The question is—will you take it?"

CHAPTER 17

eanna examined the progress her volunteers were making with stripping the old beat-up chest of drawers she and Wyatt had found at the flea market. "That's looking really great. See that gorgeous woodgrain?" She trailed her finger along the length of a drawer front and tried not to remember Wyatt doing the same to her. "It's going to be fantastic with new stain."

After a few more words of encouragement and instruction, she moved down the line, checking on each of the pieces they'd picked up from the barn and moved to this workspace at the back of Restoration Station. Carson Colwell was currently playing the role of fairy godfather in the movie of her life, and Deanna was probably going to kiss him before the week was out. The old cuss had jumped at the trade she'd offered. If they pulled this insanity off, it would be because of him. Him and the dozens of volunteers who'd answered the call for aid.

"Deanna!"

She turned to find Fiona Gaffney jogging down the aisle. "Hey, honey. Here to pitch in?"

"Yeah. I just came from Blackborne Hall. Went to drop off food for Simon and the others."

"Oh?" Deanna wondered if the girl noticed her focus sharpening like a dog on a scent. "Was there much of a crowd?"

She had no idea what was being done at the house. That would've required being home or actually talking to Wyatt, which hadn't happened since their fight. He hadn't been there when she'd brought a team to load up the furniture from the barn, and he hadn't reached out to her at all in the intervening days. The only reason she knew he'd been back at all was the incessant drone of industrial fans and dehumidifiers. She'd resisted the urge to do more than use the cameras to confirm he'd come back and started a fresh round of demolition. If he wanted to talk to her, he'd call. If he didn't—well, she was banking on his mood improving once she showed up with the cavalry.

"He put out a call to his foster family, so there's a team of other contractors and construction folks who came in to help pull out the damaged floors and drywall and make whatever underlying repairs are needed."

A knot of anxiety loosened. He'd asked for help instead of insisting he could do everything on his own. With more help, they might make it.

"Do you know how far they've gotten?"

"Ripped out the ceiling and got the pipe fixed and the last of the plumbing updated. They were starting on the floors when I left, but moving at a pretty good clip. They're expecting things will be dried out enough to start the actual repairs tomorrow."

"Good." Deanna nodded to herself, running mental calculations. "That's good. They'll be ready for this by the time it's ready tomorrow morning."

"Ready for what?"

She led Fiona to another part of the Restoration Station complex, where more of the team of volunteers painstakingly removed nails from reclaimed floors before running each plank through a planer to clean it up. They had a hell of an assembly line going. "We needed to replace the flooring with basically no budget. Carson found an abandoned school a couple of hours west of here that was scheduled for demolition. The whole place was full of variable width oak. We got permission to bring in a team for salvage. It's period appropriate, and the price was certainly right. They've been working round the clock to get it out, get it here and prepped."

She'd done her own stint over there at the start, putting in a solid four or five hours she still felt in every inch of her back.

"Wow. This is impressive. Wyatt didn't say anything about this when I was there."

"He doesn't know. I didn't want to get his hopes up unless we actually pulled it off." For all of fifteen seconds, Deanna wrestled with herself before she finally broke down to ask the girl what she really wanted to know. "How is he?"

Fiona studied her with an expression that said she saw way too much. "Focused on the job. Definitely in go mode. Which isn't surprising under the circumstances."

Did he say anything about me? Deanna wondered, but didn't give voice to the thought. It was no one else's responsibility to keep her apprised of his mental state, and she could have just as easily picked up the phone herself. Except she hadn't been able to make herself. What if he didn't take her call? No, it was better they have that conversation in person. Maybe by the time they managed it, his temper would've cooled.

"Simon said he's been miserable since you left."

Deanna's gaze snapped to Fiona, hating the sympathy in her expression. "It's going around. We'll sort it out once this disaster is over." She had to hang on to that as a possibility, or she couldn't keep going.

Clearing her throat, she jerked her head. "C'mon. Let's put you to work on this other project."

They strode past all the furniture in various stages of refinishing to the bigger project spread out on massive worktables they'd erected in an empty corner of the warehouse.

"What on earth am I looking at?"

"There's no opportunity to actually stain and seal the floors before the TCN party, so we're going to cover most of them with custom painted canvas rugs. I brought in several area artists to help out with design and painting, and there are a few that I designed myself. It's a budget friendly option that will give us a more finished look in a short time frame. On most of them, we're down to putting on the several coats of polyurethane."

A familiar head popped up from the nearest rug. "Deanna!"

"Mom? What are you—"

Kyra, one of the artist volunteers, spoke up. "I drafted her when she came in a couple of hours ago. You looked tied up with other stuff."

Deanna stared. "You've... been helping?"

Valerie beamed. "I have! This is such a clever concept. It was your idea?"

Should she be offended? Defensive? Was there judgement in her mother's tone or was that just her own innate assumption of her disapproval? "Um... yes. It was the most affordable option for custom floor coverings in a hurry."

"So smart! All day I've been hearing about the different projects you have going on. Walked by some of them on my last break. I think I never really understood just how talented you really are." Her mother actually beamed.

Had Valerie been huffing paint supplies?

Confused, Deanna could only blink. "I... thank you. I appreciate that acknowledgment. After the other night it's... unexpected."

Valerie grimaced and stepped close, laying a tentative hand on her arm. "Your dad and I... we just worry. We shouldn't have laid into you like we did. You're a grown woman, and a talented one. You have a right to live your life the way you see fit. Even if it's a lot more risky and exciting than we imagined. We just want to see you happy."

Emotion swelled in her throat, such that she had to swallow several times before replying. "This makes me happy."

Eyes a little shiny herself, Valerie nodded decisively. "Then I'll do whatever I can to help. Including working on bringing your dad around. He's got his boxers in a twist over the cohabitation." She rolled her eyes, even as Deanna felt her face flame.

What was she supposed to say to that?

"It's been a long, long time since we've seen you happy. He makes you happy. We worried about that, too, because you thought Blake made you happy. But Wyatt looks at you in a way Blake never did. That man thinks you hung the moon. Who are we to stand in the way of that?"

Because she needed a moment to hide her face and wrangle the tears, Deanna pulled her mom in for a hug. "Thanks. I really appreciate that."

As they hugged away all the lingering animosity, Deanna felt hope, for the first time, that maybe her parents were finally coming around to seeing her as the capable, independent woman she was. Or at least to accepting her right to make her own life choices.

She wished she could tell Wyatt.

Knowing that even if they were on site together, she could no longer just walk into his arms and tell him about her day, the loss of him swamped her all over again. They had to talk at some point. But neither of them could risk breaking this detente if they were going to make their deadline, so the fate of their relationship would have to wait a while longer.

Releasing her mother, she stepped back. "Fiona, I'm leaving you in their capable hands. I've got a table to refinish."

∾

EARLY MORNING SUNLIGHT streamed into the room as Porter Ingram used a pry bar to rip up the last piece of warped flooring in the front parlor. "That's the end of it. Damned shame about losing those original floors."

Wyatt swiped a tired hand across his sweaty brow and surveyed what felt like acres of empty floor joists. All traces of the temporary kitchen and lounge they'd been living with for months were gone, the stuff relocated upstairs, along with all the sodden boxes of Deanna's things. He hadn't opened any to see if anything was ruined, and as far as he knew, neither had she. He couldn't blame her for not wanting to face that, either.

"The whole damned thing makes me just sick. I keep kicking myself for not making absolutely sure all the plumbing was updated."

Landon Bane, one of the crew who'd come with Porter from Eden's Ridge, shrugged a philosophical shoulder. "You don't know what you don't know. And it's all updated for sure now."

It had taken extra time, but Wyatt wasn't risking a repeat that might destroy even more of his work. The entire process had gone a hell of a lot faster with professional help. "I can't thank y'all enough for coming."

Porter snagged a bottle of water and took a swig. "It's no problem. That's the whole point of my taking Mia on as a business partner. So I have more flexibility to do the things I want to do."

Wyatt looked askance in his direction. "Working forty-eight hours straight on a project you're not even being paid for is on that list of wants?"

"Helping family is. Besides, Faith isn't sleeping right now because she's cutting teeth, so taking a few days away from my darling daughter is keeping me sane. And if you tell my wife I said that, I'll call you a dirty liar."

Huffing a laugh, Wyatt guzzled his own water. "Well, at this point, shower and shut eye are more or less the order of the day. The drywall mud still needs to finish drying before it can be sanded and painted, and I don't know what we're doing about floors yet."

And why the hell was he still talking in "we"? He hadn't seen Deanna since their fight. She hadn't contacted him, and she'd taken the dog wherever she'd disappeared to. To his mind, it was a sign that she was over and done with all of this. Including him. He'd need a lot more time and space to process that rejection, but he wasn't going to abandon his investment. God knew how he was going to get that money back without forcing her to sell, but he'd figure that out later. He'd made a promise, and he was going to keep it. Somehow. Because, for better or worse, this whole thing had become more about her than the house or the show. After all these years of pouring in his blood, sweat, and tears, he hadn't even been able to make himself look at social media or the website. Why torture himself with the disappointment of fans too?

At the sound of a vehicle coming up the drive, they all started for the door.

"Man, I hope that's Simon with breakfast," Landon muttered. "I'm freaking starving."

It wasn't Simon.

The truck that rolled to a stop in front of the house sported the Reclamation Station logo on the side, and the trailer behind it was loaded down with a hell of a lot of something under tarps.

"What the hell?" Wyatt trotted down the steps as the driver's side door opened.

Carson slid out, tucking one hand in his red suspenders as he ambled over. "Mornin'."

"Morning. What are you doing here?"

"Oh, well, I heard about the trouble. Figured you could use a hand. And this." He flipped the edge of the tarp back to reveal flooring. Loads and loads of oak flooring.

Wyatt couldn't stop himself from stepping forward to run his hands along it. Planed smooth as a baby's butt. "Carson, this is… I can't afford to pay you for this."

The old man grunted. "Nothing to pay for. It's reclaimed from a demolition site. There was a whole team of volunteers who pulled and prepped it for you. All you've gotta do is put them in." He checked his watch. "Reckon it'll be cutting it pretty close, but you'll have something for those network suits to stand on."

Wyatt offered a sad smile, torn between grief and gratitude. "It's too little too late. Deanna cancelled the party."

Carson smirked. "You sure about that?" He nodded toward the driveway, where a whole long line of vehicles were turning in.

Deanna's car led the pack. She parked to one side and got out, opening the back door for Casper, as she waved everyone else past the house to the field in the back.

The sight of her was a sucker punch. Everything in Wyatt pulled toward her, needing to eradicate the distance and the hurt. He wanted to pull her into his arms. Stroke that messy hair back from the beautiful face that looked as exhausted as he felt. But he did no such thing.

She didn't acknowledge him as she began issuing orders to the people who spilled out of cars and trucks. "Start setting up the tents in that open space on the other side of the barn. We should be able to run power from the house. We'll offload everything from the trucks once those are up."

Somehow, without being aware of it, Wyatt had closed the distance between them. "What's going on?"

She finally turned her attention to him, and he noted the skin beneath her eyes was bruised. But there was an almost fevered brightness there that told him she'd hit a second wind. "We're finishing the house. It'll be down to the wire, but I think we'll make it. At least if you and your team can get those floors down."

"We can get them in, but they can't be finished. And there's still no furniture. You were right. There's not enough time." He hated admitting it, but facts were facts.

Deanna pressed her lips together, as if she didn't dare unleash what she was actually thinking. When she finally spoke, there was a reserve and professional distance in her tone that he hated. "We're not giving up now. Get the floors installed. I'll take care of the rest."

She started to walk away, leaving him with a distinct sense of being dismissed. He'd put that distance there by lashing out and hurting her. Treating her as if she were a project, not a person. He wanted to apologize. To talk things through and find that way his mother never had to overcome hard words. But they needed time and privacy for that. Right now, they had neither. So he nodded. "We'll get it done. Just one more thing."

She paused, brows arched expectantly as she looked back at him.

"Who are all these people?"

Her gaze slid past him to Porter, Landon, and their crew, who watched the unfolding chaos with interest. "You have your army, and I brought mine."

Someone called her name. After one more long, humming beat, she walked away to command her troops.

Porter wandered over. "So I'm thinking that sleep is no longer on the table."

"Looks like no."

"Alright then. Let's get to it."

CHAPTER 18

*D*eanna eyed her reflection in the bathroom mirror and winced. "Well, that's as good as it's going to get."

She'd pulled out every trick in her arsenal to make herself presentable—tea bag compresses and hemorrhoid cream for the suitcases under her eyes, a revitalizing face mask to add a bit of a glow to the skin that looked just a little sallow, the caffeinated moisturizer to perk up her whole body, and a bold red lip to draw attention away from the eyes that were just a little bloodshot. There was only so much that could be done to hide the fact that she'd had only about twenty hours of sleep in the past week and had been subsisting on energy drinks, fast food, and sheer, unadulterated stubbornness.

But they'd done it.

Their people had still been tearing down the work tents when the caterers arrived, and the last of the fans and dehumidifiers got adiosed a mere half an hour before the first guests were due to show. The only reason she wasn't greeting people in ratty jeans and a filthy t-shirt was that Bennet had shoved her toward the stairs with a promise to set up the TV and video equipment for the screening. Deanna hadn't had a chance to preview their pilot, so she was having to trust that her girl had her back. Maybe if she'd trusted more before now, she wouldn't be in this untenable situation.

She'd thought bringing a veritable army and a plan and pulling all this off would fix the strain between her and Wyatt. She'd thought her actions would prove she *did* believe in him, in them. That it would make up for her initial reaction. But they'd barely exchanged a dozen words since she'd showed up yesterday. Of course, they'd been moving at a hundred miles an hour, not even stopping to sleep. But she thought there'd be... something. A word. A look. A touch. Something that would let her know they'd be okay. But there'd been no chance for that either. As staging was primarily her responsibility, he'd gone up to shower first. She'd been in the other bathroom when he'd headed down to greet the initial guests, so they hadn't even had a moment alone.

No time for it now. Despite their current estrangement, they needed to present a united front for producers tonight, or the support for their show would likely be dead in the water. Resigned to her fate, she went back to the bedroom for her heels. Her gaze landed on the bed and spawned a wave of intense longing. She'd done her job. She'd made the house pretty, met the deadline under impossible circumstances. Surely no one would notice if she skipped the party to fall face first into bed. She was so tired, she was pretty sure she'd be unconscious before hitting the mattress.

Except her job really wasn't done. She still needed to rub elbows and name drop the people and businesses who'd made tonight possible. The list was extensive and the good word and exposure was the thing she'd promised many of them in exchange for the help. So on a deep sigh, she slipped on her heels, put on her game face, and prepared to dazzle.

Low strains of easy jazz floated up to her at the top of the stairs. For just a moment, she held there, out of sight, and remembered her first view of this staircase. She'd known then it was meant for making an entrance. Some of that fanciful excitement leeched into her as she descended, feeling a little like Cinderella at the ball. Maybe she'd finally get the moment she'd been waiting for with her prince. She'd bought this confection with him in mind. The same bold red of her lips, the body-hugging lace cocktail dress had a curve of chiffon across the wide neckline, clipping at the shoulders to leave gossamer tails fluttering behind her arms. She'd fallen in love with it on the spot, imaging how it would make her a focal point for exactly this entrance. As she hit the landing, faces below turned up, studied her dress, and she automatically paused to let them as she sought one particular face.

Wyatt stood in conversation with a man she didn't know. He looked as at ease in the charcoal suit as he did in work clothes. It was the first time she'd seen him in a suit, and damn, he cleaned up well. As if he felt her gaze on him, he stopped speaking and turned, lifting his eyes to hers.

For a beat—two... three—she stood frozen as something pulsed between them. Then those unfairly long, sooty lashes swept down, and he turned away, murmuring an excuse to his companion before he walked out of the room.

Deanna's hand curved tight around the banister. That was it then. He was well and truly done with her. There'd be no Prince Charming moment for her. No reunion on the other side of the struggle. The pain of it lanced through her, almost buckling her knees. But she still had a job to do before she could fall apart. Drawing on all her years of pretending things were fine when her world was falling apart, she released her death grip on the railing and glided down the foyer.

Patrick snagged her immediately. "And here's our lovely hostess. Darling, let me introduce you."

She played the game, smiling, nodding, making small talk and answering questions. When a glass of wine made its way into her hand, she made herself sip instead of gulp. At this level of exhaustion, the alcohol would go straight to her head. "Thanks."

"You looked like you could use it."

Wyatt's low voice had her head whipping toward him. But he was already leaning toward one of the producers, smiling and laughing at something the other man said.

What was this? A peace offering? A way to present that faux united front? Deanna didn't know.

"—find this gorgeous rug?"

She dragged her attention to the woman she thought was an associate producer. "It's custom painted. Several area artists pitched in to help make all the canvas rugs you'll see tonight. Are you familiar with Ruby Lindon?"

"*The* Ruby Lindon?"

"The very one. Turns out she's a fan of *DIWyatt.*"

For nearly an hour, she chatted people up, played the game. Wyatt joined in conversations, and anyone who didn't know they'd been involved would have thought they were professional friends. Good colleagues. They answered questions about the house and restoration as the team they'd been. But it wasn't the same. They weren't the team they'd been, and her heart wasn't in it. She just wanted to get through the night and get him his show. She'd deal with the devastation later. Her price to pay for this adventure with him all these months.

"Patrick's been talking you two up. I'd love to hear your ideas about the premise for the show."

Deanna smiled at the suit—she couldn't remember his name. "In fact, we have a mini pilot pitch we've put together. If everyone could turn their attention to the TV." She wished there was time to do something about this. To make it focus on him, not them. But it was what they had. She'd find a way to salvage it. Somehow.

From the other side of the room, Bennet sent a thumbs up and started the video, raising the volume until they all could hear.

It began with stills of the original exterior in all its faded, awful glory and rolled into a montage of interior shots that played up exactly how bad things had been. Bennet had spliced in a voiceover of one of Deanna's interviews, talking about all the potential she saw in the house. Then came Wyatt, with all his practicality and confidence that they could make the house a home again. In the footage that followed, she saw what Bennet had seen in the way she and Wyatt looked at each other. That tension and attraction had been simmering from the beginning. The cut was masterfully done, weaving together dual love stories of the two of them and that of the house itself. Hers wasn't the only sigh as the tale unfolded.

When the flood footage filled the screen, Deanna slowly backed out of the room. She didn't want to see it again. Didn't want a front-row seat to the end of them or she'd never be able to make it through the rest of the night.

Edging free of the crowd, she hurried down the hall and out the back door in search of some air.

WYATT'S SMILE weighed a thousand pounds. Keeping it in place for this houseful of people who held power over his future felt about like trying to bench press Blackborne Hall in its entirety. Every muscle ached, and every fiber of his being wanted these people gone. He just needed to talk to Deanna.

She'd come through in the end, doing what she had to in order to give him the dream she'd promised. And she'd done it after he'd implied she was some broken thing. A fixer upper he'd taken on. There was so much to say, and he hadn't even managed the barest, "I'm sorry." Saying it without addressing all the rest felt like a copout somehow. So he'd said nothing. He'd realized the mistake of that once he'd seen her tonight, seen the hurt in her eyes.

But they both had to play the game, schmooze the producers they'd done all this for, or all their hard work would be for naught.

On the flat screen TV, the pilot episode Bennet had developed continued to play. Watching the outsider's view of their romance made him ache, wanting to hold Deanna, to face this pitch truly together as they'd intended. Could the powers that be sense the rift between them? Would they attribute it to nerves or to relationship problems? Would it impact what they thought of the show? They weren't just selling him anymore. They were selling them.

Would there still *be* a them after this?

The flood footage had guests murmuring in alarm and surprise.

Someone nearby gasped. "That was last week?"

"Yep," Wyatt muttered.

"How on earth did you pull this off?"

As if in response to the question, Deanna's face filled the frame.

"*DIWyatt* fans, we need your help."

What was this? Wyatt dragged his flagging focus to the TV as she outlined what had happened and the appalling deadline they were under.

"What you've seen so far is all there is. The team is Wyatt, Simon, me, and the handful of volunteers you've seen in various episodes. We don't have a full crew. This isn't some bait and switch where we claim to do it ourselves and secretly have an army off camera. That's not why any of you watch the show. It's just us." She paused, and he recognized she was taking the time to carefully word what she was going to say next.

"I've made a lot of mistakes in my life, but falling in love with this house and with the man who's helped me bring it back to life isn't one of them. We have a chance to save his dream. But I can't do it without all of you. So I'm begging—if you're in the Nashville area and love the show, come volunteer your time and your backs to save it."

Wyatt couldn't breathe. The gut punch of her words nearly sent him to his knees. She'd made a public declaration that she loved him days ago, and he'd said nothing. Because he didn't know. Because he hadn't been on social media for the last week, even for his normal duties, because he'd been so focused on trying to do the work. To get the house done.

Shit. No wonder she'd looked so hurt. He was an ignorant asshole.

Frantic, he turned, searching for her tumbled blonde waves in the crowd. But she wasn't in the room.

At the back, Bennet jerked her head toward the door.

Wyatt cut through the guests, making a beeline in her direction. Despite the fact that he wanted to shout, he kept his voice low. "Where is she?"

Bennet gave him the long, studied look of a friend looking out for another friend. Apparently satisfied, she nodded. "Saw her step outside. Kitchen door."

He left the party, moving fast. That was probably violating some kind of host rules, but he really didn't give a damn at this point. This was way more important. *She* was way more important.

The night air was cool as he stepped out, his eyes automatically searching the reclaimed sun porch. But she wasn't there. Had she headed out to the barn? Around front?

In the end, it was Casper who alerted him. The dog's soft woof pulled his attention to the lone figure who stood beside the pond that had finally been uncovered by part of the army of volunteers. Moonlight cast a halo over her hair, washing out the vibrant color of her dress. Everything about her seemed muted, like something out of a dream. Or a ghost story. The erect carriage and flawless poise she'd displayed inside were gone, replaced by bowed shoulders and arms crossed tight over her middle. As she caught sight of him, her whole body curled in on itself.

Love and guilt tangled inside him, invisible vines wrapping around his feet as the need to fix warred with a desire to comfort.

Wyatt's heart hammered against his breastbone as he closed the distance at a stumbling run.

She didn't move as he approached, and that was almost worse because he could see defeat written all over her face.

No. No, this had to be fixable. He could still salvage it.

"I'm sorry." The words came out in a breathless rush, feeling entirely inadequate as she turned to look at him with wounded, cautious eyes. "I didn't know what you'd done. I haven't been on social media since last week. I didn't see the point because I was too focused on trying to figure out how to fix the problem and thinking you were done with me."

Her eyes widened. "I thought you were finished with me. That's why I stayed away. You were angry, and I wanted to prove that I don't think you're a mistake. That I still believed in this project. In you."

Even after everything she'd proved with her actions, hearing the words released the teeth of doubt that had clamped around his heart.

"I mean, you pulled that off in spades. I cannot believe how much you managed to orchestrate in so short a time. It's nothing short of miraculous."

"I'm not great at rolling with disaster in the moment, but I'm the person you want in the aftermath to pick up the pieces."

Wyatt couldn't stop himself from reaching out to stroke her cheek. "You're the one I want for the all the time."

Deanna turned her face into the touch. "You do?"

"Yes." The word came out rusty because so much emotion caught in his throat as she looked up at him with tremulous hope. There was no more caution, no more reluctance, only pure depth of feeling in her eyes. And with it, he realized just how much he'd hurt her.

He stepped into her, framing her face and dropping his brow to hers. "God, I'm so sorry you even have to ask that. I'm sorry I lost my temper. Even in all the chaos, I should have made the time to talk to you. I never meant to make you feel like you were a project."

Deanna huffed a laugh. The sound flowed over him like gentle hands smoothing over tense shoulders. "Well, you weren't entirely wrong. You effectively restored me. Gave me a dream I'd never even allowed myself to have. But it doesn't mean anything if you aren't here to share it with me."

"I'm not going anywhere. I love you, too. I want to build that life we talked about. To finish the house. To do the show if you still want to do the show. And it's fine if you don't because you'll find something else that makes your heart sing. None of it matters in the end, so long as I still have you."

"Wyatt." His name sounded like a prayer.

And then her mouth was on his, and she was, at last, in his arms again. The foundation of his world resolidified. He didn't give a good damn about any of the rest of it because they were okay, and he hadn't lost her.

Deanna dropped back to her feet, breathing hard. "God, I missed you."

"I missed you, too." Needing to touch her, he ran his hand down the skin of her bare back, absorbing her shiver of reaction. "And I can't wait to go to bed and pass out for about seventeen hours so that we both have the energy for the makeup sex we deserve."

Her laughter soaked into him like sunlight. "I am on board with that plan. But we have to survive to end of the party. To that end, we should probably go back."

"Sometimes I really hate being responsible."

"Just a couple more hours and we can find a horizontal surface."

"From your mouth to God's ear."

Hand in hand, with Casper on their heels, they returned to the party. The pilot had apparently concluded, and Bennet was holding court with all the producers. As all eyes turned in their direction, and more than one eyebrow cocked up at the sight of them, Wyatt wondered if he was wearing some of Deanna's lipstick. Was hers smeared? He didn't look because there wasn't a damned thing he could do about it at the moment, so he kept his hand in hers and played it cool, flashing what he hoped was an easy, charming smile.

Myron Boroughs, who Wyatt dimly recalled being introduced as one of the head, head honchos, returned the smile. "Well, I think I speak for all of us when I say that it is, in general, amazing what the two of you have done with the restoration of this house. But seeing what you pulled off without a crew, without production funding, without anything, just to make everything ready, or as ready as it could be to host us tonight, was essentially the last thing we needed to see."

Deanna squeezed his hand as Myron continued to speak.

"We love the concept. We love the two of you together, and we want to sign you both for a pilot season of a new show on True Country Network. What do you say?"

"We'll have to talk contracts and all that jazz but," Wyatt turned his gaze on Deanna, who beamed back at him. "It sounds like I'm getting everything I ever wanted."

EPILOGUE

"Don't you open that oven door!" Deanna leapt across the kitchen and hip-checked Wyatt out of reach, just in case. "Athena said the turkey has to stay in for exactly the length of the timer to get the perfect crispy skin."

"But it smells so good!"

"Don't care. I have never cooked a twenty-pound turkey before. We have seven guests, plus the rest of the crew stopping by to film the last shots of the finished house. I'm not leaving this to chance."

Wyatt heaved a beleaguered sigh. "Fine. I'll just nibble on you instead." He snagged her around the waist, hauling her in to run his lips down the column of her throat.

Torn between a giggle and a moan, she tried half-heartedly to shove him away, even as she dropped her head back to give him better access. "Don't you be writing checks with your mouth that you can't cash."

"Oh, I can cash them in spades." His growled promise had warmth pooling between her thighs.

"Not for another several hours, you can't."

"I bet we can make fast use of the butler's pantry."

Before she could consider the offer, the timer went off for the turkey. She swatted him away and reached for the oven mitts. "Behave. There are guests to entertain."

"Remind me again why we invited all these people to Thanksgiving?"

She hauled the giant roasting pan to the trivets on the island. "Because we have a lot to be thankful for. Go take everybody's drink order."

Much like the show, it took a crew to haul all the dishes to the long table that was the centerpiece of the finished dining room. Deanna took in the spread with the gigantic bird, the sweet potato casserole, the dressin', the green bean casserole, the deviled eggs, the hot pineapple salad, and the fresh rolls and heaved a satisfied sigh. This whole feast looked like the cover of a magazine. It did her designer's heart proud.

"Wait, wait! Let me take a picture first before everybody sits down. I need to commemorate."

She framed the shot, already imagining the blog post in her head. As soon as she was finished, everybody dropped into a chair. When she didn't sit, they all turned in her direction.

"The turkey still needs to rest for a few minutes, so before we start with the carving and all the passing of plates, I wanted to propose a toast and have everyone go around the table and say something they're thankful for."

"I'm down for that." From his position halfway down the table, Scott carefully lifted his glass of iced tea. "I'm thankful to be here celebrating the success of my baby brother and his phenomenal taste in women." As everyone's laughter died down, he sobered. "And I'm thankful to this man right here for his patience and fortitude and sometimes outright bullying to get me to the point where I got to walk this whole house on the tour."

Alton clinked his glass to Scott's, his eyes soft. "I'm thankful you finally graduated to a new physical therapist, so I can flirt with you openly."

Deanna grinned as he leaned over to give Scott a quick peck that had him blushing.

Beside him, Marjorie cleared her throat. "I'm thankful that I have both my sons back in my life." She lifted her glass and shot a watery look at Wyatt, who sat at the opposite end of the table.

He angled his head in acknowledgement. The two of them still had a lot of healing to do, but it had been his idea to invite her today. Deanna considered that major progress.

Simon raised his glass, a wide grin taking over his face. "I'm thankful that I finally asked out Fiona, and she said yes."

"We are *all* grateful you finally asked out Fiona," Wyatt announced.

Simon winked. "What can I say? You and Dee are inspiring."

Deanna winked at him. "Flatterer."

Valerie went next, looking caught somewhere between nervous and proud. "I'm thankful we have such a brilliant, talented daughter."

"And I'm thankful that our daughter was strong enough to make her place, even when it was the harder road to take," Phillip rushed to add.

Throat tight, Deanna raised her glass in acknowledgement. It meant so much that both her parents were finally on board with the dream she and Wyatt had worked so hard for, and the public declaration was icing on the cake.

Bennet lifted her glass. "I'm thankful that I'm finally getting my shot as assistant producer on this new show." She'd charmed the TCN execs the night of the party. They loved her vision, and she was pumped to be working with one of their best senior producers.

"Here here," Deanna crowed.

"You totally deserve it. We wouldn't be here without you." Wyatt turned his gaze on Deanna. "I'm thankful that this brilliant, beautiful woman took a chance and bought a house with a busted kitchen faucet, such that she fell into my life. That she agreed to come along with me on this crazy ride. That our show is proving to be a raging success. And that she's going to be with me every step of the way as we keep moving forward."

Lucky. She was so very lucky.

Beaming back at him, Deanna clutched her own glass. "I'm thankful that this monster turkey is actually cooked. That we managed to more or less get all the food ready at the same time. I'm grateful for friends, family, our sweet pooch, Casper. That we had a successful renovation of Blackborne Hall. For the nearly wrapped current season. And most of all, for Wyatt, for taking a crazy deal and a chance on something more. Cheers!"

The cry echoed around the table, and glassware clinked as everyone toasted their neighbor.

"Holy shit."

Deanna narrowed her eyes, spotting the screen in Bennet's hand. "Did you seriously bring your phone to the dinner table?"

"I did, and I apologize, but this may be the biggest thing to be thankful for today."

"What is it?"

She lifted her head, dark eyes wide. "Blake and Mercy Lee eloped."

No way had she heard that right. "They did what now?"

"Went to Vegas. There are pictures and everything." She held out the phone, which did show Mercy Lee coming out of a chapel on the Vegas strip on Blake's arm.

"Pictures prove nothing. They could be out of context." God knew Deanna understood that after all her years in PR.

Bennet swiped at the screen again. "They could be, but the exclusive interview just posted on *Countrified* confirms it."

Her heart began to pound as she considered the ramifications. "He really married someone else? I'm really done with paying that rat bastard alimony?"

Bennet reached out to squeeze her hand. "Girl, you're free at last."

Relief had Deanna's knees going weak, and she flopped into her chair. "Oh, thank God."

Cheers rang out around the table, with hoots, hollering, and fist pounding. As the noise died down, Deanna took a long drink of her wine.

"On that glorious note, let's eat!"

The meal was full of talk and laughter, exactly the kind of celebration she'd imagined in this room on her first walk through the house. How far they'd come since then. She met Wyatt's gaze from her end of the table and lifted her glass once more with a secret smile in a silent toast to him.

Well after dinner was over and all the dishes were cleared away, the crew had arrived and was starting on the footage that would become the last episode of *DIWyatt*. The network had opted to keep the name they'd started with for this brief season special about the renovation of Blackborne Hall. They'd be announcing the new name of their new show at the end.

As she followed them through the house, idly listening to everyone describe their favorite room or feature. Who knew her mom would appreciate the vintage tile surround she'd laid herself on the fireplace in the study? Or that Simon was so attached to the sun porch glider he'd refinished with Fiona? She was a little sad that things would be emptied out tomorrow. An enormous chunk of the furniture had been rented and staged for the big reveal, and they'd definitely needed somewhere for everybody to sit. But she and Wyatt would fill it again over time, with special projects and pieces that fit the space and overall look they wanted.

Deanna leaned against one wall, listening to Bennet corner Wyatt for the call-out segment.

"My favorite part of the house is definitely the master bathroom shower."

Her cheeks flushed hot, though he didn't so much as glance in her direction. They'd spent many, many happy hours beneath the spray of that shower.

Though it was hardly efficient, the crew trooped upstairs so that Wyatt could show off all the swanky features he'd installed. When he was done, the crew finally turned to her.

Knowing her role in this, she put on her hostess smile. "My favorite feature of the house has to be the kitchen overall and the custom island Wyatt built me in particular."

"I added a feature to one of the drawers."

"You did?"

"Mmm. We should go check it out." He had that vibrating excitement again.

As they all trailed back downstairs to the kitchen, she wondered what custom thing he'd added. The built-in knife block, maybe? Some kind of utensil organizer?

"Which one?"

"Top center," he told her.

Deanna narrowed her gaze at him. "What did you do?"

"Open it and see."

Beyond curious, she tugged open the drawer, only to find it empty. Not understanding, she frowned at him.

He leaned forward, peering inside. "Must've slipped to the back. Open it all the way."

Tugging it open the last couple of inches, she found a small, square wooden box. Everything around her seemed to hush. When she didn't move, Wyatt reached for the box himself.

"It's custom. I made it from some of the original American walnut we salvaged from the house. Couldn't help myself. But it's really what's inside that matters." He dropped to one knee and flipped it open.

The diamond nestled inside was a glorious twist of antique filigree around a princess cut stone.

Wyatt took her hand and grinned from his position on the floor "I'm gonna need you to breathe, honey."

Deanna sucked in a squeaking sort of breath.

"We fell in love over restoring this house. We've done everything together since we fell into each other's lives, and we're setting off on a whole new adventure with a brand new show. It only seems fitting that we take the biggest adventure of all together. Will you marry me?"

There was only one possible answer.

"Yes."

Wyatt slid the ring onto her finger and launched to his feet to kiss her. Deliriously happy, she melted into the kiss and into him. She'd never imagined being here again. Never imagined the life that she'd built with this wonderful, perfect man. And she was looking forward to another fifty years of surprises.

The rousing cheers reminded them both that they had an audience and the rest of an episode to film. Breaking apart only enough to pivot and face the camera, they launched into the final spiel.

"I'm Wyatt Sullivan."

"And I'm Deanna James." With a grin, she pressed a smacking kiss to Wyatt's lips. "For now. And we hope you'll join us for our brand new show next year where we'll help you Romance Your Renovation."

Choose Your Next Romance

Next up in the Men of the Misfit Inn series is Griff Powell, who we first met in *Our Kind of Love*. I paired this former Marine up with Samantha Ferguson, who some readers my remember as Audrey's best friend in *Second Chance Summer*.

> Griffin Powell has avoided his hometown since he left it in the rearview years ago. But the former Marine understands duty and promises, and that means dragging himself back home as part of his brother's wedding party. Which gets him thinking about a promise he made to a woman, after the best night of his life.

When she, too, shows up as part of the wedding, it feels like a sign.

Always a bridesmaid, professor Samantha Ferguson is dreading this bachelorette weekend. She's the one of the lone single ladies, and the matron of honor is her high school nemesis. Sam figures she can suck it up and deal, until she comes face-to-face with the big, sexy ginger mistake from her past. Can this trip home get any worse?

Turns out it can. Not only are she and Griff paired up for all the bridal party bonding activities, forcing her to relive high school hell, but Sam's best friend goes missing. When no one takes her concerns seriously, she starts a search herself--and ends up with an unwanted bodyguard whose very presence reminds her of a hot Vegas night she's tried hard to forget.

Come a Little Closer releases in January.

While you're waiting, why don't you go acquaint yourself with Sam as she cheers on her one of her BFFs in embracing a grown-up summer camp fling with the hot firefighter who saved her life? *Second Chance Summer* is waiting. It was the 2018 RITA® Award winner for short contemporary romance!

Or maybe you've blown through all my Eden's Ridge series and you're looking for something else to sink your teeth into. Did you know I have a whole other, complete, twelve book series set in Mississippi? The Wishful Romance series begins with a fish-out-of-water, opposites attract love story featuring a shero who... honestly should be really good friends with Deanna. You can find *To Get Me To You* here.

Can't decide? Keep turning the pages for a Sneak Peek of them both.

SNEAK PEEK SECOND CHANCE SUMMER

A SUMMER CAMP FLING ROMANCE

Professor Audrey Graham shouldn't be alive. But she didn't walk away from the accident that should've taken her life. She shouldn't have ever walked again according to the doctors. But after two years of physical therapy and countless surgeries, she's got a second lease on life. First stop? Camp Firefly Falls to try and catch up on some of the living she never did before her accident.

Firefighter Hudson Lowell shouldn't be alive. In the wake of losing two members of his team in a structure fire gone wrong, he's been unable to work, unable to pull himself out of the survivor's guilt. In a last ditch effort to snap him out of it, his family surprises him with a 2 week reunion session at Camp Firefly Falls, reminder of a simpler, better time. The last thing he expects to find is the woman he helped cut out of a snarled up wreck of a car two years before.

As sparks ignite between rescuer and rescuee, Audrey finally gets the chance to repay her hero. But can she convince this proud, stubborn man that life is still worth living? Or will Hudson let this chance at happiness slip through his fingers?

"*I*'VE NEVER SEEN ANYBODY so excited to ride a bus before."

Audrey Graham gave a little bounce on the vinyl-covered bench seat, strangely delighted with the squeak of springs. "I've never been on one. I mean, not a school bus. Just the public transit kind."

Beside her, Samantha Ferguson, her partner in this adventure, chuckled and grabbed hold of the seat in front of them for balance as the bus lurched through a pothole. "Whatever floats your boat, sugar."

"If you're looking for an authentic school bus ride, I can always start a spitball fight." This came from the guy who'd twisted around from the next seat up. The mop of sandy hair and smattering of freckles across his cheeks made him look several years younger than he probably was. He stuck out a hand. "Charlie."

Was this what camp was like? All first names all the time? It was so different from the formality and pretentiousness of academia.

"Audrey. And this is Sam." They all shook hands.

"Where are you from?" Charlie asked.

"Little bitty town in northeast Tennessee called Eden's Ridge," Sam replied. "Though most recently Chattanooga. I teach at a small, private college there. So does Audrey."

For now. "I'm originally from Kansas City, though."

"Long Island. I work in Manhattan these days."

"Yeah? What do you do?" Audrey asked, unable to imagine this golden retriever of a man amid the stiff suits and stuffed shirts.

"I'm an assistant editor at Macmillan."

Sam brightened. "Yeah? What genre?"

"Don't laugh. Romance."

"Now you've done it," Audrey warned. "The book monster has awoken. Sam's an English Lit professor and romance aficionado."

"Really? I'd have thought you'd turn your nose up at romance."

"No way. I love it. I even teach a class on the development of the genre and its relation to feminist theory."

Audrey hid a smile as the two launched into an animated discussion of favorite authors. She had no idea if there were any prospective sparks there, but at least Sam had found a kindred spirit.

"Are you two returning campers to Camp Firefly Falls?" Charlie's question pulled her attention back to the conversation.

"First timers," Sam told him. "Audrey here is a summer camp virgin."

Audrey felt her cheeks heat with a blush and had no idea why. It wasn't like she was *that* kind of virgin.

Not exactly far off... her brain reminded her.

Shut up.

"No shit? Well, the Retro Session is definitely the way to go to get the experience," Charlie said. "I came here every summer, when I was a kid. Got super pumped when I found out it'd been turned into a camp for grown-ups."

"Me too I'm tackling some entries on my bucket list lately, and when I heard about Camp Firefly Falls, it seemed like an opportunity to knock a few out in one fell swoop." Which was the most understated way Audrey could possibly explain her reasons for being here. But spilling her guts to a complete stranger on the camp bus as they drove up from New York was not one of those bucket list items.

"So you've never been to camp, and you went to camp somewhere else?" Charlie asked, looking from Audrey to Sam.

"Hale River Camp and Farm, in North Alabama," Sam replied.

"That's a long way from the Berkshires. How'd you hear about Camp Firefly Falls?"

The flash of phantom pain in her legs kept Audrey from answering immediately. Riding the wave, she forced a smile. "Oh, someone I met once mentioned coming here as a kid. I guess the name stuck in my head."

"I'm just along for the ride and to get my nostalgia on," Sam put in. "I *loved* camp. Went every year, from the time I was seven—camper through counselor."

She and Charlie fell back into easy conversation, and Audrey let them, focusing instead on breathing through the ache. The novelty of the bus ride was wearing thin. She'd been sitting too long and her legs were beginning to cramp up. A walk would be in order as soon as they got their stuff dumped at the cabin. Maybe a stroll along Lake Waawaatesi. It had looked so picturesque in the promo photos online.

From the back of the bus, someone began to sing "She'll Be Comin' Round The Mountain" as they turned onto the long, winding road that would, according to the map Audrey had studied, lead up to Camp Firefly Falls. They were nearly there. Then she'd have two, long, glorious weeks with no cell phone, no email, no reminders of the career decisions she still needed to make. Two weeks to relax. Two weeks to take life by the horns and really live it. Which meant pushing herself out of her comfort zone. She'd become an expert at pushing herself the last two years. More than she ought to, according to her parents, but what did they know? If she'd listened to them, she wouldn't have anything resembling a life anymore.

Well, okay, that wasn't entirely fair. They meant well. They'd always meant well. But it was her life, and she was finally going to live it. Going to camp was just the latest in a long line of small rebellions. Who knew that she, of all people, would develop a taste for defiance at the ripe old age of twenty-seven? But was it enough to change her life over? That was part of what she was here to figure out. Maybe, by the end of session, she'd finally know what she wanted.

Abruptly, the lush green trees opened up and the bus turned beneath an arched sign that read *Camp Firefly Falls*.

"We're here!" Audrey couldn't keep the excitement from her voice.

A cheer swept the bus as they pulled into a gravel parking lot, where a blonde woman with a boathouse stood behind a folding card table, surrounded by a handful of staff members in Camp Firefly Falls t-shirts. Audrey was on her feet the moment they rolled to a stop. Her legs protested the rapid movement, and she had to grab Charlie's seat to catch her balance.

Sam slipped an arm around Audrey's waist to steady her. "Okay?"

"Just stiff. Let's get out."

They edged into the aisle and filed off the bus with the other campers. A couple of other staff members circled around to the back and began offloading luggage as Audrey, Sam, and the others got in a loose line at the table to register and pick up their cabin assignments.

"Hi!" The blonde offered up a wide smile. "I'm Heather Tully. My husband and I own the camp. Welcome!"

"We're so excited to be here. I'm Audrey Graham, and this is Samantha Ferguson."

"Excellent. You're in Cabin 7."

"Lucky number," Sam pronounced.

If this were one of the camp movies Audrey had binge watched before coming, some guy would make a crude joke about getting lucky in Cabin 7. Apparently, the Camp Firefly Falls alums were a little more discreet. Or maybe real life was less salacious than the movies.

"Now, if you'll just turn in your cell phones. We'll keep them locked up at the lodge, so no worries something might happen to them." Heather held out zip top bags with their names scrawled out in marker.

"No cell phones?" Sam asked, digging in her purse.

"It's a new rule we're trying out for the Retro Session. Cell phones weren't a thing back when we were kids at camp, and we're trying to get back to that feel as much as we can."

"Sign me up. I can't remember the last time I went a day

without hearing a phone ring." Sam slipped her phone into the bag.

Audrey sent one last text off to her mom. **Arrived at camp safely. No phones allowed. I'll talk to you in two weeks.** Then she powered down and slid her phone into the other bag. Two whole weeks where her parents couldn't pressure her about Berkeley. That sounded like heaven.

Heather pulled out a map for each of them and circled Cabin 7. "If you head just up that trail and take the left fork, past the dining hall, you'll find your cabin ready and waiting. Dinner's going to be served at six, and we're having a little opening night mixer at the boathouse starting at seven-thirty. Come ready to dance!"

Audrey took her map. "We'll be there with bells on."

AT THE SIGHT of the bus turning onto the final road to Camp Firefly Falls, Hudson Lowell grimaced. The last thing he wanted was to get caught up in the crazy of drop off day with all the other campers. Was it even called drop off day now that they were all adults? Didn't matter. Either way, there'd be enough excitement and good cheer that he'd be liable to deck somebody. Better to kill a little time and circle back. There'd be no avoiding the walk down memory lane the next two weeks, but he could ease into it rather than leaping feet first. So, he drove on past the turn and kept heading north, wondering if Boone's was still in business.

Part gas station, part general store, part diner, Boone's had always been an official stop before his parents dropped him off to camp as a kid. Located halfway between camp and Briarsted, the nearest town, Boone's was the last bastion of civilization before two weeks of unfettered, summertime awesome. Ten minutes later, he pulled his Jeep into the lot. The whole complex was smaller than he'd remembered, but the scent of freshly brewed coffee was the same. It drew him back into the diner, where he settled into a booth and grabbed the laminated menu from between the napkin holder and the ketchup. He looked at the options without much interest.

A gum-chewing waitress appeared at the table, a pot of coffee in her hand. "What can I getcha, hon?"

"Just coffee. And a slice of pie." Pie was always a good idea.

She turned over the cup at his elbow and filled it near to the brim. "Apple or peach?"

"Peach. With ice cream."

"Comin' right up."

As she disappeared, Hudson slipped his phone out. Might as well make this last call before he got on up the mountain. Reception would probably be spotty.

"Hudson!"

"Hey Mom."

"Are you there yet? Is it fabulous? I'm so curious what all they've done to change the place since you were a boy."

He gritted his teeth against her cheer. "I haven't quite made it to camp yet. I stopped in at Boone's."

She laughed. "Of course. Couldn't go to camp for two weeks without your Twizzlers."

Had he even had a Twizzler in the past decade?

The waitress returned with his pie a la mode, and Hudson nodded his thanks.

"I just wanted to check-in one last time, before I got up there. Cell coverage will probably be lousy. You've got the number to the camp office, in case you need to reach me for anything." Translation: In case there's any change in John's condition.

"Got it right here. But sweetheart, I really want you to give this a chance. Embrace the whole camp experience. You used to have such fun up there. Unplugging from things will be good for you."

Unplugging. An unfortunate word choice. Hudson closed his

eyes as his brain conjured the tone of a flatlining heart monitor. His hand fisted around the fork. "Yeah. I'll try."

By the time he got off the phone, he'd lost whatever appetite he'd had for the pie. He ate it anyway, a mechanical shoveling in of food that had become habit the past few months. Food was necessary fuel, whether you tasted it or not. Leaving some cash on the table to pay his bill, he gassed up the Jeep. Then, remembering the promise to his mother, he bought a couple of packs of Twizzlers for nostalgia's sake and got back on the road to camp.

The bus crowd had cleared out. A lone blonde with a ponytail sat at the registration table. She looked up at his approach and broke into a grin. "Why Hudson Lowell. Didn't you grow up nice?"

"Don't know about nice, but I grew up. So'd you. Heard you married Michael."

"I did. We run this place together."

"Suits you," Hudson said. Heather Hawn had been one of his first camp crushes, but she'd never had eyes for anybody but Michael Tully. She looked happy. The kind of down-to-the-bone happy that exhausted him just from looking.

She checked her clipboard. "You're in Cabin 16 with Charlie Thayer. He got here about an hour ago from New York. You're in Syracuse these days?"

"I am."

Seeming to sense his reticence to talk, Heather turned all businesslike. "Not that I think you'll need it, but here's a map of camp and our list of available activities. Dinner's at six, and we're having an opening night dance at the boathouse at seven-thirty."

He'd rather be shot. But he took the handouts and thanked her before turning toward the Jeep for his gear.

"Oh, Hudson, I'll need your phone."

"Sorry?"

"We're banning them for the Retro Session. This is a technology-free zone."

"Not happening, Heather."

"You don't strike me as the type who'd be addicted to Candy Crush."

"I've got family in the hospital. They need to be able to reach me if things take a turn for the worse."

Her smile faded. "Oh, I'm so sorry. Well, keep it, then. But I'll warn you, reception is spotty, at best."

"Noted."

Charlie—whom he had dim memories of from years before as someone they'd short-sheeted once—wasn't at the cabin when Hudson arrived, though he'd already claimed the right side for his own. The cabin was still rustic in appearance, but the Tullys had done quite a bit more than spruce the place up. Instead of the old-school bunk beds with room to sleep eight, there were only two twin beds with quality mattresses, already made up with real bedding instead of lying bare and waiting for a sleeping bag. Hudson shoved the one he'd brought beneath the bed. The bathroom was small, but functional, with hotel-style towels and travel-size toiletries. They definitely hadn't had AC back in the day. Curious despite himself, he headed out to see what else had changed in the past seventeen years.

The lodge was the most obvious difference. A grand structure of wood and stone, he'd read that it now housed five-star dining with an honest-to-God chef in residence, along with conference rooms, staff quarters, and luxury suites. Hudson guessed there was a market for those kinds of amenities, but he hoped there'd be some straight up burgers cooked over a campfire while he was here. He was more a pot of chili kind of guy, or he could go for a vat of spaghetti, served family-style around the long table at the firehouse. Not that he'd been doing any of that lately either.

They'd added a ropes course—a big, sprawling labyrinth of ropes and platforms. It was the kind of setup that looked more intimidating than it actually was. Climbers would be strapped into harnesses and attached to guide wires the entire time. Probably the liability insurance for the place wouldn't allow for anything else. But still, he'd check that out, at some point. Maybe he'd see if they had gear for some rock climbing, too. That kind of physical exertion suited his desire to push himself to exhaustion in hopes of maybe sleeping. He might not be out with his company, but he'd kept himself in top shape since he recovered from the fall.

The wooded trails crisscrossing the grounds felt the same, as did the long pier that branched off to the boathouse. Hudson could see racks of kayaks and canoes. He followed the pull toward the water. The gentle lap of it against the wooden pilings soothed his nerves a bit. He had definite plans to grab one of those kayaks and disappear. There were countless inlets to explore along the length of Lake Waawaatesi. He might even do some fishing while he was here. Fish didn't talk or expect you to talk back. He figured that made for much better therapy.

As he started to turn back toward camp proper, he caught a flash of fire. A woman strolled along the bank on the other side of the lake, her face tipped up to the sunshine, a gorgeous fall of red hair rippling in the breeze. From this distance, Hudson couldn't see her face, but he knew she was smiling. Everything about her posture suggested absolute peace. He found himself watching until she disappeared into the trees.

Shaking off the vague ripple of envy, Hudson decided to curtail the rest of his tour. Better to unpack and settle in before dinner, get a little quiet. He'd have to deal with people soon enough.

Grab your copy of *Second Chance Summer* today!

SNEAK PEEK TO GET ME TO YOU

WISHFUL ROMANCE # 1

Just a city girl, living in a lonely world

Displaced Steel Magnolia Norah Burke doesn't know the meaning of failure. But when she threatens to blow the whistle on some shady business practices at her Chicago marketing firm, she gets fired fast as all get out. Licking her wounds, she heads back below the Mason-Dixon for a little home-grown Southern comfort.

Just a small town boy

With his iron-clad Mississippi roots, Councilman Cam Crawford is a man who values tradition, preservation, and the love of a good dog. When a big box warehouse store tries to capitalize on his hometown's economic downturn, it seriously burns his biscuit. He's not about to let anyone's ambition destroy what he holds dear.

A David vs. Goliath story with a side of grits.

This unlikely pair just might be the perfect allies—in war and out.

But as the battle to stop GrandGoods heats up and sparks of attraction turn to something more, will Norah's bigger-picture perspective go with Cam's "keep it as it is" attitude? Are they meant to be like biscuits and gravy? Or are they just as wrong as un-sweet tea?

Chapter One

*T*HERE WAS NO ESCAPING now.

As the steady click of sensible heels on asphalt grew ever closer, Campbell Crawford shut his eyes and repressed a curse. Where the hell had she come from?

To give himself another few moments to arrange his face into something resembling polite civility, Cam ducked back into his truck.

"Mr. Crawford, I need a word." Agnes Crockett used the same stern tone she used to call his name when she'd taught trigonometry back in high school.

Resisting the urge to hunch his shoulders, Cam tucked a cardboard tube of landscaping blueprints under his arm and turned to face her. "Yes, Mrs. Crockett. What can I do for you?"

Mrs. Crockett peered up at him from beneath her umbrella, a bright floral affair completely at odds with her no-nonsense demeanor. "I have a matter that needs to be brought up at the next City Council meeting. It's about that stoplight at Market and Spring Street."

Not again. If he had a nickel for every time somebody griped about that stoplight, he could buy a round of drinks for everybody waiting inside the Mudcat Tavern.

"The city needs to fix the sensor. Cross traffic from Market Street gets stuck entirely too long, when nobody's even coming the other direction. Why, I sat there for a full *five minutes* today without a soul passing by on Spring Street, and I was late to Bitsy Elliott's daughter's baby shower. When is that sensor going to get fixed?"

Cam privately thought that, given the state of the city coffers, it would be more likely the stoplight would be entirely decommissioned and they'd go back to the four-way stop, but that wasn't something he was about to share with this particular constituent. "I certainly understand your concern, Mrs. Crockett. Now we talked about this the last time—"

"You said I had to fill out this form." She dug around in her purse and came up with a sheet of paper that she thrust at him. "I want that traffic light fixed."

Cam took the paper. She'd filled in the blanks by hand, her slanted scrawl covering most of the page. He bit back a sigh and refrained from mentioning that it was a web form she was supposed to submit online. "Ah, yes, ma'am. I'll see that it's put on the agenda for our next City Council meeting."

"See that you do. I've been put off for the *last time,* young man."

Aware that his shoulders had hunched up by his ears, Cam forced them down. "Yes, ma'am. Now, if you'll excuse me, I've got to go meet a client." He tapped the blueprint tube and softened the diplomatic brushoff with a smile. "You have a good evenin', now."

He called the escape good when he made it to the door of the Mudcat without pursuit or an order to detention.

Somebody had Garth Brooks playing on the jukebox. The hot fiddle licks of "Callin' Baton Rouge" were punctuated by the crack of billiard balls from the far side of the bar. Christmas lights still twinkled around the perimeter, as they probably would until Valentine's Day or Easter. Cam felt some of the stress of the day leech out as he crossed to the high-top table in the corner, where his cousin, Miranda, was already taking a pull on a Sam Adams.

"You're late." She set down the bottle. "Had a real pisser of a day at the clinic, so I started without you. Two days after

Christmas and there's already an outbreak of flu. And *not* the strain they were predicting when they formulated the flu shot this year. You have a client meeting?"

Cam laid the blueprint tube in another chair. "No, this was just cover. Got ambushed by Mrs. Crockett in the parking lot."

"The stoplight again?"

He cocked thumb and forefinger at her. "Got it in one. I'm late because I was working on mixing potting soil today, and I figured you'd appreciate me showering and changing first so as not to smell like manure."

Miranda leaned over and gave an exaggerated sniff as he shrugged out of his wet coat. "Much obliged then, cuz." She settled back in her chair. "Did you hear about Travis Hugget?"

"What about him?"

"Remember he's been dating that girl from college—Gwen something or other—long distance for more than a year, since she took that job in New York? Apparently, right before Christmas, he went up there to her fancy Wall Street office and proposed, right as the entire company was coming out of a staff meeting."

Poor bastard. He had plenty of reason to know that was a disaster waiting to happen.

"Not only did Gwen say yes, she quit her job right then and there, and they eloped."

Cam swiped Miranda's beer and tipped it back to wash the sour taste of envy from his mouth as he revised his opinion. *Lucky bastard.* "Good for them."

Aware of his cousin's *I shouldn't have said that* expression and sensing an imminent and entirely unnecessary apology, Cam wiped the scowl from his face. Christ, when was his family going to stop pussyfooting around it?

Miranda's phone rang and she glanced at the screen. "It's Norah. I need to take this. Go get yourself a beer and bring me another since you polished mine off. And put in an order of cheese sticks while you're up there. I'm starving."

"Your wish." He saluted and headed for the bar, sending a silent thank you to Miranda's old college roommate for the distraction.

Adele Daly, the opinionated owner of the Mudcat, worked the taps as she chatted with Abe Costello about Ole Miss's chance at making it to the Final Four.

"I'm tellin' you, if they can just take out Emory, they've got a shot," Abe insisted.

Adele slid a glass of IPA down the bar into a waiting hand. "My money's on State. They've been burning up the courts this season."

Easing between two stools, Cam propped himself on an elbow and nodded a hello to Abe. "Adele, would you be so kind as to get me a Killian's and put in an order for cheese sticks and another Sam Adams for Miranda?"

"You want a bottle or tap? Keg's fresh."

"Tap then. And better add some chili cheese fries to that order. Miranda doesn't strike me as being in a sharing mood tonight."

"You got it, sugar pie."

Cam lounged back against the bar and took note of the glass of scotch Abe was nursing. "Are we celebrating or commiserating?"

"Little bit of both. I got an offer on my land."

"That acreage over by Hope Springs?"

"Yep."

Cam straightened in surprise. Abe was a local man, born and raised in Wishful. That land parcel had been in his family for generations. "You're selling?"

"Thinkin' 'bout it. It's a damned good offer. Well above market value." He sipped the scotch and grimaced, more a testament to the situation than the drink.

"Who?"

"Nobody local."

Cam had figured that. Nobody local had that kind of money to throw around. In the wake of the plant closing, a lot of people didn't have any money at all. Heirloom Home Furnishings had been the primary employer in town. When they'd opted to move their operations to Mexico eight months ago, it had gutted the town's economy. That was just the latest blow in a long line of economic downturns over the last few decades. Their population was shrinking as more and more good people were forced to go elsewhere to support their families.

"But you can't sell. That land's part of your family history. Part of Wishful's history."

"History don't pay the bills, son."

It was an unfortunately familiar story. Loss of workforce and population also meant loss of business. Abe's farm supply company took a hit when Cam bought the nursery five years ago. Cam had a wider variety and better stock, and with local propagation, he was able to offer better prices than the other man. But nursery and garden stock wasn't Abe's bread and butter. If the farm supply was suffering, this was the first Cam had heard about it.

Adele set Cam's beer on the bar. "It's too bad the city can't make an offer on that parcel. Be nice to make a formal park out there by the springs. Like that plan you drew up. It'd be a great addition to the town."

Cam's mind started to spin. "Who's brokering the sale?"

"Sally Forester on my side. Other folks got an attorney from out of town."

"Hold off on making any final decisions, Abe. If anybody's gonna buy that property, the city ought to have first crack at it."

Abe grunted in acknowledgment, but it was a hollow victory. Buying more land was only one of many things the city couldn't afford to do. The truth was, the town he loved was dying, and Cam didn't know how much longer they could limp along as they were. What they needed was a miracle, and despite the holiday season, those were in pretty short supply.

❧

"AND HOW IS my sister from another mister?" Miranda's voice rolled out of the car speakers, a welcome breath of the South that made Norah Burke ache with homesickness.

"Tired. It's a long drive back from New York."

"Why on earth didn't you fly?"

"Because nobody's invented a teleporter yet. Flying would take just as long, and I'd be one of a hundred other irritable sardines, who want to be home already. At least on the road it's quiet."

"You totally live in the wrong city for quiet. Are you home yet?"

"Got a couple more hours. But I'm about to break it up a bit and make a stop in your honor."

"Off I-90? Oh my God, are you in Morton? You're going to Have Your Cake, aren't you?"

Norah laughed at the mix of accusation and longing in her friend's tone. "Guilty."

The stretch of road immediately off the interstate had mushroomed in the past three years with the usual contingent of fast food restaurants, gas stations, and a couple of chain hotels. Pleased at the evidence of growth, Norah bypassed them all, following the signs for downtown and sending up a silent prayer that Have Your Cake would be open until six.

"Best road trip discovery *ever*. I love their caramel cake. The perfect marriage of salty and sweet, with four layers of lovely, moist cake…What made you decide to stop?"

"I was missing you." It was the truth, even if it didn't touch on all the whys. "How is everybody?"

As she navigated through town, Norah listened to her friend's account of this year's holiday hijinks. It was almost like listening to the summary of a Hallmark Channel movie, for all she could relate to Miranda's sprawling family, with aunts, uncles, and cousins galore. They were as close to normal as Norah ever got.

"—oh, and the boys had a poker tournament to decide who got the last slice of Grammy's chocolate pie."

Amusement and envy warred. Grammy's chocolate pie was a thing of legend. "Who won?"

"Reed, who was totally the dark horse in that race. Everybody assumed Mitch would win because he always does. He said to tell you hello, by the way."

"Tell him hi back and ask him when he's coming to Chicago again for another architectural convention."

"I still can't believe you went on a date with my brother."

"It wasn't a date. It was a pity tour of the city, since you didn't warn him you wouldn't actually be able to leave the hospital to see him."

"That's why they call it residency. And anyway that's not the way *he* tells that story."

"Then Mitch is a liar liar pants on fire."

"Why don't you come down here and tell him that yourself? You keep promising to visit."

"I know, I know," Norah groaned. "It's been way too long. But work's been *crazy*. I had a hard enough time getting off to go to New York for the holiday. I can't possibly ask off again so soon. Maybe closer to summer."

"Summer? You *do* remember what Mississippi is like in the summer?"

"Honey, given the winter we've been having, I'd relish the chance to wear some short shorts and a tank top instead of a winter coat that makes me look like the Michelin Man."

"I'll remind you of that when you come and do your impression of the Wicked Witch of the West. How did Christmas go on your end? Was Rockefeller Center fabulous? I'm getting my vicarious white Christmas fix through you."

"It was gorgeous. The Plaza was amazing, and midnight mass at Saint Thomas was simply beautiful. Christmas in Manhattan is definitely a unique experience." And she'd have traded it all for one zany family dinner with the Campbells.

"Did your dad manage to refrain from harping on you about going back to law school?"

"Actually, he's dating somebody. Some high-powered exec who looks like Hollywood's idea of Wall Street. They went to Saint Bart's, so it was just me and Mom. *She* got called in to emergency surgery, so I spent my holiday blessedly harp-free."

Miranda didn't buy her breezy, no-big-deal tone for a moment. "Wait, so you were *alone* for Christmas?"

Sensing the edge of a blistering rant, Norah felt compelled to head Miranda off. "Not all of it. Between surgeries, Mom and I had a blast shopping for Operation Santa Claus, and she got out of surgery in time for a late Christmas dinner."

"That's awful."

Norah bit back a sigh as she turned onto Main Street. Miranda's outrage on her behalf was well-intentioned, even if it solved exactly nothing. "Well, it was certainly better than if Dad had tried to include Lillian. We're a weirdly civilized modern family, but I don't think we're *that* civilized. Besides, it gave me some quiet time to catch up on this radical thing called reading for pleasure."

"You should've come here. You know you're always welcome."

Norah knew they'd fold her into the flock. It was part of the Campbells' charm. But there were a hundred reasons keeping her from following through on the invite Miranda made every year. "And I appreciate the offer. Now I'm going to let you go because I'm pretty sure I drove past Have Your Cake while I was running my mouth."

"Buy two pieces and have one in my name."

"And will those calories vicariously travel to *your* hips?" Norah circled the block for another pass.

"They will in spirit."

"Give your family my best."

"Love you."

"Love you back. Talk soon."

Norah didn't have to hunt for parking. But for a handful of cars, downtown Morton was deserted. She got out and climbed over the mounds of dirty snow to the sidewalk and took a good look around. No sign of Have Your Cake. Thinking she parked on the wrong block, she began to walk.

Maybe they're still on shortened holiday hours. Not what she'd have recommended to business owners in the wake of the holiday. They should've been taking advantage of post-Christmas shoppers with gift certificates and Christmas money.

A shop window across the street had *Going Out of Business* painted across the glass. The sign above the awning indicated it had been a florist. Even with the poor economy and reduced discretionary income, a florist should have been able to make it through the Christmas season. In another window on her side, she saw a For Rent sign. A lone, headless mannequin stood inside, one arm lifted like it was waving goodbye. One empty retail space she could dismiss, but two? That didn't fit with her expectations.

Three years ago, she'd been brought in as the voice of the marketing team that convinced the town of Morton that Hugo's ValuCenter would be a partner to the community, a harbinger of new economic growth. She'd seen their multi-phase plan for sustainable community development, had been the one to sell city leaders on the concept. So why was everything closed?

The next couple of spaces were occupied by a law office and an accountant. But the space after that had a discreet For Sale sign and the name of a local real estate company. Cold fingers walked down her spine as Norah looked into every window on the entire three block stretch.

Based on the community development plan, downtown Morton should've been a bustling retail corridor, full of local vendors and craftspeople. Exactly what it had been, at the heart, when she and Miranda had discovered the place years ago, but bigger. And yet more than seventy percent of the retail space sat empty. It was such a far cry from the bustling, quirky town she remembered, she half wondered if she'd come to the wrong place.

"What the hell happened here?"

One business still had active clientele at this hour. Crossing the street, Norah stepped inside the Five O'Clock Shadow. The bar was dim and quiet. A few people looked up when she came in, then went back to their drinks. Their low murmurs of conversation barely competed with the classic rock playing over the speakers. She noted a handful of suits and some business casual attire, suggesting that this was probably a hang out for the office workers and city government employees who worked further down the street.

Loosening her scarf, Norah crossed to the bar, where a mustached man was drying glasses.

"What can I getcha?"

She slid onto a stool. "Directions, I hope. I'm from out of town, and it's been a few years since I came through here. I was hoping you could tell me where Have Your Cake moved to."

"Didn't move. Closed along with just about everything else down here."

She'd been afraid of that. "What happened?"

"Same as happened lots of other places. We got a Hugo's ValuCenter."

Norah swallowed, her throat suddenly dry. "I'd heard that they were in to being partners with the community."

The bartender snorted. "They're like any other politicians. Telling people exactly what they want to hear to get in, then going back on their word. Within six months of opening for business, they added an in-house florist, a bakery, a butcher, on top of all the other products they already carried. They undercut local prices, all in the name of *value*." The word rolled off his tongue like something foul. "Local businesses couldn't compete. Those of us still standing are the ones who aren't in direct competition. Everybody else...*poof.*"

Numb, Norah thanked the bartender for his time and headed back to her car. Her stomach roiled.

Hugo's had done exactly what she'd promised the town they wouldn't do. She'd *seen* the proposal, *seen* the plans to integrate, not overtake the community. Was there a statute of limitations clause she'd missed? Had they performed some kind of bait and switch with the final contracts? Had her partner failed to do proper due diligence on the company? She had, in effect, lied to the townspeople. Used all her skill in persuasion to talk them into something that had decimated the character of the town.

How did this happen? Where did I screw up?

She didn't know. But as soon as she got to the office in the morning, she was going to find out.

Try the Wishful Romance series today! Grab *To Get Me To You* wherever ebooks are sold.

OTHER BOOKS BY KAIT NOLAN

A complete and up-to-date list of all my books can be found at https://kaitnolan.com.

THE MISFIT INN SERIES
SMALL TOWN FAMILY ROMANCE

- *When You Got A Good Thing* (Kennedy and Xander)
- *Til There Was You* (Misty and Denver)
- *Those Sweet Words* (Pru and Flynn)
- *Stay A Little Longer* (Athena and Logan)
- *Bring It On Home* (Maggie and Porter)

RESCUE MY HEART SERIES
SMALL TOWN MILITARY ROMANCE

- *Baby It's Cold Outside* (Ivy and Harrison)
- *What I Like About You* (Laurel and Sebastian)
- *Bad Case of Loving You* (Paisley and Ty prequel)

- *Made For Loving You* (Paisley and Ty)

MEN OF THE MISFIT INN
SMALL TOWN SOUTHERN ROMANCE

- *Let It Be Me* (Emerson and Caleb)
- *Our Kind of Love* (Abbey and Kyle)
- *Don't You Wanna Stay* (Deanna and Wyatt)
- *Come a Little Closer* (Sam and Griff)

WISHFUL SERIES
SMALL TOWN SOUTHERN ROMANCE

- *Once Upon A Coffee* (Avery and Dillon)
- *To Get Me To You* (Cam and Norah)
- *Know Me Well* (Liam and Riley)
- *Be Careful, It's My Heart* (Brody and Tyler)
- *Just For This Moment* (Myles and Piper)
- *Wish I Might* (Reed and Cecily)
- *Turn My World Around* (Tucker and Corinne)
- *Dance Me A Dream* (Jace and Tara)
- *See You Again* (Trey and Sandy)
- *The Christmas Fountain* (Chad and Mary Alice)
- *You Were Meant For Me* (Mitch and Tess)
- *A Lot Like Christmas* (Ryan and Hannah)
- *Dancing Away With My Heart* (Zach and Lexi)

WISHING FOR A HERO SERIES (A WISHFUL SPINOFF SERIES)
SMALL TOWN ROMANTIC SUSPENSE

- *Make You Feel My Love* (Judd and Autumn)
- *Watch Over Me* (Nash and Rowan)
- *Can't Take My Eyes Off You* (Ethan and Miranda)
- *Burn For You* (Sean and Delaney)

MEET CUTE ROMANCE
SMALL TOWN SHORT ROMANCE

- *Once Upon A Snow Day*
- *Once Upon A New Year's Eve*
- *Once Upon An Heirloom*
- *Once Upon A Coffee*
- *Once Upon A Campfire*
- *Once Upon A Rescue*

SUMMER CAMP
CONTEMPORARY ROMANCE

- *Once Upon A Campfire*
- *Second Chance Summer*

ABOUT KAIT

Kait is a Mississippi native, who often swears like a sailor, calls everyone sugar, honey, or darlin', and can wield a bless your heart like a saber or a Snuggie, depending on requirements.

You can find more information on this RITA ® Award-winning author and her books on her website http://kaitnolan.com.

Do you need more small town sass and spark? Sign up for her newsletter to hear about new releases, book deals, and exclusive content!